CHEEKY ROYAL

NANA MALONE

Cheeky Prince and Cheeky Royal

Photography: Wander Aguiar

Cover Art by: Amy Daws

Edited by: Angie Ramey, Sara Lunsford, Keyanna Butler

Published in the United States of America

PENNY...

"Do not embarrass me in front of the king."

I glared at my father as he frog-marched me down the enormous gilded hallway leading to the king's personal office. My heels made a clop-clop sound that echoed right along with the sound of my father's making a similar click-clack sound on the polished marble.

I'd been summoned by King Cassius.

I'd *never* been summoned by the king before.

"Thanks for the vote of confidence, Dad."

"Sweetheart, stop. You know I believe you can do anything. But this is important. This is *His Majesty*. Do not embarrass the family. Keep your mouth shut. Try not to twitch too much. Don't fidget. Stand there, listen, and nod your head. You can handle that?"

I nodded slowly. "Yes. Keep my mouth shut, show no personality, and act like a robot. Done."

As we passed the Fountain Garden, I gasped. I'd forgotten that this part of the palace had floor to ceiling windows looking out on the garden. Outside the birds of paradise were in full bloom. The colors of the Hibiscus and Bougainville, and the Caribbean Lilies should have clashed, but the gardens were done so elegantly that the different flowers wove together and told a story. As the palace sat on top of the hill, the azure- blue waters of the Caribbean were visible.

If I had this view I might never get any work done. *Not that you do anyway.*

The question was, just how much trouble was I in?

Had Kind Cassius possibly heard that I was the worst Royal Guard in the history of man? But if that were the case, he wouldn't have sent for me, right? Or was he calling me to fire me personally? But why not have my father do it?

Was he pissed about the ball? That was months ago. I hadn't set any dukes on fire since then. Honestly, it wasn't my fault the Duke of Essex caught on fire. And I'd *had to* tackle him to put him out. Besides, he was fine. Maybe a little scared, and sure, the flames had gotten rather close to him. Again, not my fault...*entirely*.

Since then, my father hadn't let me near anyone remotely related to the royal family. I was still relegated to the Queen's offices. But now they didn't even allow me to talk to any dignitaries. I was nothing more than a glorified secretary. And I was miserable.

My family had been in the Royal Guard since the 1700s when King Jackson had first come to the Winston Isles. Granted, he hadn't been king then. He'd been a commoner, escaping his own king in England. He'd been put on a ship headed to the Americas that had instead crashed on the Winston Isles. Because he had no papers and no family, he'd been taken in as an indentured servant by the duke who ruled the island.

But then he'd organized the other indentured servants, slaves, and the indigenous people on the Isles to rise up against the aristocracy.

From the stories that had been passed down in my family, I understood that the war was fought dirty. Jackson had refused to see people enslaved— refused to watch and stand idly by as anyone was mistreated. When the war ended, the people made him king. And he promised his subjects that they would all be free and that the laws would be fair.

As a kid, I'd thought the stories of some great-great-great-grandfather fighting next to King Jackson were merely stories that the old folks told. But as I got older, I realized that they weren't stories; they were history. My ancestor was one of the indigenous people of the Winston Isles. He'd fallen in love with a slave that worked in the plantation houses, and all he wanted was freedom. So he joined Jackson's cause and eventually became one of the king's trusted advisors. And ever since then, a member of my family had been in the Royal Guard.

Including myself.

My grandfather was Royal Guard. My father was Royal guard. Hell, my mother was Royal Guard, as was my older brother. It was sort of expected that I would be Royal Guard as well.

I'd enjoyed the training. It had been rigorous physically. The history and the studying part had been easy and fun. I liked history. But when it came to practical application of everything I learned, I was a walking, talking Calamity Penelope.

I had the best of intentions, but everything always went wrong. And that's why getting summoned by the king wasn't something to be excited about. I just knew I was about to get sacked.

We paused outside the king's office, and I drew in a deep breath before knocking quietly.

The booming command from inside had me shaking, but I clasped my hands together behind my back to quell the movement. I could do this. I *had* to do this. Because, if I didn't do this, I was afraid it would show that I didn't belong here. Didn't belong as a member of the Royal Guard. Didn't belong anywhere.

When I opened the door, King Cassius stood immediately on the other side, and I stared. Up close he was even more imposing. Proper breeding eventually won out, and I curtsied. "Your Majesty."

His voice was as kind as I remembered. His was a mix of

almost undistinguishable island lilt, a crisp British clip mixed with an odd occasional flattening of vowel sounds that spoke to the influence of the States over the years. But no mistake, he was all aristocracy.

"Penelope?"

I nodded. "Yes, Your Majesty."

King Cassius glanced over my shoulder to my father. "Ethan. Come in."

My father shook his head. "Sorry, Your Majesty. I'm actually needed in security. Cancun didn't pan out, but we may have another sighting."

The king nodded gravely. "Then by all means. Go. See if you can locate my son."

I swallowed hard. My father was one of King Cassius's closest advisers. He was also the head of security. When Prince Sebastian left six months ago, my father was charged with finding him and keeping tabs on him at all times. Though, as it turned out, the prince was a little difficult to keep track of.

The prince employed a series of doubles and scattered them to the far corners of the earth. So one day there'd be a story of the prince in Mallorca making out with some heiress. And the next day, there'd be a story about him in Thailand, chilling on the beach with some American tourist. The paparazzi followed after him like flies to honey.

"Come in Penelope. Have a seat."

Surprisingly, everything in the king's office was quite understated. It looked like the office of a CEO. Dark oak table; dark leather; dark wood paneling. It was oddly *normal*. Still, though, I knew I was sitting in front of royalty. And so, I eased myself down into the chair he indicated and sat on the very edge, trying to remember all the etiquette my mother had pounded into my head.

Edge of the seat. Knees together. Ankles crossed. Shoulders straight. Head at an incline of 45 degree angle to show interest. Wow, it was exhausting.

"You wished to see me, Majesty?" My voice sounded strange in my own ears. Warbled. Like I was fighting back tears. Well, I *was* fighting back nerves.

"I guess you're wondering why I've asked you to come."

I braced myself. "Yes, sir. I can assure you, any mistakes I made in the past have been rectified. And I've tried not to embarrass —"

He put up a hand. "I assure you, you've done nothing to embarrass me. Or your father. I wanted to ask a favor."

I stared at him, my mouth open. "A favor. From me?" I snorted with laughter. Okay, admittedly, not my finest moment. "What favor can I do for my king?"

His smile was kind, but his eyes were fierce. "I need you to become Prince's Guard."

I shook my head. "I'm afraid I don't understand."

The king sighed. "As soon as your father locates my son, I'd like you to go undercover. Every time I get someone close to Sebastian to provide him protection, or try to talk to him, he manages to evade us. But, the queen pointed out that I may be approaching this all wrong. So, I figured if we have someone undercover, someone he can *talk* to, he might be more inclined to listen. My hope is you can provide that service. A *twofold* service. First, keep him safe. You've been trained as all members of the Royal Guard have. But you can also get close enough to convince him to come home. It will take a lot of convincing, as my son is quite angry with me."

I stared at him. Honest to God stared. Then my gaze flickered to the portrait on the wall of the royal family. With this dark hair and eyes that matched the color of the Caribbean water, Prince Sebastian was hot. Hotter than hot. Panties on fire hot. And his voice, when he was making a woman—

Yeah, never mind how I knew that. It wasn't like I was eavesdropping that one time at the ball. He wasn't exactly being discreet.

As children, we'd played together sometimes. He'd always seemed like a lonely kid. He and his cousins had been tutored on the grounds. With only his cousins for playmates, he used to scour the castle looking for someone else to play with. He'd often found me, desperately trying to follow behind my brother. And we were close enough in age that he let me play whatever he was playing.

I'd loved those moments. But then he'd gone to boarding school at age eleven, and I never had contact with him again. At least not close-up contact.

"This sounds extremely important. What makes you think I'm the right person for the job? Honestly, it can't have escaped your knowledge that I'm a total disaster at this job. I'm quite possibly the worst Royal Guard in the history of the planet. Or at the very least, in the history of the Winston Isles."

Kind Cassius sighed. "To be honest, you're female. And you know him. I know that you used to play as children. And I saw you with the Duke. In an emergency, you stay calm. You're not flustered. You're professional. What happens before an emergency is where things seem to go a little haywire."

"A little. Besides, I knew the prince years ago. I don't know him now."

"Still, he won't see you coming. And as you know, my son has a weakness for women. I know that you have a good head on your shoulders. From what your father tells me, you take no prisoners, and you won't be swayed by Sebastian's charm. But you are a beautiful girl, so at the very least, he'll like having you around."

I knew the appropriate response. Despite how this sounded, this wasn't a request. It was a command. From my *king*. I needed to listen. To follow through. To say yes.

So when I opened my mouth, to say, 'Yes sir. When do I leave?' I was just as shocked as the King when I said instead, "Your Majesty, I'm honored that you would think of me, but I have to decline. I'm terrible at this job. Really, really bad actually. You don't want to entrust something as important as this to someone like me."

And then I did the one thing I knew would embarrass my

whole family. I stood and walked out on the king without waiting for him to dismiss me.

Penny ...

"HAVE YOU LOST YOUR FUCKING MIND?"

Yep, that was pretty much the response I'd thought I'd get from my best friend, Ariel, when I told her.

It's not like I could argue with her. I *had* lost my fucking mind.

I crossed my arms and paced the length of Ariel's living room. "I can't believe I said that. I am going to get shoved into the dungeons. I know how bad this is."

Ariel shook her head and blinked rapidly as if trying to understand what I'd just said. "Well, first of all, I want to know exactly what the king looked like when you told him no."

"Ariel, be serious. I told His Royal Majesty, that I wouldn't take a job. I am *King's* Guard. Okay, technically *Queen's* Guard. But still. I looked the king in the face and said *no*. Oh my God, he really has to be readying the dungeons."

Ariel sighed. "I hoped that it wouldn't come to this, but I will get you out of the country. Operation Condor is in effect. Let's get the passports and the cash. You can't be held responsible for your actions. If we're caught, we'll plead temporary insanity."

I halted, then stared at my friend. I was never really sure if Ariel was serious or not. "Do you actually have passports and cash?"

Ariel raised a brow. "Do you really want to know the answer to that question?" She'd always said her father knew some unscrupulous people, so it was possible she'd picked up a thing or two from him.

I held up my hands. "You know what? No. Don't tell me. But I know the code word Condor. And no, I can't run from this, because if I run, that's bad for my parents."

"So what if it looks bad for your parents? You don't want to be Royal Guard anyway."

This was true. Just because I'd gone into the family business didn't mean I loved it. *But there's no way you're telling your parents that you're quitting the Royal Guard.* Dear Lord, the disgrace that would bring to my family. A member of my family had been in the Royal Guard since the very beginning. Since King Jackson. It was a great honor. *Then why don't you want it?*

I resumed pacing. "Maybe I'll just go back and tell him that I'm really sorry and clearly I had lost my mind. And maybe he'll just give me the job, and I'll find Prince Sebastian and bring him back."

Ariel smirked. "You mean His Royal Fucking Majesty."

I giggled. "Yeah. His Royal Fucking Majesty." He was every bit the cocky, bad boy. I remembered him boning the Duke's daughter. But there was another side to him. I'd seen him with the people. He often drank at the local pub and bought the whole place pints. But not to be flashy. More like so everyone could enjoy themselves for one drink with no worries.

He gave generously to dozens of charities and especially championed charities for educating youth. Hell, I'd won a full academic scholarship paid for by the royal family to go wherever and study whatever I wanted. If my parents had paid, I likely would have been *encouraged* to study something practical like political science or criminal justice. At any rate, thanks to the prince I'd had a little freedom. But amongst the guard, he was known as His Royal Fucking Majesty.

He was never rude to any of those charged with protecting his family, but the rumor was there was a lot of dick swinging going around. Some of which I'd seen personally. He was in charge, and he knew it. No one dared tell him no. And uh...also the *literal* dick swinging. Every member of his personal guard had seen him in various stages of undress with his infamous women.

"Have you talked to your mom? Maybe she'll have insight."

I stopped pacing and joined Ariel on the couch, flopping onto it. "I didn't dare go home. I was too terrified. I knew my father would bring the roof down screaming at me for being such an idiot."

"We both know your father would never call you an idiot."

I sighed. "No, you're right. He wouldn't. But man, he would give some serious disappointment face. That's worse. And then my brother would start on me."

Arial set up straighter. "Michael?"

I bit the inside of my mouth to keep from smirking. Ariel had been half in love with my brother for ages. But Michael, of course, was oblivious. He was all Prince's Guard, all the time: rigid and all about the job. He wanted to move up the ranks as quickly as possible. He had a steady girlfriend, Emily, who he ignored most of the time.

She wasn't particularly nice, and really was too much of a doormat for my brother. And the funny thing was no one ever believed that Michael and I were brother and sister. I took after my mother, with my tawny skin and curly corkscrew hair. Michael took after our father, looking every bit the European aristocrat with olive skin and straight dark hair that he kept military short. Genetics were a funny thing.

"Okay, if I'm destined for future in the dungeons, I want to go out in style. Let's make my twenty-second birthday count for something then. Just uh, keep Operation Condor on ice. I have a feeling I'll be needing a bailout soon.

"You got it. You know I'm ride or die. You and I are like Thelma and Louise."

I shook my head. "Why is it ride or die? Why must we always die in the end. Money and passports are good enough. Honest."

Ariel winked. "Okay fine. We'll be Thelma and Louise before driving off a cliff. We start tonight with an epic birthday celebration and then tomorrow, we figure out how to fix this. You and me. But tonight, we drink!"

2

PENNY ...

"WHAT DO you mean you're not staying?"

I stared at my boyfriend Robert and blinked. "It's my birthday. You know how much I *love* my birthday."

Robert slid his gaze around as if terrified I was going to make a scene. And why shouldn't I? We were at the bar. All my friends were inside. It was my birthday and he was trying to weasel out of it.

"Look, it's not that I don't want to celebrate your birthday. And I swear to God I will make it up to you, but I do have to work. King Cassius has a lead on the crown prince. I need to go to Barbados tonight. I'll be back in the morning. And we'll do this tomorrow, just you and me."

I tried not to let my anger simmer over. How many times had he cancelled something with our friends, or my friends, in *favor* of doing something with just the two of us? It was almost as if he were embarrassed to be seen with me. But that couldn't be true because he always took me around his parents and his friends. It was just *my* friends he didn't want to be around.

"You can't keep doing this to me. You're always backing out on things that are important to me. But if it's your favorite football team, God help me if I'm not right there next to you between your father and your brother watching as a family, and that's a first game match. This is my *birthday*."

He frowned. "You know how seriously my family takes its football."

"You don't even *like* football." I threw up my hands. This had to be a joke. This couldn't be real. He was not trying to abandon me on my birthday. "Robert, tell me this is a joke. That you've cooked up some elaborate ruse with Ariel and Michael to surprise me or something."

He frowned and looked at me as if I had three heads. As if such a thought would never have even occurred to him. "But I don't like surprises."

Oh God, why was I dating him again?

"See, here's the thing, it's not about *you*. It would be a nice surprise for *me*. *I* like surprises. I like any time that my boyfriend shows me he cares about me. It's a nice thing to do."

"Penelope, you're being absurd. Look, today or tomorrow, it doesn't matter. I'll see you tomorrow, you know, on your *actual* birthday. Right now, duty calls. You should know about duty. You're a member of the Royal Guard too. You know how important finding the prince is."

I tipped my chin up to glare at him. "Something tells me you volunteered for this particular duty. Anything so you wouldn't have to spend time with me." I shook my head. "I'm starting to think that maybe you and I together isn't going to work out."

The words left my mouth dry like sawdust, but lately it had just felt like a lot of work trying to keep us together. Robert had been a part of my family unit for years. He'd just always been around as my brother's best friend. He was handsome, smart, and a Royal Guard. My parents respected him, and my brother adored him.

And he was good-looking.

He'd started showing interest in me. Finally, after years of crushing on him, he liked me back. It was like something about going to university had changed me. Oh yeah, I'd grown breasts. So that was helpful. I'd thought everything would be perfect.

But it wasn't. For starters, he never actually seemed to want to have sex with me. It was just bogus. Such bullshit. Why was I the one begging for sex?

It wasn't that I didn't want all those things. Marriage, kids, raising another generation of the Royal Guard … and, well, orgasms. I would actually like some non-self-administered ones again though.

Ariel always made a face about that, as if there was something wrong with him. But I thought it was great. He had conviction. That was one of the things that drew me to him. He took his work seriously. He took his family seriously. He took everything seriously.

Except for our relationship.

Robert's eyes went wide. "Penny, you know you don't mean that. You know how I feel about you. Don't do this because you're being childish."

The thing was, I wanted to do just that. Let my anger take over. Scream, and wail, and throw things. But that would have been conduct unbecoming of a lady, let alone conduct unbecoming of a Royal Guard. My parents would have flipped.

"I don't know what I'm supposed to do because it feels like you don't make me a priority."

For the first time, he looked panicked, like I'd finally gotten through to him. "This is important right now, but not more important than you, okay? The unit leaves in an hour. As soon as I'm back I'll come find you, okay?"

I didn't really have a choice, did I? He had been given orders, and my being pissed about it wasn't going to change anything. "Yeah, I mean if you have to go, you have to go."

"Look, we'll talk tomorrow, okay? I'll pick you up and we'll do something all day that you adore. You call the shots. Anything you want."

"You don't get it, do you? I want *you* to think about all the things that I love and plan it all out."

His brows furrowed as if I'd started speaking Greek. "I don't—"

I shook my head at Ariel when I saw her drive up to the bar and climb out of her Fiat. She gave me a big wave until she saw who I was talking to. Then she marched over like she was on a war path.

We'd always had each other's backs since school. For her, things weren't always great at home, so my house had become a sanctuary. She always said, my house was how she pictured a real home. I knew she didn't always want to go home, thanks to things with her folks, so I had her over as often as possible.

And well, she was loyal to a fault. If she had her way, she'd start a fight with Robert and knock his ass out just to protect my feelings from his assholery. But that's not what I wanted. What I wanted was for everyone to be happy to celebrate my birthday.

But you don't always get what you want. "Go. Do what you need to do. I guess I'll see you tomorrow."

Robert leaned over and brushed a kiss on my cheek. "I really am sorry."

"Yeah, I hear you."

Ariel bounded over. "Why did that look so intense? Please tell me it was because he got you the wrong present and not because he disappointed you again."

I was always comforted by having her near. We'd had each other's backs since we were six and Jamison Briggart made it a point to steal our plantain chips every snack time. Alone we cried, but together we stood up to him. We'd been besties ever since.

I wrapped my arm around her and let her squeeze me tight despite her deceptively petite frame. "Yeah, I've always been a shitty liar, so I can't tell you what you want to hear. And I just had a really long day."

"You don't need him. You have me, and half the Royal Guard

is inside. So we're going to let the cute boys buy us drinks until you forget your problems, okay?"

I loved her. Tonight, we'd celebrate. Tomorrow, I'd face the music. "Sounds like a plan."

I tried not to look back at the retreating form of my boyfriend. Was there something wrong with me? Was there a reason why I couldn't have my own prince charming? I mean, he was perfect, wasn't he? So why wasn't I awesome enough for him?

Ariel snapped her fingers in front of my face. "Hey, don't let him do this to you. You are awesome. Now, let's get a drink. We'll do a lot of shots, dance on the tables, and let the cutest members of the guard flirt with you. We'll celebrate your twenty-second birthday. Sound good?"

I gave her a determined nod even though I wasn't feeling it. "Yep, sounds good."

3

PENNY ...

I'D SET out last night to drink my troubles away...and I had. Now a couple of elephants were trying out aggressive sexual positions in my skull. But forgetting about my troubles for a night... #worthit.

I reluctantly left Ariel's in the morning and took the quarter-mile pathway from my friend's up to my parents' place. The sun beat down on my face, trying to make me atone for every single shot last night with its rays.

The grounds just below the palace were massive, sporting more than twelve gardens and the accommodations for the Royal Guard.

A series of interconnected walkways linked the fifty or so accommodations that were actually on palace grounds. The lesser guards lived off-property and commuted in daily.

I had lived on these grounds since I was little because of my father's position. *And you fucked up his whole career by saying no.*

I opened the door to my parents' place and searched for my mother. I didn't find her, though. Instead, as I wound my way through the living room into the kitchen, I found my wayward boyfriend. Robert was pushing my brother up against the sink and shoving his hands into his hair.

All I could do was stand and stare as their lips crashed together.

As my stomach plummeted, all I knew was that Robert had never kissed me like that. When they parted, their lips swollen and their breathing harsh and choppy, Michael's gaze lifted and met mine.

PENNY ...

I wasn't sure how long I stood in my bedroom, frozen numb in shock, but in the distance I could hear my brother's voice. I could hear the pounding on my door. Hell, I didn't even know how I'd gotten there.

I didn't know how long it was before I snapped out of it. But when I did, I used my door to the back patio and was out the back gate in seconds.

I didn't think I consciously knew where I was going I just knew I had to get out of there. I took the winding path up to the stairs that led to the palace.

I had taken this route so many times. Maybe several thousand times throughout my life.

My leaden steps took me past the Rose Courtyard. I'd played in this courtyard so many times, teasing the koi in the pond, even though I knew I shouldn't. This was my home, but it didn't feel that way right now as the fog of confusion and betrayal brought on a swirling nausea.

Yes, I'd left to go to university. I couldn't believe it when my father had let me go to the Chicago Institute of Art. But I had a feeling that was my mother's doing. My last chance at fun before I had to return home and take on the family's mantle: *Royal Guard*. That was the only time I'd ever been away from home. And it terrified me. Just like now. But after what I'd just witnessed ... I couldn't stay.

"Well, well, if it isn't the favorite pet's street urchin."

I rolled my eyes and ignored him. Prince Ashton was a grade A asshole. He'd forever tortured me when we were children. Once, he'd locked me in a closet during a game of hide-and-seek. No one had found me for hours. I'd never been so terrified.

It was finally Prince Sebastian who found me and let me out. I was so relieved I forgot myself and hugged him fiercely. I still remembered how he hugged me back, tentatively at first and then tightly. I was sobbing hysterically because well, I'd been locked in a closet, convinced I was going to die in there. My voice was hoarse from all the screaming for someone to let me out.

Sebastian had soothed me, stroked my back, and told me he was going to make Ashton pay. He'd promised me his cousin would never hurt me again as long as he was around. I'd felt safe in his arms. It was so against all the protocols in every book. Sebastian was a royal. It wasn't proper to hug him like that. But I'd been a terrified little girl who had been rescued. As far as I was concerned, he was every fairytale prince rolled into one.

I wasn't sure what had happened, but Ashton had never bothered me again. Though, unlike Sebastian, Ashton hadn't been shipped off to boarding school at age eleven. He'd gone to a prestigious private school on the island, but it still wasn't as good as Eton. Even his brother Aidan went to Eton. He'd gone off to university in the UK and come home three years ago showing all his royal asshole colors. "Is there something you need, Your Highness?"

Prince Ashton leered at me. "Yes. You, on your knees, with that pretty mouth of yours around my dick."

I didn't even break stride. This was not the first time he'd made some lewd suggestion. I knew he wouldn't dare carry it out because at the end of the day, he was a coward. And he knew that if he touched me, my father would have his hide, prince or not. "It's nice to dream."

"You know what? One of these days, you *are* going to suck my dick."

I laughed. "And I see we've gone from dreams to delusions. As always, not nice to see you, Ashton."

"You forgot to call me, Your Highness."

"You mean Your Dickhead Highness, right?"

I easily sidestepped him. He was no better than a schoolyard bully. When I reached the king's office, I could hear my father and the king inside. My palms were sweaty as I wiped them on my pants. *Are you sure this is a good idea?*

Good idea or not, I was doing this. Now or never. I knocked softly, and from inside the king called, "Come in."

Pushing the door open, I took a deep breath.

My father's eyes went wide. "Penny, is something the matter?"

"No. Everything's fine." I shifted my gaze to the king. "Your Majesty, I apologize for my earlier departure. I've had some time to think about it, and I'll do it. When do I start?"

PENNY ...

THE KING NODDED a dismissal to my father, who narrowed his gaze at me. I'd be in for an earful later.

Once my father was gone, King Cassius spoke. "Your life is your own. I know you were probably terrified when you walked out of here and said no. But honestly, that is exactly the reason I want you for this job."

I licked my lips nervously. "Your Majesty, if you don't mind me saying, I'm a terrible King's Guard. You know what happened with the duke, of course."

His lips twitched. "The Duke of Essex is an ass."

My mouth dropped open. "Your Majesty?"

The king laughed, and I didn't know if I'd ever seen him so candid before. "It's true. You didn't do anything wrong. Hell, you probably saved his life. Of course, outside of these doors, I can never say that. But it was the most entertainment I had all night."

I flushed. "Noted, Your Majesty."

He sobered. "Listen, I know what I'm asking you to do is difficult. But I need someone who can tell Sebastian no. I need someone who isn't *afraid* to stand up to him. I need someone who can actually bring him home."

"How?" I didn't understand.

"Look, I won't send you alone. You can select one person from the Royal Guard to go with you. I know he'll be difficult. But if he suspects at all who you are, he'll bolt. And it's been hard enough trying to locate him. My understanding is you played together when you were children but you haven't seen him in some time. So to him, you would just be a girl that he is meeting for the first time."

I frowned. "I understand, Your Majesty. But—" I sighed. "May I speak freely?"

He nodded. "You're free to speak your mind."

I inhaled deeply. "Okay. Can I ask why? Why do you need *me* to go after him? Why not just ask him to come home?"

"Because Sebastian is going to earn his grandfather's Regents Council votes on his twenty-sixth birthday. He will have the most powerful voting seat on the council. And right now, his life is in danger."

I frowned. "Are you sure?" My heart thudded against my ribs. *In danger?* Just what the hell was I walking into?

"Yes, I'm sure. I'm also sure someone will make an attempt on his life. So, Penelope, I need you. And Sebastian can never know who you are. Because I'm afraid if he does, he will put himself in more danger."

I swallowed hard. I knew what I had to do. "In that case, I know just the person to take with me."

SEBASTIAN ...

"Your Majesty, you have to forgive me. I wasn't informed that you were coming to town." Noah Blake glanced over my shoulder and frowned. "I would have set up security protocols. You don't seem to have a Royal Guard with you."

I shrugged. "No one knows I'm here. You may have seen the reports of me partying it up everywhere. Doubles. I needed to be a little incognito. I need help finding someone."

Noah frowned.

Over the years, I'd learned to respect Noah Blake. When I started at the university, my father had hired a different security company. They were competent, but old guard, old school. They didn't understand that I needed more freedom of movement. So, eventually, my father switched to Blake Security. At that time, Noah and his crew were untested; his company just started. But they had been good. They kept me out of trouble for the most part. I only managed to give them the slip once or twice. And that was because there were only two of them at the time and they didn't have enough coverage. I'd never managed it again, though.

"Who do you think *we* can find that *you* don't already have the resources to find?"

I sighed. This was where things got delicate. "His name is

Lucas Newsome. I've spent the last six months tracking him down. I've managed to track him from Mexico City to here, but my other resource is tapped out. They can't find him. I was hoping you could be of service. I know you've got a hacker on the payroll. I'm sure just a quick tap to the keys and I'll be on my way."

Noah rubbed his jaw and leaned back in his chair. "Your Majesty, of course we're happy to assist. And as you have us on retainer, it's not a problem. But I'm concerned about your … stealthy arrival. How long have you been with no guard? Do you have a death wish?"

I laughed. "Is someone trying to kill me?"

Noah frowned. "No, that's not what I meant, but you're royalty. Do you know how much you're worth?"

I shrugged. "None of that matters right now. I just need help finding this kid. Can you do it or not?"

"Yeah, of course, I can do it. Who is this kid to you?"

"I thought one of Blake Security's cornerstones was discretion."

"It is." Noah nodded. "But, as I told your father, I don't do anything blindly. I went down that path once. I'm not one of those guys who you can get to do some dirty work and then ask questions later. Integrity is our cornerstone too. So I have to point out things like the Crown Prince of Winston Isles running around without Royal Guards, looking like an American civilian to boot. It looks like you're hiding. Are you hiding? Is there something you're not telling me?"

And that was the problem with Noah Blake. He was too astute. From what I'd gleaned from Dad, he was a former special operations guy. Black Ops stuff, the kind of stuff that nobody wanted to acknowledge. He was technically on the Winston Isles' retainer, so he worked for me. "Since you're on retainer, and you signed the nondisclosure, I can tell you. He's my brother. I need to find him."

Noah's jaw dropped. "Excuse me?"

I rolled my eyes. "I know I didn't stutter. *Brother*..." I said more slowly. "I need to find him."

The muscle in Noah's jaw worked. "We'll find him, but allow us to at least put a guard on you. I wouldn't be doing my job if I didn't suggest it at the very least."

"No, no guard. This way I'm able to walk around freely. And honestly, no one has recognized me because I'm just walking around the street like a normal person. No one cares. Right now I'm just Sebastian Westmore, and I kind of like it. Haven't you ever needed to disappear and not be you for a minute?"

"I guess I have."

"Not to mention, there are people who don't want me to find Lucas. All the more reason I need to. So what will it be? Will you help me or will you not?"

Noah sighed. "We'll do it. And for what it's worth, I don't think you're trying to do anything to the kid, but I'm still concerned. I get what you're saying. You want to blend. Fine. I have guys that can blend. All-American-hero types. They'll play your best friends. Just let me get those set up—"

I shook my head. "No. If I wanted a guard, I would have brought one with me. I need to do this unencumbered, which means I may get an occasional scrape or two. I don't want your guys or Royal Guards getting caught in the crossfire, or messing up my chances. This is important."

"Fine. Since you've gone back to the Sebastian Westmore name does that mean you'll be working at the old bar? Are you sure there is nothing you need?"

I trusted Noah. If he wanted to rat me out to my father, he could. But I was hoping I'd be able to buy a little time. "I appreciate it, but no. I'm doing this on my own. And yeah, I'll be taking up my old job at the bar."

Noah nodded. "Okay, fine. Do you need a place to stay? We have some great safe houses—"

I shook my head. "No safe houses. Not to worry. I have a place to stay." I stood and extended my hand. "Thank you for your help."

"You're welcome. But I wish you'd tell me what the hell is going on."

"I can't. There's too much at stake."

Penny...

"CAN you help me understand what's happening right now?"

I sighed. I knew my mother would have questions. She wasn't blind. She could see how unhappy I was as a Queen's Guard. "Mom, this is a request from the king. I have to go."

She narrowed her gaze at me. "The hell you do. Just tell me what's happening. Is your father making you do this?"

She knew as well as I did that my father would never force my hand. But he made it plain how proud he was that both his children served at the pleasure of His Majesty. "This has nothing to do with Dad. I want to do this. I think I need a change of scenery."

"Is this because Robert didn't show for your birthday? You're running?"

No. It's because Robert was kissing my brother. The betrayal twisted deep. But as pissed off as I was with Michael, I wouldn't out my brother. I needed some distance before I could even think about him again. "This has nothing to do with Robert. I was just thinking it was time I lean into this job more. I haven't really given it my all."

I had. I'd just been bad at it. My mother wasn't buying that line of bullshit either. "Penny, you don't have to do this to try and make us proud. We already *are* proud."

I finally gave up and told her what I thought would make her back off because, damn it, I needed to pack. "When His Majesty first asked me, I thought I might be doing it for the wrong reasons too. That's why I said no."

Her eyes bugged. "You said what?"

I avoided her gaze. "In my defense, I was nervous. And there he was, the king, asking me for a favor. One, I might add, that I didn't think I could carry out. I don't know what happened, because I was going to say 'yes, of course I'll figure it out,' but instead out came 'no.' Then I left without waiting to be dismissed. I was sure there was a beheading in my future."

My mother chewed her nail. "So you said no. We'll address that little issue later. Then you said yes. What changed your mind? And you can cut the crap about wanting to lean into the job."

I sighed then stopped packing to face her. Her shrewd, hazel eyes bored into me. I could see her assessing every inch of my face, trying to determine what was up with me.

"Okay, the truth is … It's not working out with Robert. I've needed to figure out my life for a while, and this is a good opportunity at a good time. I'll have Ariel with me, and it's pretty much a babysitting job. I need this right now."

For a moment I thought she would stop me. I thought she would see me for what I was: a liar. But she didn't.

"Oh honey, I know how heartbreak can be. But I never saw him as right for you anyway. Yes, he's part of the family, but I never saw him as right for *you*. Besides, he's not the kind of guy to give a girl multiple Os. And every woman deserves that."

The giggle escaped before I could stop it. My mother was outrageous, and it was best not to encourage her. Mom still looked radiant, and her cocoa skin gleamed in the sunlight that was pouring into my bedroom. Her wide, dark eyes were often full of mischief. I'm pretty sure it's why my father loved her so much. She was the perfect foil to his always-serious demeanor.

"Mom!"

She shrugged innocently. "What? It's the truth. And also he can be an asshole. So there's that."

My mouth hung open.

"Like I didn't know he opted out of your birthday?" She rolled her eyes. "He never did deserve you. Besides, you can't be in a relationship where you have to direct the other person on basics. Imagine that in bed. 'To the left, to the left!' Sex is not a Beyoncé song. Unless it's 'Drunk in Love.' That's different."

Oh my God. Ground, swallow me up now. She was impossible. But as always after five minutes with my mother, I felt better ... lighter.

There was a knock at the door, and she answered before I could. It was Michael, and he froze in the doorway when he saw my mother. "Oh, Penny, I didn't realize you were in here with Mom."

What he wanted to know was if I'd told her or not. I'd never hated my brother more. And considering I'd spent most of my childhood and adolescence being insanely jealous of him for how much better than me he was at everything that was saying something. "Well, I am. What do you need?"

His eyes settled on me and shifted quickly. Yeah well, if I'd been caught kissing his boyfriend, I'd be embarrassed too. His gaze finally landed on my suitcase. "Are you going somewhere?"

"Yep." Let him and his new boy toy speculate.

But my mother was too helpful. "Your father has given her an assignment."

His eyes went wide. "Dad has a job for *you*? This is a joke right? I mean I love you, but you're not exactly the best Royal Guard."

I pinned my brother with a glare. He wasn't wrong. "You can go."

He looked like he might refuse for a minute but then left.

Mom sighed. "I wish you two got along better."

He was my big brother. I used to adore him, but now I didn't know what I felt. "Yeah, understatement of the year. I'm sure he's on his way to talk to Dad and expound on my many shortcomings in an effort to have me removed from this job."

My mother sighed. "We are all proud of you, Penny."

"You're sure Dad is? Because earlier today he couldn't remind me more times to not screw up in front of the king."

"You only disappoint your father if you don't try. He's proud of you. He loves you."

"The love, I believe; the being proud of me, not so much. Even as he walked me to the office he told me not to mess it up."

Mother cursed under her breath. "I swear that man. He makes my life more difficult every day. No matter what he says, he loves you and he *does* believe in you. He just doesn't know how to articulate that properly."

Mom took a deep breath. "Sweetheart, look at it like this. This is your opportunity to break out. You can write your own ticket. I know that the confines of a palace life, the etiquette, and the rules, they chafe at you. You've never liked them. You wanted to run around the palace barefooted. You've always danced to the beat of your own drummer. So, who better to take on a specialized job like this? You can protect the prince. I know you can."

I lifted my lashes and met my mother's gaze, so like my own. "It's not protecting him that I think will be the problem, it's the getting close to him. Getting him to talk to me. To listen to me about coming home. That's the other part of the job that the king commands."

Her mother grinned. "Talking has never been a problem for you, my darling. I'm pretty sure you came out of the womb talking a mile a minute and asking questions about everything and nothing. I think you can handle that part."

"But you're always telling me to try and be meeker. Talk less. Listen more. Not be so crazy."

"And I fear that I've shoved you into a box that you didn't really belong in. I think that all you need to do is be *you*. That's how the prince will trust you. If all else fails, flash him."

"Mom!"

"Oh my God, I'm kidding. Relax. Have fun with this. Show everyone what you're made of."

I just hoped she was right and I wasn't making the biggest mistake of my life.

6

PENNY ...

"Mr. Blake, thank you for seeing us. As I'm sure King Cassius told you, we've been trying to track down the crown prince for several months. The last intel we have said he was here. It seems we need a little help." I tried to remember everything my father ever said about speaking to intimidating people. *Look them in the eye. Do not waver.* Too bad Dad didn't tell me what to do when they were hot *and* intimidating. "Thanks to you, we know exactly where he is. But we want to make sure that he doesn't get wind that we're here, so we might need some assistance."

Noah Blake watched me carefully, and then his gaze skimmed over Ariel. He was shrewd, watchful, and hot as hell. "The prince came to see me. Imagine my surprise when he came without any Royal Guard."

"Did you assign someone to watch him?"

Noah shook his head. "I strongly suggested he needed that, but he declined."

I sagged in relief. "Thank God."

He frowned. "Thank God? You realize that you're *supposed* to be concerned about his safety?"

"Yes, I realize that. More importantly, my assignment from

King Cassius is to bring him home. If he catches one of your goons watching him, he'll be in the wind."

The big, blond Viking guy leaned forward. "I'd hardly be called a goon. The suit is Armani." He inclined his head towards the dark-haired, good-looking one behind the laptop. "Him? Totally a goon. DeMarco over there—" He indicated one of the men to Ariel's right. "—absolutely a goon." He shrugged. "Me, not so much. I'm too good looking."

I blinked. He was right. No way this golden god was a goon. "Sorry." I was fucking this up. My first assignment and of course, I was a dumb ass, a screw up. Ariel knocked her knee to mine, and I took a deep breath. "That's not what I meant. As you know, the crown prince is notorious for slipping his guard. Except this time, he's been gone for six months. King Cassius wants me to bring him home. If Sebastian even so much as catches wind that we're watching him, he'll bolt."

Noah leaned forward. "I'm starting to understand why the King picked you to come for him."

I tilted my chin up and glared. "Because I'm good at my job?"

He grinned. "Sure. I've met the King. He never would have hired you if you weren't. But also, you're determined. And you don't scare easily. Also, the prince has a soft spot for beautiful women, so it makes sense to send you. Prince Sebastian was here, obviously. He just wanted assistance in finding someone. He wasn't interested in our security services."

"Well, Prince Sebastian isn't in charge here. Until he is king, he doesn't call the shots. King Cassius does. And he was clear. No bodyguards: just me, Ariel, and our wits. But if you can help me in any way in finding him and keeping him safe, we're happy to have it. We'll need to work out some kind of discreet rotating tail."

"We'll give you what you need. Since there are only two of you, maybe you'll allow me to use two of my guys." He put his hand up before I could even protest. "They're young, like college kids. They blend easily and will serve as surveillance *only*, unless you need more. They'll hang back and stay out of your way. You probably won't even know they're there. Does that sound like something you can agree to?"

I studied him for a moment then slid my gaze around to the rest of the men in the conference room. Next to me, I could feel the heat of Ariel's gaze. *Shit.* I knew that we'd need the help. There were only two of us, and we could only watch him so often. "I think rotating in your men is a good idea, so we can, you know ... sleep. We'll discuss the schedule with you."

Noah nodded. "As you wish."

Oskar Mueller, the big, blond guy, flashed a devastating smile, and Ariel clasped a hand on my leg and squeezed tightly.

Yeah girl. I feel you. Jesus Christ, that one was dangerous. Even *my* stomach fluttered a little bit.

Noah took his seat. "So, I'm to understand that you don't want Blake Security running point on this?"

"That's correct."

"And you don't need the tactical assist?"

"I am more than proficient with a hand gun. I think I can hold my own tactically."

Noah blinked. And then he nodded his head. "Okay then. Then what else can we help you with? The Winston Isles have us on retainer. Whatever you need, we'll provide."

Ariel leaned back. "For starters, I need to piggyback on your system. I know that you piggyback off super-secret satellites and I want access."

Matthias angled his head as if looking at her for the first time. "It's a closed system. You won't be able to —"

Ariel smirked. "Check. I'm already in."

Matthias frowned and glared at her, then start typing furiously.

A low string of curses fell out of his mouth, and Ariel grinned. "It's a lot easier if you give me access as opposed to me taking it."

The guys glanced between Noah and Ariel and back to Noah again.

Noah nodded. "If you're that good, are you sure you need us?"

Ariel shrugged. "Yes. We do. Like you said, there are only two of us."

Noah grinned. "You know what? The two of you apparently have balls of steel." He nodded at Ariel. "And you have some serious skills if you can keep Matthias on his toes. Awesome. If you are looking for a job outside of the Winston Isles, I'm willing to give it to you."

I squared my shoulders. "Thank you. But we'll be sticking with our employer for the time being."

"Anytime you change your mind, I think we can use some fresh blood in here."

Penny ...

I SHIFTED the curtains aside and stared at the apartment across the street.

"You know, someone will call the cops because they see you peeping out like a crazy person." I slanted Ariel a little smirk before I went right back to staring. Tomorrow was my official *move-in day*. We'd been lucky that Blake Security had checked the IDs Sebastian had used when he went to university in the States.

Sebastian *Westmore* lived across the street.

I needed to start recon on the Prince. Part of me still wasn't sure this was the best idea I'd ever had, but right now, there was only the one option. If I wanted to make my parents proud of me, I had to prove that I could do this mission. After all, how many times did the king personally send anyone on a mission? "I'm not being a creepy stalker. I am keeping an eye on the place. Seeing what exits I can see from here. Seeing how well covered I'll be by you."

"You can relax. I'll have you covered. Between the mic, the cameras I've already tapped into for the front and the back of the building and your hallway, I'll see anyone going in and out anywhere near you and the prince. Not to mention, you hardly need back up." Ariel nodded encouragingly.

"You're kidding, right? I am Calamity Jane. Calamity Penny in this case. I'm a walking, talking disaster."

"Well, I don't believe that. Apparently, neither does the king. Otherwise he wouldn't have sent you. And clearly, he thinks you can handle yourself because he asked you to protect the prince."

I turned and sat on the windowsill. "Yeah well, I've got a theory about that."

Ariel chuckled, leaning back in her desk chair. "This I've got to hear."

"Well," I started, crossing my arms. "First of all, the prince hardly needs a security detail. Just like all the men in the royal family, he spent two years in the Winston Isles Guard as a soldier. You and I have both been through the training. Worst-case scenario, he knows how to take care of himself. Plus, we're both well aware of his reputation for fighting and getting in trouble before he went to uni."

Ariel rolled her eyes. "Yes, he has *some* skills. In a bar fight, and maybe even in some short-term, hand-to-hand combat. But tactical?" Ariel held up her hands. "Okay yes, I'll concede he did get some strategy training. After all, he's the prince, and at the end of the day, he commands the military. But for detailed, tactical work, he needs experts."

"Fair enough. But hear me out. I'm a disaster. Of course I can shoot, when I don't have an actual target coming at me. I'm decent at hand-to-hand. But let's face it, if I had an opponent that had thirty pounds on me and was as well-trained as I was, I'd be toast. And if the prince is in danger like his father says, I'm the last one anyone wants to send after him. I have a feeling the boys at Blake Security are already on the case. Probably have been for weeks. But they can't get close enough."

Ariel conceded slightly. "Yes, I do think that the king possibly wants to use you because you're a woman. But you need to look at it like you're the secret weapon. And you have to show Noah and the super alphas over there what they don't have."

I inclined my head. "An ounce of fat?"

Ariel grinned. "Me."

I returned her smile with genuine enthusiasm. "That's right. I do. And the two of us together, we make one hell of a team. God, I loved the look on Matthias's face when you told him you were already in the system. That was freaking priceless."

Ariel said. "I'll tell you now, it wasn't easy. And to be honest, I had just barely breached. I slipped in like the thinnest of tapeworms. And his systems were already on the lookout for me. It was mostly luck. And he happened to notice that I was there just at the right time. I let myself get caught and asked for permission nicely. His systems would have kicked me out eventually anyway, and then it would be next to impossible for me to get in. He's that good."

"Yeah, let's not tell them that."

"Nope, we sure won't. So did the pep talk suffice?"

"You mean am I ready to engage in my somewhat open-ended mission to keep the Crown Prince of Winston Isles safe from harm?"

"Yeah, that."

I shrugged. "Yeah, sure thing. Never mind that I have absolutely no idea how to do that."

"Lucky for you, I do. And it starts with getting you closer to him."

I pursed my lips. Ariel seemed far too chipper about the prospect. "Something tells me I'm not going to like this."

Ariel placed a finger over my lips. "Shhh, just let it happen. Best if you don't know what I have planned."

7

PENNY ...

"YOU'RE sure this is the path you want to take?"

I set my drink down and studied Ariel over the rim of my glass. "Well, I don't have many options. I think the lonely, stranded neighbor who wants to be his friend will actually work."

Ariel rolled her eyes. "Am I the only one who's going to point out the obvious?"

"What's that?"

Ariel groaned and shifted on her seat. "Look, you're cute. The prince is smokin' hot. Ergo, you need to use your assets to bag— er, I mean, *protect* the prince. How is it that you haven't even thought of this yet?"

I glared at her. "I haven't thought of this yet because it's not what I intend to do. I'm a professional. I don't have to sleep with him to get close to him. I want to use the whole like-friends thing. I mean, I'm sure as a prince he's had more than a few women trying to get close to him. Trying to sleep with him is the easy part. Trying to get him to *talk* to me, now that will be difficult. And it will be maybe *more* difficult if I'm doing it naked. I personally think this is the better angle."

"I have to disagree. Do you know how many men get caught all because they were having sexy pillow chat with their new girlfriend? All kinds of criminals. Men tell women who they're sleeping with all kinds of things. Their guard is down. They've just had an orgasm. No blood in their brains. It's the perfect opportunity for you to slide in and plant your little seeds. Like, 'Hey, wouldn't it be great if you went home to this island I know nothing about?'"

I couldn't say she didn't have a point. Hell, I'd considered it. And to be perfectly frank, that's what I thought the king was asking of me. You know, 'Hey, go to America and date my son. Not for real of course, but just to get him to come home.' But as the king hadn't come right out and said that, I couldn't make any assumptions. "I get what you're saying, and it would be easy. But hello, you don't even know if I'm his type … which I doubt."

We both slid our glances over to Sebastian as he worked the bar. A number of women had made their approaches to him, clearly flirting, writing things on napkins and sliding them over to him, but he ignored them all. For the last hour and a half since we'd posted up at the bar, he'd been legitimately working. Which, I couldn't understand. He was the bloody crown prince. He didn't have to work. So what was he doing here in a bar in the middle of the Village?

Slumming it?

But why? "I mean look at him. Do you see how many women have made their approach? He's clearly not interested. And the crown prince we know would have been all over that. If I come on too strong like those women, I'm going to blow the whole operation. I will be on a plane back home having failed. Which, might I remind you, is not an option. So friends it is."

Ariel rolled her eyes. "Fine, we'll do it your way. I still say a little skin wouldn't hurt anybody."

"You're so interested in showing skin, why don't you show your skin? Nothing about the rules that were given says you can't be the one to talk Sebastian into going home. You're cute. You can do it." Suddenly the idea sounded more appealing. That would mean that I could go back to being normal and deal with my

Robert-and-Michael situation. My stomach twisted just thinking about it. Michael was my brother. That hurt more than the shit with Robert had. There had always been a part of me that knew Robert maybe wasn't the right guy. But Michael, he was my brother. He was supposed to love and protect me always.

But that's not the kind of relationship you have.

"Um, no. Besides, we already agreed. I need to stay out of sight. There's an off chance he's seen me before. I did some military training ops with him. Not directly on his team, but it's entirely possible he might remember having seen me from somewhere. And we don't need any of that, 'Hey, haven't I seen you somewhere before?' kind of conversation. Not when this op is strictly need-to-know on the clandestine tip."

"Yeah, okay. You have a point. But I'm still not going to use the whole sex-him-up angle. It's not even my thing."

"Penny, your thing right now is adorable, and klutzy, and also hot. We need to work all those angles, especially the hot part."

I still shook my head. "Nope. That's not going to happen. At least not until we try it my way first. If it doesn't work, fine. Then I'll put on some sexy heels and beg him to fuck me. Sound good?"

Ariel laughed. "Now you're talking."

I frowned as Sebastian kept checking the pool table in the far corner.

Ariel turned around to check out what he was staring at. "That guy has been with that group for an hour now. Could they have caught on he's hustling them?"

"I don't know. But if they do, it's going to turn nasty." I turned my attention back to Sebastian. The way he was looking over there, I had the feeling he knew what that hustler was up to. And God help us if Sebastian planned to stop them because then *we'd* have to stop him. "Do you see what I'm seeing?"

I could see Ariel nod on my peripheral vision. "The crown prince about to put himself in harm's way? Yeah, I see it. He's about to break up those shenanigans by the pool table. So do we break it up first?"

One of the guys sank the eight ball, swore loudly, and then banged his pool cue on the floor. The guy who had been hustling them was really good looking. Tall. Lean. He looked like a soccer player with just enough scruff on his chin to make him a little bit edgy.

He was sexy. Objectively speaking, I could see the appeal. The problem was he was a flirt. He'd been flirting with one of the girls by the table. And as it turned out, she was the girlfriend of the guy he was playing. So that clearly wasn't going to end well. Next to me, Ariel groaned. "Oh no, he's going to do it. Do you want the little guy on the left, or the big guy on the right?"

"Oh, this time you're giving *me* a choice? I'll take the big guy."

"Just because I'm five foot two doesn't mean I should always get the little guy." She had a point. She might be little, but in hand-to-hand combat, Ariel was badass. But even though I knew better, I still wanted to protect her. Though technically, she was here to watch *my* ass.

The good looking guy leaned over and gave the girl a kiss on the cheek. The guy he'd been playing cursed mildly, and Ariel groaned as she pushed to her feet. "Looks like we're on."

I groaned too, because just as we stood, Sebastian hurled himself over the bar. We were in for a night of trouble.

Sebastian ...

THAT WAS HIM.

It had to be him. I hoped Blake Security had given me the right guy. Who was I kidding? They never got it wrong. I made an approach, looking for signs of my father in the kid. But I didn't see any. Maybe he looked like his mother?

Even after nearly six months, it still tripped me up to think that I had siblings. And that for years my father had been lying to me. That was the part that stung the most; the years of condemnation and looking down on me when after all, the apple didn't fall far from the tree.

When I left the Winston Isles six months ago, I didn't take much with me. Just the money I had in my personal accounts, some clothes, and a few books. Overnight I'd gone from a prince who had everything to a pauper who had nothing.

That is of your own doing. Yeah, it was. I didn't want anything my father had to give. So I gave all my credit cards and access to my royal accounts to the two doubles that had often been employed to help keep me safe.

They had only one directive now though: to keep the Royal Guard as far away from me as possible. They had carte blanche to sleep with as many women as possible, to party as much as they wanted, and to spend the royal coffers.

And from what I could see in the papers, they were making one hell of a show of it too. Good for them. Someone should enjoy it. As soon as I arrived in New York, I'd gotten my old job back. Thanks to my time spent at uni, I had a social security number.

The stab of pain I felt in my chest whenever I thought of Dad burned. My whole life, my father had been this paragon of virtue. I knew I would never live up to him, but it didn't hurt to believe that it was *possible* to become that man. My whole life, I had thought him a good king, a good man. Someone who loved deeply and cared about his people. How could that man abandon two children? How could that man cheat on his wife?

Thanks to Blake Security, I'd found my brother. My sister was proving a little more elusive, but they'd find her eventually. I knew if push came to shove, I could always call my father and ask where she was located.

I knew when I was done in New York my next stop would be her, wherever she was. The vote was scheduled in six weeks though, so I didn't have a lot of time. But at that moment, it looked like my brother might need me. I watched from behind the bar as the dark-haired guy in the corner played pool.

Then he leaned over and grabbed the brunette next to him,

planting a sloppy kiss on her cheek. She giggled but shoved him away. Then her boyfriend stepped in.

Shit. This was going to get ugly quick. I looked over at the other bartender, Jason. "You mind covering? I have a feeling I need to break this up."

Jason eyed me up and down as if doubting my ability to kick ass. But when it came down to it, I knew how to handle myself. Granted, that was mostly from years of anti-kidnapping training, but I wasn't planning to disclose that to Jason.

In a blink, I was up and over the bar, narrowly avoiding the drinkers with their craft cocktails and peanut butter-flavored beer. In a few strides, I was at the back of the bar. The boyfriend was big, tatted, and looked pissed, but he wasn't moving like someone who knew what the fuck he was doing. So, bonus points.

He got up into Lucas's face. "Did you just fucking kiss my girlfriend?"

Lucas gave a shit-eating grin. "Not the kind of kiss she wanted."

Aaand it was on. The guy made a wild swing, which Lucas ducked easily, and then he punched the bigger guy in the gut. I cursed under my breath, even as I jumped into the melee. "Take this shit outside."

The tatted guy was more than happy to oblige. He took Lucas by the collar and practically lifted my brother off his feet, tossing him at the nearest exit. The problem was, while Lucas might have been able to handle the guy on his own, three of the idiot's friends followed. The girlfriend too. Though I wasn't sure exactly what she would be doing to help the situation.

I was out the door, and before one of the guys could even think about it, I stepped in front of him. He scowled and took a swing, but I wasn't having it. I blocked the shot and landed a straight jab to the nose. Blood spurted everywhere. And what do you know? I wasn't the least bit rusty.

While the guy howled and sank to his knees, trying to stem the flow of blood, another one jumped in to help his boy out. The girl, as I'd assumed, stood there screaming at us all to stop it. None of us listened, and then she made things worse by trying to jump in and pry us off each other. I wasn't quite sure who she wanted to win, and I wasn't taking any chances that she would get hurt or do or say something that got Lucas's ass kicked even worse.

I pulled another guy off Lucas. This one was the better fighter, like maybe he had some boxing experience. I took one hit to the jaw and a gut shot. That wasn't good, but that shit also woke me up. This was not a game. I needed to save Lucas's ass right now. Because I was here with a plan and I needed him.

With two quick jabs, I popped the guy in the nose and in the chin. His head snapped back, but I wasn't done.

I finished the combination with a left hook and he went down like a sack of potatoes. The blond guy was the only one left until two more guys stepped out of the bar. I turned to help my brother, but Lucas already had a guy on the ground. He was holding him with his left hand dug deep in his hair and raining a series of punches down with his right hand. When the guy finally sagged out of his grip, Lucas stepped back, sucking down gasps of air.

Behind the last two guys that had stepped out to join the fight, there were two girls teetering on their heels. *Shit.* That was the last thing I fucking needed right now.

And to make it worse, Lucas was goddamn showboating, laughing like a crazy person. Yes, okay, there had been a point in my life when I loved to fight. Getting drunk in a bar, getting in a dustup with my mates, it was fun. But this situation was different. There was a lot riding on this.

"You girls get back inside," I shouted.

The girls didn't listen to me though. Instead, they staggered on over just as another group of guys exited the bar and approached the alley, coming toward me and Lucas. One of the guys broke off like he planned to circle around from a different direction.

Shit. Shit, shit, shit. "Look man, we gotta go," I said to Lucas.

The girls kept coming closer, too, leaning on each other,

giggling and swinging their bags. That was the last thing I fucking needed. I feared one of them was going to get hurt with this crew.

These morons didn't exactly look like paragons of virtue who would be concerned with hurting a girl. *Now, now, that's judgmental.* Okay, fine. Just because they had tattoos, bad attitudes, and had been slapping the asses of the waitresses inside didn't mean they were sexist pigs.

Fair enough, but it didn't preclude them from wanting to kick my ass or Lucas's. My brother was still having the time of his life, going pound for pound with one of the bigger guys that I'd shoved outside.

The guy that had called out had convinced one of his buddies to come along with him, and they were right in front of the girls. When one of the girls lost her balance and tripped into him, he turned to scream at her, "What the fuck is your problem? If you can't fucking hold your liquor, don't drink." Then he shoved her.

Shit. With an elbow, I delivered one across the face of the guy I was currently beating down. He sagged onto the ground, and I went straight for the girls. I needed to get them back inside where it was safer. And I had to deal with the asshole that shoved the little one too. But before I could reach her, the little one weaved on her heels. Her friend tried to catch her but instead caught her purse, and the little one fell right over into the big guy. But something happened as she tried to right herself: her foot caught with his.

As she was grasping for purchase, she managed to somehow grab hold of his belt. One pull and the damn thing came flying off in her fingers. She was headed for a hard landing on her face, but she managed to put her arms down as protection and turned her face to the side.

I squinted. That was a fall break, a classic one they taught in self-defense. Was that automatic? Or had she been lucky?

Not everyone is a suspect.

As far as I was concerned, everyone was. But no matter, the guy whose belt she'd grabbed lost his pants. They immediately sagged below his ass, making it more difficult for him to walk. As he brushed past her, screaming his head off, she grabbed hold of his foot, as if trying to use it to help herself back up. Instead, *he* tripped.

He apparently had never learned how to fall break because he fell flat on his nose, howling all the way down. The other girl with the long, silver wig giggled and then teetered over to the big guy's friend. "Oh my God, do you know how to get to I-bar? I heard it was really cool, and I just really want to go there with my friend as soon as she gets back up again. Do you know how to find it?"

The guy lifted an arm to brush her aside, but she raised an arm as if to protect her face. The movement caused her purse to swing upward, and it clocked the guy in the face.

I didn't know what the hell she had in there, but the guy staggered.

She squealed. "Oh my God, are you okay?" She went for him and somehow instead of helping him, she managed to shove him backward until he fell on his ass. He was clutching his head and then she leaned over him with her knee directly in his sternum. "Oh my gosh! Are you okay? I didn't mean to do that. I've got water bottles in my purse. Do you know where you are? Do you know what year it is?"

The guy swore but didn't answer her question.

"Come on, you need to tell me what year it is because that means you don't have a concussion or something. Hold on. Let me call 911." She reached for her purse and lifted it as if trying to find something inside it like her phone. And then she dropped her purse on his face repeatedly. "Oh my gosh, here it is. Let me call 911 for you. You hold still." With her hand, she reached out for his face and managed to push his head down hard.

It was like I was watching a Jackie Chan movie on how to drunken box. Both of these girls were a wreck, completely wasted. I'd been feeding them drinks all night. But somehow, they still managed to take down two guys twice their size.

"You guys get back inside. I'll call the cops."

The girl with the silver wig didn't turn around to face me, but instead she stood, putting her full weight on her knee into the guy's stomach. Or at least that's what I assumed, because the guy *oophed* and grabbed his gut. "Are you sure? Oh my God. Yeah, that would be awesome. I don't feel very good. I think I need to vomit. Come on, honey."

She stepped off of the guy with his nose spewing blood and ran over to her friend, reaching for her hand, but the friend needed no assistance. She managed to push herself up on her heels, staggering slightly. For two girls that seemed wasted and uncoordinated, they still managed a hell of a lot. I could only stare as they wandered arm in arm back down the opposite end of the alley.

"Who the hell were they?" Lucas asked.

I turned to face him. "No idea, but we need to move."

We headed down the alley and around the corner. When we were alone, I shoved him against the wall. "Are you fucking serious?"

Lucas gave a nod and a smirk. "Thanks for the assist, man. Although I probably could've taken them."

"They were going to kick your ass. You would be the one lying bloody in the alley if I hadn't been there."

Lucas shrugged. "Maybe. But that was a good fight though."

I could only stare at him. "Don't you give a shit? That could have been bad."

"But it wasn't. Thanks to you. I owe you a beer or something. What's your name?"

I sighed. "Sebastian."

He grinned. "I'm Lucas. C'mon. Let's have a beer."

8

SEBASTIAN ...

THE FOLLOWING MORNING, there was a clattering and a banging outside in the hallway, accompanied by a series of inventive curses from a soft, feminine voice. With a frown, I tugged open my door and was met with a sight that had me both grinning and shaking my head.

It looked like I was getting a new neighbor.

She was bent over, trying to pick up a box and shaking her ass. "Back, back, back it up. Three, six, nine, damn you're ... " She hummed and sang as she picked up one of the boxes.

It was kind of unavoidable, but my eyes strayed to the way her jeans stretched tight across her ass. And the view made me wonder what the rest of her looked like.

Unfortunately for her, the jeans hung so low, they also exposed her electric blue thong. Despite myself, I laughed. "Looks like you could use a hand with that."

She stood abruptly and whirled around, and some kind of lamp went flying. I lunged for it, catching it in the nick of time. "Holy shit." She clutched a hand to her chest then tugged out her earphones. "Where did you come from?"

I hitched a thumb toward my door. "From there." I frowned as

I stared at the thing in my hand. When I shook it, the boobs jiggled, as did the hips. "Is this seriously yours?"

She grinned and gave a nod. "That's Lola. My lucky charm. I know she's tacky, but I picked her up at this artist's display a couple of years ago. I love her. And when I take her somewhere, I have the best kind of luck. So when I moved to New York, of course the lamp came along because I need all the luck I can get. Going out on my own, moving to New York, it's crazy. So … " She shrugged. "Lucky charm."

I stared at her, dumbstruck. She was pretty, beautiful even. Her skin was a luminescent, sandy brown, and her hair framed her face in a wild array of curls. Several locks were green and purple. I wanted to play with them, and watch them bounce back into place.

Her eyes were wide and dominated most of her face. In this light, they looked hazel but with flecks of green. My gaze dipped to her lips. They looked soft and full and I couldn't look away while she chattered on.

They looked tempting enough to kiss or to wrap around my—

No.

More like *hell* no. I was not going to go there. That was the man I used to be. The new version of me didn't do that. The new version of me didn't have time. I needed to get Lucas on board and head home. Get the old man to push the vote then I could abdicate my fucking throne in time for my opening. *Easy.* Lucas could be king, and I could be free. But my plan hinged on my brother. Or my sister if I failed here.

I resented my instant reaction to this girl. I'd spent the last six months trying to prove I wasn't what everyone thought. A lazy, selfish layabout who fucked anything that moved. I resented her for tempting me.

I refocused my gaze on her face and not the full swell of her curves. "Do you always talk this much?"

She nodded enthusiastically, and her curls bounced up and down. "Yes. Usually. I can't help it. Nervous habit when I'm excited, sometimes when I'm sad or totally spiraling out of control. So, pretty much all the time." She shook her head again. "Okay, let me start again. I'm Len."

Christ church. I couldn't help but laugh. She was cute. Clearly kind of a disaster, but cute. "Okay, Len. I'm Sebastian. Let me help you with that." I took the box from her easily with one hand. Our fingers brushed and I froze. The zing of electricity surprised me and I snatched my hand back.

What the hell? I stared at her for a moment, trying to figure out what was so familiar about her, but I couldn't place it. Maybe I'd seen her around the building? Or maybe I'd seen her this morning. I hadn't been paying attention because I'd been focused on my Lucas problem.

Whatever. Shut that shit down. I cleared my throat and forced my mind and expression into neutral. "Welcome to New York, Len."

"Thanks. I'm really excited. It's my first time in the city." She talked *a lot*. With the box no longer blocking my view, my gaze swept over her. I was already a fan of the hair. And, yeah, the face was beautiful. Heart shaped with high cheekbones. And when she talked, they dimpled. When she smiled, they deepened even more.

Jesus, she was adorable. She wore an off the shoulder T-shirt in gray that said, *I'm an artist, so I'm sensitive about my shit*. The thing was meant to be oversized and have a bohemian look, but all I could focus on was how it clung to her tits.

You do not have time for this. And I didn't. I had a plan, and I had to work fast. I had zero time for this, but it was like she'd been sent here by a really twisted deity to tempt, seduce and punish me.

This girl was everything my type. *You mean breathing?* She was sexy, adorable bait, but I wasn't biting the line. I had more important things to do.

Hell. I'd managed to keep shit wrapped up for six months. I hadn't slept with anyone. I'd been too busy traipsing all over the

US, Canada and Mexico looking for my brother. Well technically, I'd been tracking Lucas's mother and her longtime boyfriend. But the investigator I'd hired had led me here.

The girl had a strip of belly showing. It was flat, taut. Like she worked out. She was probably into classic yoga—a 'look into your inner eye' kind of girl. And her legs were amazing, even though she wasn't excessively tall. Probably around 5'7", but her legs … *Wow.* All toned and lean. She looked like an athlete.

She turned around to the door, kicking it open. "Could you help me carry it in here? Please?" As she turned, I noticed she had paint on the hem of her shirt back.

Okay then. She also had a streak of badass. "So, I guess from your T-shirt that you're an artist?"

"Yeah, good guess." She directed me where she wanted the box. "I just graduated from the Chicago Institute of Art. I think my father thought it would be a passing fancy. That I'd give up and study engineering. You can imagine his face when it wasn't. So he's given me a whole four months to figure out this artist thing. If it doesn't work out, then I have to get a real job."

"That's one hell of a Faustian bargain."

"You don't know my father. He has this way of getting what he wants. So I moved out here to get away from him and his influence. I'm starting fresh, and he's footing the bill."

"Four months isn't very much time."

She gave a winning smile, and for a second all I could do was stare at her. Jesus, she looked like some kind of angel. A cherub without all the baby fat. She looked far too cute to be locked in an engineering lab. If I'd gone to school with her, I would have spent a lot of time trying to get in her pants and very little time studying.

Keep it in your pants. Put the box down and run. I made a vow in that moment to spend as little time as possible with my new neighbor. It would be far too easy to forget what I came here to do.

"It's plenty. Good news is I'm just like my dad, and I have a way of making things work out. Thanks for the help."

The urge to stay and help her was strong. And even though I tried to fight against it, the next words out of my mouth tumbled out on their own volition. "You need help moving any more stuff in here?"

"Thank God. I thought you were never going to offer. Come on."

I shook my head as I followed her back out the door. As I watched her ass, I wondered if this was what it was like to follow the Pied Piper.

9

SEBASTIAN...

IN THE DARKROOM I hung my latest developed prints and studied them closely. Would any of these be good enough to exhibit? Since leaving the island, I felt like that endless well of creativity was dying.

Like somehow removing me from the place I loved had shut me off entirely. My camera was usually my center. With it in my hands, I usually felt like I knew who I was.

But that was all different now. Everything had changed that day. And I didn't know how to get any of it back.

6 Months Ago...

Sebastian ...

No guy in his right mind said no to a hot girl who wanted to suck him off. But somehow, as Bridget's hair fanned across my lap in a golden cascade, and her lips encased my dick in warmth, I couldn't get into it.

She was beautiful and ... enthusiastic, but my mind kept wandering to all the shit I needed to get ready for my first big gallery opening. I'd just gotten the news. All the hard work I'd put in was paying off and I had an opening in ten months, just after my birthday, for the Piques Gallery's Fresh Young Talent exhibit. So instead of focusing on the woman with my dick in her mouth and my balls in her hand, I kept wondering if any of my pieces were good enough.

Clearly something was fucking wrong with me.

I loved women. All kinds of women. Tall women, short women, waiflike women, and curvy women. I'd never met one I wanted to say no to.

Bridget Lennox had tits so perky they defied gravity and an ass so tight someone should make a bronze casting of it. But she was just like everyone else: more than eager to get in my royal pants but lacking any real substance or desire behind her eyes.

None of what was happening was about me. And I'm just enough of an asshole not to care. There were three very distinct reasons for my ambivalence.

For starters, she wanted to bag the prince. I got that; I really did. Because ... well, I was the prince, Crown Prince of Winston Isles. And as much as I hated it sometimes, the crown came with some perks.

The second reason I knew this enthusiastic display of oral skills wasn't about me at all was that she had some daddy issues. Her father was the Duke of Essex, and fucking me would piss her old man off.

Ever since my failed engagement to Lila DuPont, the French duchess, it was open season on me, the eligible prince. Lila, it seems, didn't want a royal life. Or at least not one with me. As it turned out, I wasn't royal enough. After all, I wasn't European royalty. My father hadn't been pleased about the whole situation, and I knew he blamed me.

After Lila walked away, I went a little off the rails and became the kind of prince who made any royal father nervous.

I apparently had a bit of a reputation. So sue me.

The final reason for my ambivalence about Bridget's performance was my awareness that she'd likely heard the rumors and wanted to test them out for herself.

I knew what women said. 'Incredible stamina and unparalleled knowledge of the female form.' There were many rumors; like I once went down on a woman for an hour and she passed out from too many orgasms. Oh yeah, and my personal favorite, that I was packing a ten-inch cock.

Neither of these were exaggerations.

Bridget had been trying to find out if I rocked boxers or briefs for the two years since I'd returned from my military service, and lost my would be princess. She wanted to know if I went commando.

I did.

No, I was lying. It was boxer briefs, but commando sounded better.

Bridget tilted her head forward, sucking me deep and forcing the tip of my cock to the back of her throat. Holy shit. Oh yeah, that got my attention.

Get your head in the game. You have a reputation to protect.

I let my eyes close and surrendered to pure sensation as she deep-throated me. There was almost something poetic about the way her hair brushed over my thighs.

As I gave in to the sensations, I let myself pretend that she was someone who could matter—that I was someone who could matter as more than just the crown.

The only warning I had that we were about to be interrupted were the footsteps at the door. My Royal Guard would never think of walking in. Only one person would turn that knob unannounced.

Shit.

My father was supposed to be in meetings with the Foreign Secretary of Labor. He wasn't scheduled to be back for three days.

Bridget's eyes widened, and she released my dick abruptly with an audible pop before scrambling under my desk.

Fuck me.

I pushed to my feet and winced as I shoved my dick back in my jeans.

Dad stopped short inside the door, glaring at me before narrowing his gaze at the massive oak desk in the center of the office.

Behind him, Roone gave me an apologetic shrug. Roone had been my best friend since I was eleven and sent off to boarding school, and now he was in charge of my security detail. He'd probably done his best, but my father was the king.

With a straight, stiff back, my father stepped inside and abruptly turned and shut the door. When he spoke, his voice was low and irritated. "Ms. Lennox, I'm sure you and I are going to forget this ever happened. No reason for me to discuss any of this with your father?"

From beneath the desk, I heard Bridget shuffling around. Presumably, getting her clothes on as quickly as possible.

She scurried out from under the desk when she was ready. "Your Majesty. Yes of course. No, we weren't—I mean—" She stumbled through a response before grabbing her shoes.

Then with a quick wave to me, she ran past my father and out the door. When she was gone, Dad turned around. "Sebastian, you have got to be shitting me."

I couldn't help myself. I laughed.

Fuck.

I was in enough trouble as it was. Dad rarely swore. After all, it wasn't very royal. So, every time he did, I laughed, which he hated. "Dad. No, it's not what it looks like."

"So, you're telling me that wasn't Bridget Lennox half-naked in your office fellating you?"

My lips twisted. "Yes, okay, it was what it looked like. But—" I stopped abruptly. What the hell was I going to say? 'She really, really wanted to suck my cock'? Nope, better not.

My father shook his head. "You know what? That is a fight for another day."

For real? Score. He must have been exhausted because he let me skate.

Just when I thought I'd escaped a boring lecture, he slammed down his tablet with so much force I worried it might crack. But it didn't. On the screen was the promo for my gallery show. The promo clearly said, Winston. "Do you want to explain this to me?"

Shit. He wasn't supposed to find out about that. I ran a hand through my hair and tried to think of a good explanation. He'd asked me to stop displaying my work six months ago. Listening was not one of my fortes. "Dad, I can explain." Maybe I should have mentioned to him I was still exhibiting my photos despite his royal edicts not to.

"We've discussed this Sebastian. The crown prince cannot run around being a photographer. And you certainly can't take lewd photos and call them art."

"My photographs are not lewd. You can't see anything in the

photos." They were tasteful nudes. And it wasn't like I only did nudes ...
"

"Oh, but it's the suggestion of nudity. I swear you are trying to rip this monarchy apart single handedly."

"No one knows I'm Winston. Trust me, the monarchy will survive. You are so melodramatic. Why can't you just see that I'm good at this? After all the years of you getting on me to focus, to find a cause to champion, I finally found something I'm really good at besides fucking."

Maybe that was going a little far. But my whole life, the old man had been after me to be better—to do better. I'd get honors, and he'd say, 'Why isn't this a distinction?'

When I had a camera in my hands, it just worked. I was not a fuckup or an embarrassment.

Dad shook his head. "You take beautiful photos. You always have, but you don't get to be this. It's time to put away childish things. You will be king, Sebastian. You have a higher calling than photographs. I've let you indulge this hobby of yours for too long."

"This hobby?" I narrowed my eyes.

"Don't act like you don't know that this can't actually be a profession. You are the prince. What do you think will happen when the world discovers you're Winston? You think they'll embrace it? Especially given the subject matter of these photographs? You need to be above it all. That is the job."

"You know, ever since I was a kid, you've been telling me what the job is. Have you ever stopped once to ask what I fucking want?"

"Watch your language."

I dropped my arms and picked up the camera on my desk. "This, I'm good at. Really good at. There are galleries that want to feature my shit."

"And that is fine for anyone other than you. But you need to set that aside. You can support the arts as much as you want. But Winston has to go." My father sighed before striding over to me and clapping a hand on my shoulder. "I'm sorry. I know this is important to you. But we all have to give up things that are important to us when that crown gets placed upon our heads."

I wanted to blurt out the truth. But even now, I couldn't bring myself to hurt him like that. So the words stuck in my throat. I don't want the crown.

He had given up his whole life to be king when his brother abdicated. To him, it was a calling. "So that's it. I'm just supposed to walk away?"

"It's what we must all do."

The crux of it was I loved the Winston Isles. This was my home. I loved the people. I genuinely wanted to make their lives better. But I just wanted to do that through photography and not through the crown. But as I was the only child of the king, there were no other options.

My father sighed. "Sebastian, there's actually something else I need to talk to you about."

"You mean besides burning my dreams to the ground? By all means. You're on a roll now it would seem."

My father shook his head. "Stop acting like a child. We have bigger things to talk about right now."

I frowned. "Like what? The fact that you want me to take on more duties?"

Father sighed. "No."

"Then what?" *I wasn't in the mood for more of his shit.*

"There's something I need to tell you."

"If this is your version of the birds and the bees, you're too late. Besides, I'm careful. I don't have any kids. Number one lesson you drilled into me the moment I hit puberty: wrap it up. Always."

Dad frowned, the expression making him look older than he was. "Must you always be so cavalier? This is important. Children shouldn't pay for the sins of their fathers."

Way to lay on the guilt. "I know the responsibility that you're placing at my feet."

His father sighed. "Yes, eventually. I'd like to see you mature more. But at the end of the day, I know the kind of man you are. I know what you're capable of. And you could do great things. The people of the Winston Isles deserve that. I know what's at the heart of you." *My father rubbed at the back of his neck.* "It's about the Regents Council and the succession law."

I shook my head. "I still don't know why you're pushing so hard to change the law. I mean, it's not like Uncle Roland's illegitimate heir could have any claim on the throne. He'd be like sixteenth in line or something."

The Regents Council was made up of sixteen members of the court or high-ranking government officials, and they helped make the laws in the islands. Unlike England, the monarch in the islands still had a say in day-to-day government. The people elected a prime minister and lesser officials. The prime minister sat on the council to speak for the people.

When it came to matters of state, I usually let my father do the voting on my behalf. Because there was nothing more boring and mind-numbing than a Regents Council meeting.

"I know they will fight me, especially your cousin Ashton. He's terrified that his father has illegitimate children floating around."

A sense of dread rolled onto my shoulders like the shadow of an elephant. "What's going on?"

My father clasped his hands. "I'd hoped to wait until later to tell you this, but it's important to do so now because the rumors are going to start flying when I start pushing for a vote."

I crossed my arms. "You're freaking me out."

Dad winced. I knew he didn't like the American colloquialisms that I had picked up while going to university abroad. My natural accent was more British than anything, thanks to boarding school at Eton, but I'd picked up an American one along the way, as well as some particular phrasings. It drove His Royal Majesty insane. "There's a reason I've been pushing for the vote. And it's not because of Uncle Roland."

I frowned. That stung. "Fuck, you really think I'm dumb enough to get some want-to-be-princess pregnant?"

"No, Seb. I'm doing it because of me. I have other children."

Sebastian ...

"DID YOU KNOW?" I fired the question at my mother before I even closed the door to her chambers.

My mother looked up from the stack of charity invitations and studied me over the rim of her glasses. "About your father? Yes."

I stared at her as I realized my entire life, my entire childhood, had been a complete falsehood. "And you're so calm about it."

"Yes, I'm calm about it. It was a long time ago, Sebastian. We didn't love each other then. Our marriage was arranged. We were two virtual strangers who signed pieces of paper and stood before the people of these islands and promised ourselves to each other. We didn't know each other. We didn't know what kind of commitment that love would take. That came later. And when you love someone, you accept their faults."

"How can you still love him after this? I have siblings out there somewhere."

"I know. I've always known about them. He's worked hard over the years to keep track of their lives. Neither one of their mothers would allow him to see them. They wouldn't take any money. He's trying to do right by them."

"What about us? Was he doing right by us by lying?"

My mother slid her glasses off the edge of her nose then placed them on top of the stack of invitations. "Yes. He lied. To you and to our people. But the important thing is he's trying to fix that. But understand he's never lied to me. From the moment he decided to commit himself to me, when we decided to commit ourselves to each other, he's been honest. I know exactly the man he is. Just because you didn't know doesn't mean he's not the same father who's loved you and tried to teach you how to be a decent human being, despite all the trappings of wealth and being spoiled rotten your whole life."

"How can you say that? Turns out, I'm just like him. All the lecturing about what it means to be king. The shitty thing is I never wanted any of this. Still don't."

"It's not about what you want, Sebastian. Your father's trying to do the right thing. I find that far more admirable than you kicking up a fuss like a three-year-old. You are cocky and arrogant and walk around here like you own the place. You want to be an artist? Great. Teach others how to be artists. Provide for others who don't have the means to be artists. But to give up the monarchy to take pictures? That's selfish."

I clenched my teeth so tightly I was worried I might crack a molar. "Why can't you see that this is my dream?"

My mother folded her arms. "It must be nice to have dreams. I don't want you to be unhappy, sweetheart. I don't want you to go through your whole life and wonder if there were other things you could have done, someone else you could have been. But there is a responsibility and a duty to the people who love you. If you can't see that, maybe you don't deserve to be king."

"I don't want to be."

As our gazes locked in a staring contest, it occurred to me that if my father was able to get the law passed, there would be two other legitimate heirs to the throne. And maybe, like my uncle Roland, I could find myself unfit and unsuitable to wear the crown.

I found myself just feeding that kernel of possibility; giving it sunshine, putting water on it, and letting it grow gave me hope. I realized there might be a way out of the stifling prison the crown represented after all.

If I could find one of my siblings, then I could be free.

With one text to Roone, a stop by my room for a bag, I left the only home I'd ever known without so much as a backwards glance.

10

PENNY ...

"OKAY, HEAR ME OUT."

I had a bad feeling about this. Blake Security had their eye on Sebastian who was at his apartment with Lucas. They had the exits covered, and we had our cameras, so Ariel and I had a rare night off. Or in this case, *Dancing with the Stars* on television and strategizing. The problem was I had a feeling she was about to say something crazy. Like, *extra* crazy.

And to be honest, I was already dealing with the crazy inside. Ever since coming face-to-face with His Royal Hotness, I hadn't been able to get him out of my head. He was that kind of deliciously tall that made me feel petite. And at five feet seven inches, I was tall for a girl. Obviously I knew the prince's stats.

Height: Six feet three inches

Weight: Freaking ripped ... That was accurate right?

Hair: Dark brown ... Also, incredibly glossy. I wonder what shampoo he used.

Eyes: Blue green ... And completely mesmerizing.

I swallowed hard and dragged my attention back to my bestie.

"Look, I can see your face now, but you need to hear me out." Whenever Ariel got excited, she jumped up and talked animatedly with her hands, gesticulating to punctuate every point.

"Okay look, you have a job to do that was given to you by King Cassius himself, and so far you're doing fine. Passable. Fine."

"You said fine already."

"Yes, I did. But listen, we know Sebastian—pardon me, the crown prince. We *know* him. We know how to exploit him. We know his history, his past. And it is safe to say the past can inform the present or the future, right?"

I knew where this was going. "Yes, but—"

She held up her hand. "Just listen. We discussed this, and I know you have your qualms with everything going on with Robert. But you have a mission given to you by the *king*. This is a royal edict. And we cannot bail because, according to the king, he is in danger. And we've already seen some evidence of this, like the fight in the alley with those guys. So at the very least, even if someone isn't actively trying to kill him, he is at least putting himself in dangerous situations. So it's in his best interest to at least be at home where he'll be someone else's problem."

"I don't want him to be someone else's problem. I want to do my job well. That is the ultimate goal."

"Yes it is. The ultimate goal is to protect him and to get him home where King Cassius wants him, correct?"

I nodded.

"Okay, then. I'm not suggesting you have to sleep with him." She rolled her eyes. "But I do think it's time to give the suggestion that he could look at you as more than the friendly neighbor a chance."

"Ariel, you never use this many words to explain anything. You're more of a blunt instrument. So stop talking around it and tell me what you think I should do."

"Well, I think you need to start flirting with him. I think you need to put the pressure on him to see you as a woman. Make him a little more uncomfortable; make him interested. No one's saying how far you have to carry that out, but it would make your job a hell of a lot easier. Because this whole good neighbor routine isn't getting you where you need to be, which is in his apartment, planting bugs."

"It's been two days. We just met. You need to give me time. Besides, we can plant bugs without me flirting with him. All we need is time when he's away from the apartment."

"The key element here is time. Something we have very little of. With our watch schedule and you not being quite close enough to him yet to guarantee that he'll be out long enough for me to plant bugs, it's risky. You need to get closer to him, and you need to do it quickly because we will run out of time. King Cassius wants Sebastian home in a matter of weeks. We can't play the slow game. We don't have time to screw about where you're his neighbor who gives him some casseroles and fresh baked cookies or whatever. You need to get close to him—and quickly. You want him to *want* you close, where you can protect him better. I'm saying flirt. Not screw. You can do that, can't you?"

I sighed as I pondered this. Sebastian was notorious. Many women far and wide had lost their panties in pursuit of the crown prince. Could I hold on to mine? Could I keep the job and my personal feelings separate? I hated it, but Ariel had a point. I did need to get closer to him, and he was keeping me at arm's length, which meant I had to rely on Blake Security more than I was comfortable with. And as good as they were, he knew them, so they couldn't get any closer than I could. "Okay, I'll hear you out. What do you suggest?"

Ariel grinned and clapped her hands, looking every bit a pixie fairy, which I happened to know she was not. This girl was all badass. She was just wrapped in a cute little package. Unfortunately, this package was also diabolical as hell.

"Don't worry. It won't be so bad."

"I wish I could trust you."

"For starters, we need him to think about you naked. So my first suggestion is that I tamper with your water heater. Then you're going to go over there and have a shower. Make sure you wear your silk kimono. You know the one that hugs your body.

We'll get you wet first, so it clings to you. He'll see the outline of your boobs that way."

My bottom jaw unhinged. "What?"

She shrugged. "Now is not the time to get squeamish. Now is the time to suck it up and throw on your big girl thong. We can do this. You just have to make him see you as a woman. Because even something as innocuous as that will make him start thinking about you naked. He's a guy. The more he thinks about you, the more he wants to be around you. It's easy as that. All you have to do is hold him at bay, which, as a woman, you've had a lot of practice at. How many guys have we bummed a few drinks off of in our lifetime?"

I started to retort that what she was suggesting was sexist and wrong, but she sort of had a point. "So that's your big plan? I go over there and get him lusting after me? What if I'm not even his type?"

"Um, let me point out you're a woman, so you're his type. It'll be easy. Besides, while you're in there, you can plant a bug, hopefully more than one. At least that will give us his movements. So if he says anything about where he's going and how long he is going to be out, then at least we know the time frame that I have to plant other bugs."

Unfortunately, that sounded like it might actually work. "Great. What else?"

"We're also going to have you play a little damsel in distress. You know, bitten by a spider. Ooh, even better, you see a mouse. Scream, have him come running over and 'save you.' Guys love that shit."

I shook my head. "You want me to get on a table and scream because I see a mouse?"

Ariel grinned and nodded. "Exactly."

"I have a feeling I'm going to regret this."

She shrugged. "Possibly, but you will get your prince."

Sebastian ...

I LEANED over my light box, going over the pictures I'd taken the other day. They were good. A couple of them were great. I loved shooting in the city. For the Winston show, my main focus was love in the city. Some of them included nudes, which of course the old man wouldn't be thrilled about. But I wanted to show a different kind of love, a love of the city. I'd been trying to get the photos right, but I wasn't sold on any of these. "I need something fucking perfect," I muttered to myself.

A knock at the door made me stand and frown. No one ever came to my apartment. I kept a low profile. None of the tenants here knew that I was the owner of the building. I had a property management company that handled all of it. And well, Lucas still hadn't taken me up on the offer to have another beer together, so he sure as hell didn't know where I lived. So who the fuck was knocking on my door?

I jogged over and looked through the peephole and sighed. All I saw was a mop of curly hair. Jesus Christ. Hell, I could feel it already. The twitch to be near her. Something about her fucked with my equilibrium. I just needed to keep her at a nice, neighborly arm's length. I could do that. *Easy.*

Besides, maybe she had a boyfriend. *Not that you care.*

There had been a time not so long ago that a boyfriend wouldn't have been an issue. *But then, that's not the kind of woman you want, is it?*

I sighed and tugged the door open and across the threshold stood Len. Her hair, a mass of wild curls, was pulled up on top of her head in some kind of messy knot situation. And fuck me, she was wearing a very thin kimono robe. One cursory glance told me I could nearly see her nipples through the fabric.

With more effort than I was used to, I forced my eyes to meet hers. Instead of something intelligent coming out of my mouth, I said, "Why are you wet?"

Cue Len's runaway mouth. "Oh my God. I was taking a

shower, and I think the water heater just broke or something because the water went instantly cold. And I need to wash my hair. I can't wash my hair in cold water. It's freezing, like ice. Touch me."

She reached out her hand, and I jerked back. *Pussy.* Touching her when she was wet was not a fucking good idea. I wanted to. *No. Don't do it. You cannot withstand that temptation. Jesus fucking Christ, she's wet and*—My gaze slipped to her breasts again. She was certainly more than a handful. And I had big hands. I dragged my gaze back up to her eyes, but she was still talking about needing to deep condition too, holding her shower caddy in one hand while the V of her robe slid more and more open as she waved wildly with the other.

I needed to get my shit together. "Len, stop."

She snapped her mouth shut.

"You need to use my shower?"

She nodded. "Oh my God, yes. Please … it won't happen again. I already called the property manager. They said they'd have someone come to look at it tonight, but I have to meet a new model and my hair takes forever to dry. I don't even have a blow dryer yet. Or I think I do. It's just, the boxes I have aren't unpacked, and you know how it is—"

I held up a hand. "You said you were freezing. You should probably get in the shower."

She grinned. "Thank you. Thank you. Thank you. Thank you." She shuffled past me, and I closed the door behind her. I forced myself to take three deep, fortifying breaths before I turned around. The problem was the view from the back was just as tempting. The kimono clung to her ass, accentuating her hips, and I just really wanted to know what she felt like.

Nope, no you don't. You are not curious about it at all. You don't need that in your life. This one was a handful. *Yeah, I'll bet she's a handful.*

That line of thinking was not helping me. "The shower is right through there down the hall."

She put her shower caddy on the counter and turned to face me. "Oh my God. Thank you so much. You know what? I think I owe you dinner or something. Let me repay you, okay? With more than a dodgy burrito."

"No, it's not necessary. It's just a shower."

"It's totally necessary."

Then she surprised me by jogging right up to me, and Jesus Christ, it made her tits bounce. I was a pervert, a total letch. I was going to hell. And you know what? I wouldn't feel bad about it. That's what made it even worse.

When she wrapped her arms around my neck, I thought I was going to explode right there. It was an instant shot of lust in my veins. Her body was soft and pliable. To make it all worse, she was wet and smelled like some kind of lime and mint and coconut. I wanted to nuzzle in and sniff her.

Danger. Do not sniff her. Gently, I reached behind me and unwound her arms then took a deliberate step back. "Not a problem. There's no need for payback. Just go take your shower."

She grinned and then jogged back to her caddy. "I wish I could say this was going to be quick. Hopefully you don't need your shower any time soon, because when I wash my hair, it takes a while. I have a lot of hair." And then she grabbed her caddy and disappeared into the bathroom. The knot curled on her head merrily bounced as she went.

You will not think about her naked in your shower. You will not think about her naked in your shower. You will not—

My phone rang, and I scrubbed a hand on my face. *You need to get a grip.* One girl—*one girl*—and I was close to losing my shit. If everyone back home could see me now … Hell, if anyone from the tabloids could see me now … Rumors of my Casanova tendencies had been rampant for years. No one would believe that I was trying my damn best *not* to touch a girl. What the hell was wrong with me?

I saw who was calling and grabbed my phone from the counter. *Lucas.*

I took a deep breath before answering. "Lucas, hey man."

"Hey. Got plans tonight?"

I slid my glance to the bathroom. I couldn't be locked in the apartment with her all night, thinking about her naked. "Nope, just tell me where to go and I'll be there." Everything was going according to plan. Never mind the naked girl in my shower.

11

PENNY ...

I STILL COULDN'T BELIEVE that worked. Strolling into Sebastian's apartment wearing nothing but a thin silk robe and a smile had gotten me exactly what I needed. I managed to plant one bug in the hallway by his bedroom. One was just inside his bedroom door under the lamp, and another was in the kitchen right under the counter. I honestly hadn't thought it would work. But since he was seemingly distracted by my naked wetness, he hadn't really been paying attention.

"You can go ahead and say it now: I was right." Ariel's voice came over on the comms clearly. I could see her seated in the corner at what the club called an intimate bar. Whatever the hell that meant.

"I will not say that you were right, but it did get the job done. I was able to plant bugs. So that was handy."

"Oh come on. You know you want to say it. I am a genius."

I took a sip of my drink even as I started to giggle. She *was* a bloody genius. But I didn't want her getting a swelled head about it. "What you are is diabolical. I think he was so focused on the fact that I was wet, he couldn't really process much of anything else."

"I told you. It's not about you actually doing anything. It's about getting in and getting as close as you can. Like simply give him the impression of your nakedness, and his brain will short circuit. He's a guy."

"How come you aren't using your skills to torture some guy on a permanent basis?" I wanted to recall the question as quickly as it stumbled out of my mouth. I knew why, because for as long as I could remember Ariel had been in love with Michael. I was pretty sure my big brother was the sole reason she went to the Royal Guard. When we were kids, Ariel had always talked about adventures with the perfect-looking adventurous boyfriend. She wanted to chase something grand and fun, and she'd never once mentioned being a Royal Guard, at least not until Michael joined. But then it was all she talked about. The honor, the duty ... Back then it had been kind of cute. Growing up, Ariel hadn't had it easy. She'd completely transformed herself.

As we got older, I couldn't understand why my brother didn't see how awesome Ariel was. After all, she was my best friend. The times I'd tried to fix him up with her were numerous. Before Ariel had completely transformed herself, I'd thought he was a shallow twat who couldn't look beyond the physical. Now, I knew differently.

I used to arrange to have Ariel meet me at home when I knew Michael was already there, and then I'd be conveniently late. I had her over for family dinner as often as possible. I had more of an excuse when Ariel joined the Guard with me because Ariel was all on her own on the main island. Her parents lived about forty-five minutes away by a ferry, a couple of islands over. So really, it was hospitality. But no matter what I tried, Michael wasn't interested.

Now you know why. I still hadn't figured out the best way to tell her yet. No matter what I said or did, it was going to hurt. She'd formulated her whole life around the possibility of being with my brother. No way in hell I would let her feel the same pain that I had or anything remotely close to it.

"Never mind about me torturing anybody. My plans are all centered on your brother."

"You know, you should actually date other people. I mean Michael has Emily." *And was also making out with my boyfriend.*

"You know I am a firm believer in one night stands. Nothing permanent ... nothing is gonna hold me down. So as soon as Michael is ready, I'll be there to pounce."

That was Ariel in a nutshell with her single-minded focus. For years, I've been her sidekick on the Michael chain, trying to figure out all the scenarios in which I could make my brother love her. The problem was I couldn't seem to make that happen.

"Okay, enough talk about your one day very hot relationship with my brother."

"Fine. If you insist. Can you get any closer to them?"

I sighed. "I'll give it a go, but it's really crowded."

"Welcome to the big city, country mouse. Not at all like back home, is it?"

"Yeah, tell me about it," I said. "I'm starting to miss home."

"We're not in Kansas anymore." Ariel laughed.

Penny...

"My feet hurt." I spoke into the hidden mic as I sipped my drink. I asked the bartender to give me plain apple juice in a highball glass with a couple of those big ice cubes to make it look like I was drinking something expensive and full of liquor. But alas, I wasn't there to play. I was busy trying to keep an eye on Sebastian and his new buddy. *Lucas.* The two of them had developed a real bromance, and they were hitting the club and hitting on girls.

Ariel chuckled into my ear piece. "That is the cost of beauty."

"Is it possible that the cost is too high?" I mumbled.

"This whole conversation is why I gave up on shoes, makeup and tight clothes. All that stuff screams *uncomfortable*," Ariel groaned.

"Yes well, you can say that when you have perfect skin, look like a model and don't need all the shopping because you look great in everything, including our uniforms. For the rest of us, those things are necessary. Right now I wish I had my tennis shoes on."

"Well, those wouldn't have gotten you into the club."

Ariel had a point. As it was, we'd had to move heaven and earth to make sure that we got in. Never mind. I was there, and it was pretty cool. I didn't ever get to go to places like that.

"You have our boy?"

"Yeah I've got him with his new boyfriend. They're at the bar."

Ariel chuckled. "Who is that guy to him? This is the third time this week."

"Lucas. I heard him use his name. That's all I got, but we need more information. Especially if this dude is going to spend more time with him."

"Yeah, I think one of us is going to have to follow him soon," Ariel said.

"Or we can ask the boys at Blake Security for a little help."

"Get closer. See if you can hear them."

"I'm not getting any closer," I mumbled.

"Come on. You know you want to."

And that was the thing. There was a part of me that did want to. The zing of electricity when our hands had touched the first day we met was undeniable. And now, every time he picked up his drink I watched his Adam's apple bob up and down. And when he smiled, I noticed how one corner of his lip tipped up before the other. I also spent an inordinate amount of time watching his full lips. And God help me if he laughed. *Can you say, panties wet?* My stomach clenched every time that happened.

You need to get your shit together. I was not here on a dating show. I was here to protect him. And it was time I started doing so.

"Okay. I'm going in."

"Come on, Penny. Let's get the show on the road. If you're

lucky, maybe he'll hit on you and try to take you home. Your lucky day."

No way was I telling Ariel the idea made me tingly. Because I was a damn professional.

It seemed I wasn't immune after all.

Well, I just had to steel myself against it. I had zero interest in being in the legion of his admirers. Not that I could be anyway, because I was Royal Guard and he was the Crown Prince of Winston Isles, so I needed to get my shit together and stop daydreaming.

I finally took Ariel's advice, picked up my drink and headed down to the other end of the bar. I took a seat a couple stools away from him, making sure to keep my face averted. A little redhead sent visual daggers my way as she pushed onto the stool next to Sebastian. I spoke softly against my glass. "Are you happy now? Looks like someone's making her move."

Ariel laughed. "Yep. I can see what's happening. You going to let her steal your man?"

Sebastian's friend leaned back and gave me the once over. Who was this guy? He and Sebastian were similar in a lot of ways. They were both tall and ridiculously good-looking. And there was something familiar about Lucas, but I couldn't place it. Had he been to the Winston Isles? He wasn't likely a member of court because his accent was thickly American.

But given everything the king had told me, I didn't trust him or his motives. I didn't trust anyone when it came to the prince. And that included the man himself. I took another sip of my drink and leaned over to hear more of what they were talking about. Something Lucas said made Sebastian laugh, and he threw his head back. The redhead used that opportunity to bump into Sebastian, spilling a little of her drink.

In my ear, I could hear Ariel. "She's pushy."

I didn't dare respond now that Sebastian was looking in my direction.

The redhead leaned toward him. "Oh my gosh. I'm so sorry. I didn't get my drink on you, did I?"

Sebastian's gaze slid over her. "No, you're good." He turned back to Lucas, but the redhead caught his attention again.

"Let me get you another one."

With a cough, he reassured her. "You're good. I promise."

For the next five minutes, I was forced to watch the redhead keep trying to gain Sebastian's attention. The whole flirting, hands-on handling. It made me grit my teeth, but Sebastian seemed mostly unaffected.

Before I was forced to endure more flirting, I noticed a quick slight-of-hand. At some point, Little Miss Too-Touchy-Feely had ordered the same drink as Sebastian. She fiddled with her glass one minute and the next with a nearly imperceptible movement, she switched their glasses. I blinked for a moment, not entirely sure what I'd seen. But then Ariel said, "Did I just see what I think I saw?"

Ariel jumped from her bar stool, presumably coming closer to give me back up if I needed it. I shook my head slightly, trying not to draw attention to myself. I could handle this. I made my move, spilling my drink very deliberately and precisely over the girl's lower back tramp stamp.

The redhead jumped a mile high and lost her balance, tipping and nearly falling off of the stool.

"What the fuck?"

I leaned down to give her a hand. "I'm so sorry. Oh my gosh. Are you okay? I got it all over your back."

She screamed. "You did that on purpose."

"I promise I didn't. I'm kind of a klutz. Ask him." I indicated Sebastian.

Sebastian raised an eyebrow. "Hey, Len. What are you doing here?"

I forced my expression to a sheepish one. "Meeting a friend. I didn't see you. How's it going?" I turned my attention back to the redhead. "I'll buy you another one. If you want, I can take you to the bathroom and get some club soda on the stain."

But Little Miss Touchy-Feely was it not having it. She shrugged out of my hands and stood on her own accord. "I can handle it myself." She didn't spare me or Sebastian and Lucas another look before she took off.

Sebastian grinned. "I'm pretty sure I should be thanking you, right now."

"Like I said, it was an accident." I turned away slightly and muttered into my comm unit. "Sent the girl to the bathroom, can you deal with her?"

"You got it. I'll keep her occupied and Noah's guys can grab her and wrap her up nice for the authorities." Who knew that girl was a run of the mill asshole or if she'd been sent by someone. Either way, no way I could let her slip him whatever it was she put in his drink.

When I turned back, Sebastian was laughing. "I've seen your accidents. I believe it."

I very deliberately slid my glance to his friend, and Sebastian clapped him on the back. "Len, meet Lucas. Lucas, this is my new neighbor, Len. I met her when her door was trying to best her."

Lucas's brows drew up. Then his gaze slid over me, and I met the look with an appraising one of my own. "I should meet that door."

I ignored him.

Sebastian grabbed the drink the redhead had doctored, and I warned him. "If I were you, I wouldn't drink that. I watched her. She switched your drinks. For all you know, she roofied it."

Sebastian stared at me. "Are you serious right now?"

I nodded. "Yep."

He frowned. "You know what? I'll get a new one."

"Lucky I was here."

"Yeah, lucky."

Sebastian stared at me for a long moment. "Join us for a drink."

"Nah, I'm going to find my friend. See you around." I tried to book it from the bar, hoping that Ariel had eyes on him. I needed to try and find the redhead. She'd probably gone to the bathroom. I hadn't entirely believed the king when he said Sebastian's life was in danger, but now … What had that girl put in his drink? After what I just saw, I was pretty sure the king hadn't been over-reacting all.

"Hey, wait up," Sebastian called.

I turned around. "What is it?"

"Where are you running off to? I want to say thanks."

"Told you. To find my friend. And really, it's no big deal." I shook my head.

"Oh, but it is a big deal." His brow furrowed. "That could have been bad in ways you don't even know."

"No big deal, like I said."

He stared at me. "I'm still trying to figure out what it is about you."

"Just doing a good deed for the day."

The crowd bustled us until we were forced to scuttle down a slightly darkened hallway. One of the busboys carrying a large basin ran by us. Sebastian whisked me out of the way. Unfortunately, that brought his body into direct contact with mine. *Danger, Will Robinson! Danger!*

The moment his muscles were pressed against my breasts, my whole body went to red-alert mode. Or more like hyper-alert mode. Pulse racing. Breathing erratic. Brain on the fritz. Lady parts … well let's not discuss the lady parts.

So when he leaned down closer to my face, I could only squeak in response. I stared at him as my body betrayed me, and I bit back a moan.

This is the crown prince. Get your shit together. I was his Royal Guard. I needed to remember that. Except none of that worked to cool the heat of my skin or the decidedly unprofessional tingling in my panties.

This is a job. This is a job. You will not lust after Sebastian Winston.

My body had zero interest in obeying. Our eyes locked for just a moment, and his lips parted. "You smell incredible. Do you know that?"

That? Know what? He was asking me something. I wasn't sure about the context of what he meant, or perhaps his proximity was clouding my brain. This had to be the way that he got away with murder. He would dull the senses and the rationality of any woman in a six-block radius. As superpowers went, I had to respect his. Because even though I was professional, even though I knew better, I still couldn't help myself. I nodded my head. But when he leaned closer, the rational part of my brain clicked into focus and I said, "What are you doing?"

Sebastian leaned closer still, and my eyes fluttered shut. But instead of pressing his lips against mine, he shifted his head down a little further before dusting his nose along the skin of my neck. Heat pulsed between my thighs, and my knees wobbled. *Air.* I needed more air.

He blinked in confusion. "There's something really familiar about the way you smell," he whispered against my skin, and then he backed off, deliberately taking several steps away from me. "I'm sorry." He frowned. "Now I've come across as a total creeper."

I shook my head to clear it. "I'm just going to the ladies' room."

He began to open his mouth as if he wanted to protest, but then he shook his head. "Look, if you change your mind, please let me say thank you. I'll buy you a drink."

I shoved away from the wall and forced my legs to move toward the restroom. "Nope. I'm good. See you around." And then I ran to safety. Far away from the prince. Far away from the job I was supposed to be doing. When I shoved into the restroom, it was crowded as usual.

Ariel pushed away from the sinks. "Where have you been? Your comms were down. Are you okay?"

I stared at her for a long moment. "You are not going to believe what just happened."

12

PENNY ...

I WIPED my hands on my jeans as I paced Ariel's apartment. "Okay. So, what do I do?"

Ariel just stared at me and blinked. "You mean about Prince Hot-as-Fuck sniffing your neck?" A giggle escaped her lips.

"Would you stop laughing?"

Ariel threw up her hands. "I don't have the playbook for this. I mean, he didn't sniff *my* neck."

"And if he had?"

Ariel flushed. "Let's not talk about what I would do. Let's talk about what *you* did. Looks like my plan worked."

I gave up and just flopped back on the bed. "I need to figure out how to play this. I know the directive was get close to him. But I mean, how am I supposed to do that?"

Ariel grimaced. "Well, there's the *obvious* way. It's all dependent on how far you're willing to go for the job. The shower thing got you into his place."

I raised a brow. "What exactly do you mean by how far I am willing to go for this job?"

My friend shrugged. "Well, I'm just saying. We know that Sebastian is kind of a player. You're cute, live next door, and you plan on being in his space twenty-four seven. Not to mention, I could feel the chemistry crackle the first time you met. Use it."

I blinked rapidly. "I'm not going to sleep with him. That's … " I couldn't even come up with the right word. "Unprofessional," I finally settled on.

Ariel chuckled. "That it is."

I threw a pillow at her head. "I am *not* doing that."

Ariel gave me one of those glances that said, 'oh, sure you're not.' "Seriously though. No one is saying you have to sleep with the guy, but you can flirt and throw on a little feminine charm. You said it yourself: King Cassius says he's in danger. So the sooner we can get him home the better."

I sat up on the bed and pointed my thumbs towards myself. "Have you met this girl? I have zero charm. The Duke of Essex will attest to that."

Ariel chuckled. "Yes, but even your craftiness and your general Calamity Janeness are kind of charming in a way. All you have to do is be you. Relax."

I frowned. "I'm going to need more than that. This is the prince."

"I mean obviously you're smoking hot. But the moment you get around him, you get all tongue-tied and bumbling. It's not like I didn't hear the audio from your first meeting."

That made me bristle. "Well, I was trying to play the part. And my shit was trying to run away from me."

"Okay look, maybe try and play the part. I'm not saying do anything unprofessional. But your job *is* to get close to him. You are technically here on behalf of the king. Almost spy-like. Embrace it. You're the hot new Moneypenny."

"You realize Moneypenny and Bond never actually slept together, right?"

Ariel rolled her eyes. "But you get the idea. You turn on the charm. The flirtation alone will make him want to spend time with you. It will make it easier to keep an eye on him and keep him safe. How's that?"

"Well, right about now, anything is worth a try. Because so far what I'm doing is not working. At least not how I want it to."

Sebastian ...

IT WAS four in the morning and I was knackered. Not so much drunk because I'd stopped after four. I mostly had just been keeping Lucas company, and he had been on a tear. The good news was my brother was a happy drunk and he liked his women. *Yeah, been there done that.*

I just hoped he'd be able to keep it together when he had the crown. *Maybe he shouldn't have the crown after all.*

No, I wasn't even going to entertain that thought. I'd worked too hard to get here to find him and figure a way out. He had to be what I needed. Still, as I flopped back onto my couch, I just kept wondering if he would love the people like I did. Which was bullshit because for the last three or so years, all I'd wanted was my freedom, but I couldn't seem to pull the trigger on what I knew I needed to do.

I wasn't sure what made me look out to the balcony that wrapped around and connected to Len's, but I saw the light on. Why was she still up? Maybe because some weird neighbor sniffed her neck like she was a drug?

God, why the fuck had I done that? She'd skittered away from me in the club. As well she should have.

But had she felt that tingle? This was crazy, and I knew it. I didn't need or want my body to feel the gravitational pull toward her. Why her? Why now? For months I hadn't missed the random sleeping around.

With her it wouldn't be random.

No, it wouldn't be. I would see her every day. There would be no avoiding her in the end. I wasn't sure I wanted to deal with that. And as soon as I got Lucas to agree, I'd be on a plane. But I wanted to go out there. I wanted to talk to her. I wanted to watch those dimples play in her cheeks again.

You have a problem.

I was not going out there. As tempting as she was, there were a million reasons why that was a bad idea. A million reasons why that wasn't going to work. So instead, I did something else I'd been avoiding doing. I picked up the phone not even knowing what time it was. I called the still-familiar number.

"Hello?"

I swallowed hard. "Hi, Dad."

"Sebastian, Jesus Christ! Are you okay?"

My heart pinched. Considering I'd been away for so long, I knew I'd probably put my parents through a fuck ton of worry. *And Roone. Don't forget Roone.* But my father's first question was still, 'Are you okay?'

"Yeah, I'm fine. I just—honestly, I'm not sure why I'm calling."

"Do you need a reason?"

I swallowed hard. "I don't know. I guess maybe I thought I did need a reason after the way I left."

"I wish you hadn't. We could have talked."

I shook my head even though my father couldn't see me. "I wasn't really up for talking then. And honestly, I'm pretty sure none of it would have sunk in."

"And that's fair. You had a right to take some time to process it."

What was I supposed to say this? There was no script really, so I just said it. "I found him, Dad. Lucas. I found him."

"Are you serious?"

"Yeah. He's, he's cool, kind of a troublemaker. A handful, but I can see you when I look at him."

More silence. "Did you ... did you tell him?"

"No, not yet. I'm just trying to get to know him. I want to find out who he is before I lay all this other shit on top of him."

"Maybe I could meet him."

No. "No. I'm sure there's time for that. I just—I wanted you to know that I found him."

"Thank you for letting me know. I'm just glad to hear from you, to hear that you're safe. I'm sorry all of this turned out this way."

"You felt you were doing what you had to do. And I felt the same. So here we are."

"Are you coming home soon?"

"Yeah, Dad. I promise I'll be home soon." My inability to tell my father why I'd be home stuck on the roof of my mouth.

"Sebastian, I'm glad you called."

"Me too. I'll call again soon." When I hung up, I felt oddly lighter but somehow heavier. Even as angry as I was with my parents, I didn't want to break their hearts. I heard movement around the balcony and frowned. Seriously, what was she still doing up?

I opened the door to my balcony and peeked out. And sure enough, there was Penny on her balcony, mixing paint and testing the colors on a small piece of canvas. "Shouldn't you be asleep by now?"

She jumped and turned. "Jesus Christ! You scared the shit out of me … again, I might add."

"These are wrought iron balconies. It's not like I could be quiet."

"I know. I just—I get a little lost when I start painting."

"You realize it's four in the morning, right?"

She licked her lips, and my gaze pinned to the peek of pink. "Yeah, I couldn't sleep so I figured maybe I'd mix paint colors. I don't know. There's this image I have in my head, and the color has to be just right. I don't want to start painting it without knowing, you know?"

I nodded. "I get that way about some photos too. Like, I have seen a hint of something before and I really want to replicate it. And if I can't, it drives me batshit."

"Yes, exactly. So I figured if I couldn't sleep, I'd at least get the color right and do a little test. Then I can start in the morning, or in this case, a couple of hours." She smiled at me and gave me a hint of dimple. "So what's your story? Why are you still awake?"

"Lucas wanted to stay at the club a little longer, so I just got home not too long ago." I ran a hand through my hair and cleared my throat. "I—uh—also, I feel like I should apologize for earlier." I shoved my hands in my pockets. "The sniffing thing. Not sure what came over me."

It was dark, but I was almost certain I saw her flush. Was she thinking about it? The intimate contact between us, the way I'd run my nose and lips up the column of her neck?

Dude, you're only torturing yourself. I was, but it was kind of fun.

"Forget it happened. Hope you guys had fun. "

"Listen, do you want to grab a bite to eat or something? I know this great Thai place around the corner."

Her gaze skittered over to me. "You mean like a date?"

Yes. "No." Fuck. Why was this hard? I'd never had a single problem with women. "You're new to the city, so I figured you could use someone to show you around."

What the fuck are you doing?

I had no fucking clue. All I knew was that I wanted to see that pretty pink flush again. I wanted to watch her tongue twitch over her lip. And I wanted to sniff her again, which just sounded creepy. I was losing my shit around her and it was going to be a problem soon.

"Come on, I don't bite. Unless you ask nicely."

"Sebastian … " She shook her head and cast her glance back to her canvas. "You seem really cool. I feel like I should disclose that I have a boyfriend."

Why did that make a knot form in my gut? So what if she had a boyfriend? Did she have no fucking clue who I was? Nope, she had no clue, and she just turned me down.

Okay, retreat, reassess. "Okay, I can respect that." *Like hell I would.* Okay, I would, but she had to have felt the pull between us.

"You still have to eat. And I'm pretty sure you're allowed to have some friends. You said it yourself: you're new here."

She nodded. "Yeah, I am new here, and I do like to eat. Thai is a particular favorite. But just friends, right?"

"I promise to be the epitome of a gentleman."

She laughed boldly. "Yeah, somehow I'm not sure you know what gentleman means, but don't worry, I can teach you."

"If you think I'm bad, you should have seen Lucas tonight. Even I was like, 'man, give it a rest.'"

"How do you guys know each other?"

How did I go about answering that? "Uh, it's complicated." Fuck, I needed to talk to someone. And she was so easy to talk to. She'd already tried to forcibly shove me into the friend zone, right? I could talk to her. "I found out something about him, and I'm not exactly sure if I should let him know."

"Yeah, you are." She said it with such finality.

I frowned. "How's that?"

She shrugged. "You said you're not sure, but you are. You're asking me because you're looking for permission to tell him the hard thing. But you already want to tell him the hard thing. You clearly don't want to take the easy way out; otherwise, it wouldn't be bothering you enough to ask me, a relative stranger."

Shit, she had me pegged. "I guess you have a point there."

She shrugged. "Just tell him. Whatever it is. Rip off the Band-Aid. Clean rip, otherwise it'll pull out all the tiny little hairs, and there's nothing that hurts worse than having your hairs ripped out by the roots. So don't do it slowly. And then whatever it is that's bothering you, you'll have told him. It's information you think he needs to have, so give it to him. And then stand back and wait. Give him a chance to not be so keen on hearing whatever it is you have to tell him."

I puffed out a breath. "It'll be hard to hear."

"The truth usually is."

I knew she was giving me great advice, but right now all my brain could focus on was the stretch of skin on display under her

T-shirt. I had a problem. Her name was Len Cantor. And yes, I'd looked up her last name on the lease agreement like the creeper I was.

If she wanted to be friends, we could be friends. I'd never had a female friend before, really. At least not one that didn't want to jump my bones. This would be a new experience. Besides, it seemed that Len gave great advice.

It also seemed she saw too much. Being around her unsettled the shit out of me, and I needed to be careful.

Or even better, I could stay the fuck away. The last thing I needed was this little obsession of mine growing. I needed to be singularly focused on Lucas.

Len was a distraction I didn't need.

13

PENNY ...

THERE WAS A PLAN.

I knew the plan.

But knowing the plan and executing the plan were two totally different things. I had Ariel on FaceTime as I looked into the little cage of her little mouse friend. "Ariel, I'm not sure about this. I mean, a lot of things could go wrong. First of all, I'm letting a mouse into my apartment. Second of all, I'm relying on the kindness of a virtual stranger. Third, I'm not sure about letting a mouse loose in my apartment."

Ariel laughed. "Turn the phone so I can see him and say hi."

I stared at her. "Stop being insane. I need your help and you're mocking me."

"Oh relax. It's just a mouse. Besides, that little cage you have there is state of the art. And that little guy there has been trained. All you have to do is let him out. Let him run around the apartment. When Sebastian is gone, bring out the cage again, press the little button on the side, and he'll hear the sound and come galloping for the peanut butter right into his cage. It's foolproof."

"See, first of all, I thought mice liked cheese."

"It's a common misconception. They love peanut butter."

I glanced down at Ariel's furry friend. "And what if Sebastian happens to catch him? What if he kills him?" He was kind of cute with his little whiskers and his little pink nose. Not that I wanted to touch him mind you, but he was kind of cute.

"Sebastian isn't going to catch him. These little guys are fast. He's going to call an exterminator. And that will be that. Just make sure you cause enough of a ruckus that he'll take you out of the apartment. Then I'll come back and collect your little friend before an exterminator can come over and set little mouse traps. Easy peasy."

"Seems like an awful lot of work just to catch and keep the prince's eye."

"Yes, of course. But worthwhile work because as macho or hot as he may seem, most people don't like rodents. Still, he'll feel inclined to take care of you being the chivalrous prince that he was raised to be, which gets you that much closer. And of course, then he'll remember you naked. So that helps."

"Diabolical."

"You better believe it. Now, get to screaming."

I hung up with Ariel and stared at the little mouse. "Okay, you and me, let's make a deal. You don't die today, and you don't force me to kill you today, okay?"

The little guy just wiggled his nose at me.

"I see you're mocking me too, aren't you? Fair enough, but if Sebastian catches you, that's not on me. That's on you."

For starters, I opened the French door to the balcony, knowing full well he kept his doors open. It hadn't gotten too cold yet; Indian summer was just crawling in. So it made perfect sense that we both had our doors open. The next step was releasing my furry friend. I deliberately released him deep inside the apartment away from the doors. I didn't want him escaping and actually crawling into someone else's apartment to terrorize them. Besides, if he was trained, met another mouse and reproduced, we'd have a whole epidemic of brilliant mice running around New York City, like the Rats of NIMH. Seriously, the rats were enough. I climbed up on the couch after tucking Mickey's cage in the closet, and I screamed.

"Oh my God! Oh my God! Oh my God!" Then I waited. Nothing happened. I knew for a fact that I didn't have a neighbor on the other side of me. And honestly, I didn't wanna screech. Maybe that's what it took to get Sebastian to come over. We knew from the bugs we'd planted that he was inside the apartment. So I just needed to be compelling enough. I swallowed my dignity and screamed at the top of my lungs.

That did it. It didn't take much before Sebastian was running over the joint balcony and in through my French doors.

"Len? What's wrong? I heard you screaming."

Showtime. *I had better win an Academy Award for this.* "Oh my God! Oh my God! He's over there. He's over there. He's over there." I hoped Mickey would play his part. Otherwise, it would make me look insane.

Sebastian whirled around. "Who? What? What are you talking about?"

"It's a mouse. It's a mouse. Over there. I saw him crawling. Oh my God! Please! Please! Please."

Sebastian groaned. "Fuck. This building was just fumigated. How did the little fucker get in here?"

Sebastian …

SHIT. She was really freaked out. Here's the thing: I hate mice. I'd insisted on living like a normal person when I first moved to New York for uni. The flat I'd gotten was practically infested. I couldn't stand the little creatures. It didn't matter that they looked real cute. They were disgusting. But I knew I had to man up in front of this girl, my neighbor.

She's not a girl. Well, she's a girl, but we're not looking at her like that. Whatever.

"Okay, look, you stay there. Where was the last place you saw him?"

She squeaked again and pointed in the general vicinity of the kitchen.

"Okay, do you have like a broom or something?"

Her eyes went wide. "You're going to squash him?" She looked horrified.

"Maybe I can shoo him outside, but he can't stay here. Unless you want him to stay here."

She shook her head immediately. "No. I just don't want squashed mouse guts in my kitchen."

"I'm not gonna squash him in the kitchen. I'm just gonna try and shoo him out of the apartment." At least, that was the plan. Honestly, I didn't know how to get rid of a mouse. The last time I encountered the little furry fuckers, I moved. Yes. I wasn't afraid to admit it: I moved. Because at the end of the day, it was a fucking mouse. And I could afford to. But this girl couldn't afford to. Plus, I also allowed no mice in this building. I was real clear that I would pay whatever it took to fumigate the place regularly. There couldn't be any mice in here. Maybe she was overreacting when she saw a shadow. Fuck, I really hoped she only saw a shadow.

I grabbed the broom from the kitchen and started toward the dining area where she'd set up most of her easels. I searched in the corners. Luckily, she was neat despite the paint being everywhere. All her boxes were put away now. The only hint of a mess were her easels and her paint supplies. "Okay, you saw him over here, right?"

"Yeah, I swear it. I heard a little squeak."

"Well, I don't see him now. Any chance he moved anywhere else in the apartment?"

"I don't know. I sort of ran and shouted. Then I jumped on the couch, and you showed up. So truthfully, if I'm being completely honest, I had my eyes closed. I have no idea where he is now."

Well, well. "All right. We'll get some traps, okay?"

She grimaced. "Oh my God. Not like those spring-loaded mousetraps that, like, break the neck. He's so little."

"I don't know what else to tell you. It's a mouse. It can't live here. It's not a pet, so you're gonna have to get rid of it somehow. I guess we can call an exterminator too."

"Yes, I like that one, an exterminator."

I had to chuckle. "Somehow that seems more humane to you? He's gonna gas the little fucker out."

Yeah, maybe I shouldn't have said that because her face fell. "No. I just—I just wanna catch him and you know, release him in the woods or something."

"Are there any woods around here?"

She shrugged. "I don't know. Something, anything ... I don't wanna have this little mouse's guts on my conscience."

I thought it through. "Okay, I guess, there are those like box traps or whatever. You put food or whatnot in it, and they crawl right in. It's not like those blue ones where they legit will gnaw off a limb just to get free. And it's also not like the spring-loaded traps where they break their neck or whatever. This one is humane. They go in through the locks, and then you can throw the box out, or call animal control and they take it away, or whatever." I was totally bullshitting about animal control. I didn't know what they did with those traps. I assumed they just threw it in the trash. But I supposed I'd have to figure it out for her. One neighbor ... one giant pain in the ass. But she was one giant, great-smelling pain in the ass.

Shit. I couldn't think about how good she smelled, or that creepy thing I did to her that one time. *Yeah, let's not think about that.* "Look, it'll be fine. I'll just—"

I heard the squeak behind me. Instead of turning around and bashing it with a broom, I may have yelled. Okay, I did yell. And I also jumped up on the couch with her. Before I knew what was happening, Len jumped up, wrapped her arms around my neck and straddled my hips as she tried to get even higher up off the ground.

Thought one: *Jesus, she's soft.* Thought two: *God! That was so not manly.* Thought three: *I fucking hate mice.* Thought four: *That mouse isn't so bad because now Len is wrapped around me and I think I like it.*

Thought five: *Shit, you are not allowed to like this.*

Sometimes, I hated my thought process. "Okay, okay. Settle down."

"Settle down? You're the one who jumped up here. I told you, it's an attacking mouse determined to kill me."

"He's little. He's not trying to kill you."

"Oh yeah? Then what are you doing on the couch?"

She had me there. "I—look, you looked comfortable up here. Fuck, okay. He startled me."

"You see? Now we're both going to die on this couch."

Whew! What a way to go. She barely weighed anything. She was all soft, female curves and coconut and lime-scented something that drove me insane. She smelled so good. *You will not sniff her again. You will not sniff her again.*

And I wasn't going to. But then—and it wasn't my fault—she wrapped herself tighter around me and nuzzled into my neck. And well, I couldn't help it. She was so close. Sniffing was inevitable. I did try to hold my breath. I did … for a second. And then I inhaled deeply. Every muscle in my body simultaneously relaxed and then spasmed as the electric charges hit them. And my dick, well, he made his presence known. Not that Len seemed to notice, because she was still clutching on to me for dear life.

I dragged in deep breaths, trying to think about anything other than the woman wrapped around me like a coiled snake. But oh no, every single thought was filled with Len. Len naked. Len bent over shaking her ass, wriggling at me as if in invitation. I'd already struck out with this girl, much to my chagrin. I didn't need to make it worse.

Unfortunately, I couldn't seem to make myself let her go. Her legs were wrapped around me. Her arms wound behind my neck. She was nuzzling deep inside my arms. I needed to hold her up, didn't I?

It wasn't my fault that my hands were on her ass. Really, it was her thighs. Let's be honest, though. I had to will my hand not to move because testing the firmness of her ass would have been full-on douche city. She was scared, and I wasn't going to take advantage.

"Um, well, I will call the building manager and get you a couple of those traps."

She pulled back slowly, her gaze meeting mine. Her eyes were dark pools of melted chocolate. And I could stare into them all day. She blinked rapidly and nodded. "Thank you." Then she seemed to notice that she was wrapped around me. A slight flush lit her cheeks, and then her thighs loosened their grip around my waist and she slid down. Her arms went last. And then we were standing on her couch, facing each other. Neither one of us acknowledged that my hands had just been on her ass. Because really, was there any need to acknowledge that?

She blinked up at me. "Thank you Sebastian, you know, for the rescue. Even though you ended up needing to be rescued yourself."

"Will you please tell no one? My reputation can't handle it."

She grinned. "If you get me some traps that don't involve me having to watch poor Mickey die, your secret is safe with me."

SEBASTIAN ...

As much as I didn't want to admit it, Len was right. I had to tell Lucas. Not that any of this shit was going to be easy. *Easy or not you need him. Your freedom hinges on it.*

Finding him at the coffee shop on the corner of 10th was easy. My brother was a creature of habit, and he went there every morning.

"Hey, man, what are you doing here?" Lucas clapped me on the shoulder as he ordered his sugary, girly coffee drink.

"I was in the neighborhood meeting a friend. I just popped in here for coffee." I made a production of ordering a small black coffee. I couldn't very well tell my brother that I'd had him followed by Blake Security for a month to get his routine. That would up the ante on the creep factor for sure. "Never imagined I'd run into you here." *Total bullshit.* Lucas came in here every day right after one of his classes. I might not want their security expertise right now, but the guys at Blake Security certainly had come in handy.

"I was at the library for a project."

"What do you study anyway?"

Lucas shrugged. "Business is my major. Boring, right? That

was one of those choices where I didn't exactly know what I wanted to do with my life, but I

knew I needed to make money. I'm also working on a minor in history, and a minor in French."

"You like languages?"

Lucas laughed. "I guess. They come easy to me. I'm passable in French Spanish, and Italian. So far it hasn't been of much use except for the random travel abroad." Lucas pushed open the exit and I joined him outside.

I took a seat and held onto my mug before pinning a gaze on Lucas. "Actually, I wanted to talk to you. I'm not here to just hangout."

Lucas's brows drew up. "Shit. I knew it. You're gay? I'm cool with it. But honestly, I thought that it was pretty clear that I wasn't."

I coughed. "Say what?"

My brother shrugged. "I mean. You're shifting around, looking uncomfortable. You have, like, weird tells."

"I'm not gay. Okay?"

Lucas raised brow. "Are you sure about that?"

"Yes, God damn it. I'm sure."

"I mean, the redhead was coming on pretty strong the other night and you were not interested. Although, the other girl, your neighbor, you seemed all into her. So I don't really know. Look, whatever it is, I'm cool, but I'm not interested."

I lifted my head and stared at the heavens for a long moment. "Jesus Christ. I'm straight. Not that there's anything wrong with being gay."

Lucas smirked. "Is that what people say when they think there's something wrong with that?"

"Shut up. I'm fucking trying to tell you that I'm your brother."

All of a sudden, Lucas's good mood evaporated. His brow snapped down and he scowled at me. "What?"

Fuck. That was not how I'd wanted it to come out. "I—us

meeting wasn't an accident. I've been looking for you. And I know this has to be a shock, but I am your brother."

"I don't have a brother."

"Yes. You do. I'm him. I am Sebastian Winston from the Winston Isles. Your mother and my father had a thing however many years ago. And you are the result."

Lucas laughed. "First, you want to tell me I'm your brother, and then you drop it on me that your dad and my mom had some sort of affair."

I nodded. "More or less. And you're not technically a prince yet, but our dad's trying to change that soon."

Lucas stared at me. Granted, this wasn't the sort of the reaction I had expected. In my head, I had arguments prepared. I was ready. But the dumbfounded denial was unexpected.

My brother leaned back. "You're full of shit."

"I promise you I'm not. I am currently the Crown Prince of Winston Isles."

Suddenly awareness dawned in Lucas's eyes. "Oh, are you high right now? Because whatever you're on, I want some."

I saw no other option, so I pulled out my wallet and showed Lucas my ID. Both the US driver's license and the one for the Winston Isles. It wasn't like I had a badge that said 'Crown Prince' or anything like that. But my name should suffice. "Look, I know this is a shock. I was hoping we could talk. It's been great getting to know you over the last little bit, but there are some things we need to talk about."

His frown only deepened. Somehow this was getting worse instead of better. "So, you've been acting like we were like hanging out as friends and shit, just so you could get close to me?"

That stung. "When you say it like that, it sounds shitty."

"That's because it *is* shitty. You're fucking insane. You and I, we're not brothers. I'm not a fucking prince. As much as I wish some insane shit like that were true. Maybe I could finally get those loan sharks off my mom's case. You've got no idea who I am or how I grew up. My mother hooked up with some drifter when

I was a baby. All I learned to do most of my life was lie, cheat, and steal. I'm no prince. When you met me, I was sure as shit hustling those guys. I have bills to pay. I made it to college only because I made a concerted effort to get the fuck out of that life, despite Mom and her tool of a husband Tony trying to drag me down. And I promise you, my folks would find a way to ruin this for me if they could. So I hate to break it to you, but you can't con a con man. Is that what this is? Did my mother and her good-for-nothing husband find you? Maybe you think you can shake me down and make me go back."

The flare of remorse in the center of my chest was unfamiliar. When I'd started looking for Lucas, I'd given no consideration to what I might find or who he might be. But wouldn't something like this be a welcome change?

I stood. "I promise you that is not what this is. I'm telling you the truth. You can verify with your mother if you want. Cassius Winston. Ask her if she knows him. That's all you have to do." I held on tight to my mug as if it were a lifeline. "If you change your mind, you have my number. For what it's worth, I'm sorry." I shook my head. "When I set out to find you, I never expected to like you too."

My brother glared at me mutinously. "Let's get something straight. You're a nut job. I won't be calling you"

I was getting this all wrong. This was supposed to be easier. "Okay, look. Just think about it."

Lucas put his hand up. "Dude, let me stop you now. I don't know what kind of story someone has fed you, but I don't have any siblings. My old man took off before I was even born. My mom said he was married or some shit. And he didn't want to know. So, that's that. I don't have a brother."

I shook my head stubbornly as if my mere assertion could change his mind. "You do. And I'm him."

I could only watch as my brother stalked away from me. What the fuck was that uncomfortable tightness in my chest?

It hurt. I wasn't used to people telling me no.

That's not it. No, it wasn't. I'd started to like the idea of having a brother.

I didn't want to examine any of this shit too closely. How the hell had I ended up here? The asshole son of a king, trying to right a wrong of my father's.

Trying to free yourself.

That was the plan. But that wasn't what was bothering me. I liked the guy, and I hadn't expected to. *Eyes on the prize. He'll be back.* Most people couldn't resist all the trappings that came with being royalty.

But is he most people?

Sebastian …

AFTER THE SHITTY morning with Lucas, I needed to blow off some steam and avoid my oh-so-sexy neighbor who had been painting on her balcony again.

To be truthful, I needed to put some work into the Winston project. I had another three months to deliver final images so the gallery could have them framed, but I hadn't been able to focus.

Most of my images were great, but I was looking for one signature piece and I still didn't have it. I also needed to pare down the list. The gallery wanted to show fourteen. I currently had twenty, and not one of them was a showstopper.

I was hoping the city would inspire me. The upcoming gallery show was one more reason that I couldn't get distracted by my tempting neighbor.

As I headed down to the corner, I ran smack into the woman I'd been trying to avoid. Okay, avoid sounded like it was intentional. And it hadn't been. *Mostly.*

As her breasts pressed into me, I had to stifle a groan.

"Oh my God. I'm so sorry. Of course I wasn't looking where I was going, and I was trying to carry the stupid easel. Clearly, I can't do two things at once. I should have just gotten the dolly. I don't know why I thought I could carry it by myself."

I was kind of getting used to her nonstop talking. And I liked it. I had no idea how one person could have so much to say and not filter any of it out. It was refreshing. People were always so careful with what they said to me. Either they wanted to look cool, or they didn't want to piss me off, or they thought they'd have some kind of advantage based on what they said. Len was honest. There was no pretense about her.

"It's no problem. Here, let me carry this."

She didn't let go. "No. I can do it. You helped me when I moved in. I am not a damsel in distress. I do not need Prince Charming."

The moment the word *prince* was out of her mouth, I stiffened. *Does she know?* I eyed her suspiciously. She was entirely focused on trying to lug the easel through the doors and past me. I was being too sensitive. "Come on, I insist. My mother did teach me right. Chivalry is not dead. Just let me help you take this up."

"Okay, fine, but I insist on paying you back in some way. I mean the moving in, the shower fiasco—the mouse. You need to let me *do* something."

Oh I have a couple ideas on what you can do. What? No. Not happening.

This girl did not like to accept help. Even though she clearly needed it. "It's not necessary."

"No, I insist. I like things to be even. Let me make you dinner. I mean, I can't really cook. So what I'm really saying is I'll buy us takeout. But you know what? I can bake. I make a mean cupcake. For some reason the baking gene works but not the cooking one."

I laughed. "You know baking is harder than cooking."

"That's me. If there is flour and sugar involved, I somehow get it right. When I'm cooking, I mess up every time. And unfortunately, man cannot live on cake alone. I am not Marie Antoinette."

She headed for the stairs, and I stopped her. "Why are you

taking the stairs? We live on the third floor, and this thing isn't light. Let's take the elevator."

For the first time since I'd met her, her dimples disappeared. And her lips pursed. "Uh, okay."

I pushed the button, and for the first time she was quiet. Not a peep. I slid a glance at her and noticed her stiff shoulders and the way she impatiently tapped her foot. What was wrong? Had I said something? I knew I could be an asshole sometimes, but I was on my best behavior with this girl. Mostly because I was trying *not* to fuck her.

My dick twitched as if to call me a liar.

When the elevator arrived, the doors slid open and I stepped back, letting her go in first. Her eyes went wide before she gingerly stepped in and scooted right to the back corner.

Something was off.

I stepped in after her, lugging that heavy-ass easel behind me. I pushed the button for the third floor and turned to look at her. "Okay, what gives?"

"What do you mean?" She swallowed hard, eyes pinned to the numbers above.

"I mean, I'm used to you talking a mile a minute and having too much to say. Now you're dead silent. What's wrong?"

"I don't like small spaces. A cousin of mine locked me in a closet when I was little."

Shit. No wonder she was terrified. "Fuck. Why didn't you say something?"

The elevator came to a grinding stop. The thing was old, the building was old. Everything here was old. She squeaked and tried to flatten herself even more into the corner. "Because you're right, that easel is heavy, and it was three flights of stairs, and I didn't want to look like a crazy person in front of you and tell you that I was terrified of elevators."

"So instead, you're freaking out."

Now was not the time to tease her. She needed help. And she really did look terrified. Her eyes were wide and darting back and forth. Her hands were trembling. I leaned the easel against the wall, and took her hands. "Breathe in. Breathe out."

It took her several seconds, but then she did as I told her. She finally began to relax when I rubbed circles into her back. The shaking eventually stopped, and her breathing evened out. And sure enough, the elevator started to move again. As soon as we reached the third floor and the doors split apart, she scrambled out.

I picked up the easel and followed her. "You okay?"

She licked her lips even as she nodded. And for a moment, my gaze was pinned to the sight of her tongue peeking out. "Yeah. Thank you. It seems that you are Prince Charming after all."

"Not too sure about that." But something about the way she looked at me made me want to be the kind of guy that could be Prince Charming. "Come on. Let's get your easel to your place."

"As a thank you, I offer a burrito from Angel's down the street."

The answer in his scenario should have been no. Let me list the reasons why:

She had a boyfriend.

I didn't have time for this shit.

I still felt the imprint of her body against mine from the other day. I'd wanted to kiss her so badly I had practically vibrated with it.

See, a whole bunch of reasons you have to say no. Except when I opened my mouth I said, "Sounds like a plan. Manual labor makes me hungry." I was so screwed.

PENNY ...

IT OCCURRED to me that despite all my great advice to Sebastian about coming clean and dealing with the problem, I was not doing that myself. I hadn't dealt with Robert or Michael and I needed to do something.

Ariel had a point. I could get a lot closer to the prince just by the fact that I was a woman. And wasn't that why King Cassius sent me here in the first place?

Ariel gave me a nudge. "Earth to Penny. What's wrong with you?"

Ariel had set up surveillance in the bar where Sebastian worked. And currently, he was running inventory. So we were at the café on the corner while Blake Security had eyes on him. We were close enough that we could see if anything was problematic.

"I'm sorry. I was just thinking."

Ariel stole one of the French fries off my plate. "Does this have anything to do with you getting close to a certain royal?"

I rolled my eyes. "I'm not going to do what you think I'm going to do."

Ariel just threw up her hands and shrugged. "I'm not saying anything, but the guy is clearly into you."

"He is not into *me*. He is into *women* ... *all* women, *any* woman.

There's nothing about me that makes me more special than anyone else."

"If that's the case, then why don't you use it? Look, no one's saying you need to boink the guy's brains out, even though you clearly seem like you want to. But he clearly already thinks he can talk to you so use it. Make it work. Besides, this is the gate. Get close to him, befriend him, maybe ... " She shrugged. "Maybe there's something holding you back."

I frowned. "What do you mean?"

She stared at me. "Hello, Robert."

My stomach fell. I trusted her with everything. But if something was going on between Robert and my brother, it wasn't my secret to tell, despite the slash of betrayal. Just thinking about the way they'd been kissing each other hurt. Robert had never kissed me like that before. And if I was being frank, I'd never seen Michael that passionate about anything or anyone. Especially not Emily.

"I don't know. I just need to focus on this job."

Ariel nodded firmly. "Of course you do. I'm just saying that your relationship status with Robert might be holding you back from going all in."

"And by 'all in' you mean naked with the prince? I'm not going to do that."

"Yes, I know. But whether you want to admit it or not, having things unresolved with Robert holds you back from even forming a close friendship." Before I could argue, she held up her hand. "Hear me out. Look, for the last couple of years, I've seen him keep you at a distance. I've seen him get your hopes up and then let you down. I think maybe that's stopping you from going all in. This job, this assignment, it requires a certain level of trust. Yes, you trust me. I'm your best friend so you should trust me. I will walk over fire for you. But you don't trust the prince, and, well, you shouldn't. But you have to be able to let go enough to fake it. And I don't think you can because of Robert."

I frowned. She had a point, although not for the reason she

thought. She thought my history with Robert was keeping me from even allowing someone to get close. What she didn't know was my more recent discovery about Robert that was turning me upside down. Either way, she had a point. I needed to talk to him, which unfortunately meant calling him.

"We've been here for two weeks. I haven't spoken to him since I left. I didn't even tell him I was leaving."

Ariel lifted a brow. "Okay, I get you being mad at him because he did ditch you on your birthday. But maybe you guys should talk."

I sat back and crossed my arms. "He has my number, but *he* hasn't called either."

She laughed. "Oh my God, you expect him to call? He thinks you're still mad about your birthday. But the truth is, even if you are, it doesn't matter. You have a job to do, and you have got to settle stuff with him because it's keeping you from doing that job."

I sighed. Ariel reached over to my plate for another French fry, and I smacked her hand. "No fries for you."

She pouted. "You're not eating them. Besides, surveillance is making me hungry."

It wasn't the surveillance that was making her hungry; it was our renewed workouts. We couldn't exactly be seen together, but we both had to stay in shape. So she'd gotten some workout DVDs called Insane Ridiculousness, or something. Pretty much a very good looking, abbed-out guy shouted at her in an extra perky tone about how 'you can do these sit-ups.' I did not like those sit-ups. But Ariel was committed and was in starvation mode. All she wanted to do was eat.

"Fine, take them. I don't want them anyway. Okay, you've inspired me. You have eyes on Sebastian. I think I need to make a call." Ariel dipped her French fries in some ketchup and mustard. How the hell she could do that, I had no idea. I was a purist when it came to my French fries.

"Yep. I've got eyes on him. You go make your call. Don't walk down toward the bar no matter how tempting it might be to get a good look at Sebastian, you know, using his muscles." She winked at me. I really wished she hadn't said anything about Sebastian and his muscles because they really were a sight to behold. Watching him carry that easel inside for me the other night had given me a chance to see them up close.

I deliberately walked in the opposite direction of the bar, took out my phone and dialed it, and hoped Robert wouldn't answer.

That hope died on the second ring. He picked it up immediately. "Penny?"

"Robert, hi."

"Where are you? I've been worried sick."

"So worried that you actually called me?"

"Well, I went looking for you. You know, to talk, after everything … " His voice trailed and I had to fight the queasiness as I remembered exactly why this was so awkward. "You went to my house instead of calling me. Are you sure you didn't go to see Michael?"

"Penny, about what you saw. It's not what you think. It just— happened. I don't even know—"

The sound of his lie was enough to induce a migraine. "How can you say that? Look, I can't tell you where I am, but I'm on assignment so I'm not going be back for a while. And anyway, obviously, I think maybe you and I are over. So there's that."

He didn't skip a beat. "I refuse to accept that."

"What? I just broke up with you, *after* I saw you kissing my brother. I'm pretty sure that's going to stick."

"No. We have a lot to talk about. I regret what happened, but you and I, we make sense. So why don't we just wait for you to get back and then we can decide."

I stopped walking. Pedestrians strolling through the East Village milled around me. "You've got to be kidding me. We're not going to have any more conversations. Because not only were you kissing someone else, male or female, you were kissing my *brother*. That level of betrayal is—You don't come back from that."

"I was confused, Penny. Stop being dramatic."

Oh, I'd show him dramatic. "And see, right there, that's the other reason. When I have a perfectly normal response to something, you try and act like I'm being dramatic in some way. I'm not. That was a betrayal."

He was silent for several beats before finally saying, "Look, I get it. I do. I just want us to be okay. How about we talk when you get back? Just don't abandon me."

Low blow, asshole. My heart squeezed. He once told me that one of his biggest fears was that his whole family would turn their backs on him one day. I didn't understand it at the time, but now I did.

I used to insist that they loved him. I wondered would they really turn their backs on him if they found out he was gay? It was insane. Besides, gay marriage was legal in the Winston Isles. There was no reason for him not to be who he was. But hell, what the fuck did I know about it?

Still though, it didn't mean that I could stay with him just to make him happy. Not after what he'd done.

"There's nothing to talk about. I have to go." He started to argue with me just as a street hawker nearby pulled out a bullhorn.

"Get your ten-dollar Kate Spade bags here. Kate Spade, just ten dollars, almost like the real thing." And then he started jabbering even faster. I walked further down the street so that I could speak into the phone.

"Robert, my instinct is to say that I'm sorry for hurting you or something, but I'm not the one who needs to apologize."

But as it turned out, he wasn't even that worried about my attempts to break up with him. "Are you in New York?"

I froze. How the hell did he know that? "What?"

"I just heard some guy selling kits of bean bags. Are you in New York?"

I knew the drill. When on assignment performing a royal duty, unless sent on official business for a royal tour, I shouldn't disclose where I was. "I can't tell you that."

His voice dropped an octave. "If you're not supposed to tell me, that means it's official business. The Queen is here. The King is here." *Fuck.* "Penny, did you find Sebastian?"

"I have to go. Don't call me, okay? I can't stand to talk to you." I sucked in a deep breath, unsure of why I was sweating. My heart hammered against my ribs. Had I screwed up? How had he figured out I was in New York? And how much trouble would this make for me? And why did I still feel unsettled?

Because you still have to deal with Michael.

That was another problem for another day. Right now, I'd removed all obstacles from my path. I could focus solely on the job.

Now, all I had to do was navigate my ridiculous lady feelings for Sebastian. I could do this. Like my mother said, the assignment was a chance to prove myself. And I wasn't going to screw it up by falling for the one man in the world I couldn't have.

Penny ...

I TOSSED IN THE BED. It was hot and sticky, and my mind kept going back to Sebastian. His lips so close I thought he was going to kiss me. His nose trailing along my skin.

With a groan I flipped over. "Damn it." For starters, it was far too hot for October. The heat was making me insane. It was also making me think about doing things with the Crown Prince of Winston Isles, even though I was a commoner and technically his Royal Guard. The things running through my head at the moment were not allowed.

But someone needed to tell my body that, because every time I closed my eyes, all I could see was him. Sebastian's hooded gaze, his broad shoulders casting a shadow over my body as he leaned into me. I could practically feel his nose and the shadow of his lips across my skin.

This was insane. I was just being crazy. It had been a while since I'd had sex. I tried to even remember when the last time was. It wasn't like Robert and I had never had sex. It was just that it was infrequent … *very* infrequent. *Hello, that was a sign.* Okay fine, it had been a while. We'd just go with that. That's all this was.

I was horny and strung out, and he was sexy. No one was arguing his complete and utter sex appeal. I just wasn't supposed to be susceptible to it. It was fine. No big deal. I could just think it away.

Good luck with that.

Okay, maybe not as easy as all that. My whole body vibrated … throbbed … just thinking about him. This wasn't me. I didn't lose my mind. I didn't indulge fantasies about the prince and that's what this was, pure and utter fantasy. I wasn't dumb enough to think that his attention had anything to do with me personally. He was a flirt … a renowned flirt.

You could just take care of the problem.

I groaned again. The last thing on earth I needed to do was to take care of the problem. After all, wouldn't it just come back stronger?

No. Just take some of the tension off and then you can sleep. And with a full night's rest, you can look at the scenario with new eyes.

Man, my inner voice was good at rationalizing. *But do you really have another choice? You can't sleep. You're fantasizing about someone you can't have. Take the edge off.* God, what was wrong with me? Never mind. I knew what was wrong with me. Sebastian Winston. And I knew how to take care of the problem.

With a frustrated groan, I reached into the bedside table. I'd brought my little pocket rocket from home, which was silly really because I was on a mission. Who in the world would bring a vibrator on a mission? *This girl.*

That was just good forward thinking.

I slid the tiny vibrator underneath my pajama bottoms and found my clit easily. When I turned on the buzzer to low speed, my mind instantly bloomed with visions of Sebastian. His cocky lopsided smile, the way he gazed down at me through his lashes, his strong arms around me holding me up, his hands nearly on my ass. But he'd been appropriate … mostly. He hadn't grabbed my ass. He hadn't held on to me, pressed me against the wall and ground his hips into mine.

Nope. That was just one of the many, many day dreams I've had, one of the sleeping ones too. I had to get that shit under control.

That's what you're doing. Just focus on him and then you can get back to normal. It's fine. No one will know.

And so I let the thoughts consume me. I could practically feel his lips sliding over mine. I imagined his hands roaming over my body, my breasts … holding them, weighing them, leaning forward and kissing them, licking them and then using his teeth. I could almost imagine the way he'd kiss my body, pausing at interesting spots to lick and torture me. And then he would get slower and plant his mouth directly over my clit and slowly perform some oral dexterity the likes of which I've never seen before in my life.

I let myself imagine Sebastian licking over my clit. Long strokes meant to promise orgasms, many of them. But it refused to quite draw them out as the pace was too slow. It was a tease, just like he was.

Eventually, I ditched the vibrator. It wasn't getting the job done. Using my fingers, I slowly dipped inside and moaned. What would it feel like to have Sebastian inside of me? To have his tongue, his fingers, or his dick in me? It didn't take much. Before long, with a slight flutter of my fingers, imagining Sebastian with his hands fisting my curls, tugging hard as he loved me deep, I was flying.

I knew it was a fantasy. I knew it wasn't real. I knew I was bat shit crazy for even doing this. But it didn't stop me from moaning out his name as my release hit.

SEBASTIAN ...

What the hell did she just say?

I wasn't being a pervert. I swore to God. I wasn't. It was hot as fuck and I couldn't sleep. So I opened the doors to my balcony. It wasn't my fault that my next door neighbor with the killer rat was moaning my name. And not just like *saying* it, as if maybe saying my name to a friend. She was saying it as if I were between her legs. My dick twitched. *Easy, soldier. We're not going there.* What the fuck was going on?

I meant to go back inside. I did. That was the plan.

But then she moaned again.

And naturally, being curious, I wanted to check on her and see if she was okay.

Liar.

Okay, I wanted to hear her moan, again. What were the chances that her boyfriend was also named Sebastian? It was possible. It could happen.

I leaned further out the door. I could hear her. She was making these breathy little pants. I could hear more moaning, more groaning, more of my dick turning to steel.

Holy shit, she was touching herself. And calling my name? If that wasn't the hottest thing I've ever heard or seen in my life, I don't know what was. Yes, I'd seen plenty of women masturbate. Hell, I'd even helped my fair share. But this, this was something else. Something hotter.

And this was Len, the girl with a sweet voice who talked a mile a minute and had wrapped her body around me like an anaconda just because she'd been scared of a mouse. It was bad enough that I couldn't get the girl out of my head. It was worse now that I could hear her moaning my name.

Too bad you've heard it, because you're never going to touch her. That's not the mission. It's not why you're here. Focus on that reason.

Buzzkill. I hated it when I could be rational. Because right now, there was a part of me that only wanted to focus on the beautiful girl next door who obviously had me on her mind.

But you're not supposed to be that guy anymore. You're supposed to be a different guy. I forced myself to turn around and go back to my camera and my table. I had dozens of shots from the last couple of days that I needed to go over. There were several that needed tweaks. A couple of those were good options. What was I doing standing here listening to her?

Despite the heat, I forced myself to work. If I couldn't sleep, at least I could be productive. The thing was my cock had other ideas. Little Sebastian was thick and hard against my thigh and throbbed incessantly. He knew what was up next door, and he wanted to go play.

Hell, right now he'd settle for even the suggestion that she might play with him. How long had it been since I'd gotten laid? It didn't matter. Whatever the answer was, it was too fucking long.

Len is right there and clearly calling your name.

No. Not that. She was gorgeous and stunning, and all matter of things that I could want. But I couldn't have her. Besides, she was a sweet enough girl who didn't need my baggage trailing after her. I needed to work. Easy. But I was pretty sure the wind and the heat were conspiring against me. Because as I focused my gaze on the photos I'd taken earlier that day, I heard her again, her voice calling my name on a flutter of the wind. "Sebastian!"

I was so screwed. I wanted her. And there was absolutely no way in hell that I could have her.

16

SEBASTIAN ...

THAT PROMISE I had made myself yesterday about not jerking off to my pretty neighbor next door..? Yeah, I was lying.

I'd done it again. Fuck. Okay, twice more. I'd woken up with a stiff cock and the only way to get back to sleep was to think about her and the sexy little noises she made in the back of her throat before she moaned my name.

I'd imagined her in a myriad of ways. My hands on her ass, rocking her against me. My hands on her tits, testing how full she was. I'd pictured her on her knees, writhing beneath me and on top of me. That particular mental image had been my favorite: imagining her rocking forward so I could suck on her.

Jesus.

Look, I wasn't proud of it. But it happened. But today was a new day. The shit of it was the mental image that had sent me over each time was the one of me with my hands in her hair, kissing her, like I'd wanted to do during mousegate. How could she be so damn sexy and not even fucking know it?

Easy does it. She has a boyfriend. I knew that was supposed to stop this line of thought. It had never stopped me before. And in the past, boyfriends almost made my life easier because those girls wouldn't want more from me.

Jesus, I was a prick.

So yeah, when I woke up with the memory of her moan, I wasn't thrilled. She was turning into a goddamned problem if I didn't do something about it soon. The real question was *what* I going to do about it.

Nothing. Because that's not why you're here.

I was here for Lucas. Not that Lucas had called. *I need to get shit with my brother going.*

Admittedly, I'd gone through all that went wrong in my mind. But I had wanted to get to know Lucas better. Find out the kind of man he was. Find out if maybe he'd be happier not knowing where he came from, who he was.

Lucas had a right to be pissed off. He'd felt ambushed. And he *had* been ambushed. *Fuck.* Everything was going to shit. And if I wanted my freedom, I needed to get Lucas back to the Winston Isles before the big vote. I only had two months. Two more months and I could be free. I just had to get my brother to go to the Winston Isles.

And that was the crux of it. I had to get my head back in the game. First things first, I needed to find him. I'd go to his job if I had to, but my brother had to talk to me. We were running out of time. And if Lucas was going to get to meet the old man and wrangle some votes in his favor, we needed to get moving quickly.

My dick attempted to start to life again and I growled. "We do not have time for this shit. Stop it."

Though, as it were, my dick did what he wanted to do, and right about now there was no controlling the way he responded to Len.

From somewhere in the living room, my phone rang, and I shoved up out of bed. I snatched my phone off the counter and grinned when I saw it was Lucas calling. "Hey, Lucas. Glad you finally called me."

My brother was silent for a beat. "Yeah, well, I debated it for a bit."

"But you're curious?" *Please, please be curious.*

"Look, we need to talk. Can you meet me? Joe's Café? Like around ten?"

"Yeah. I'll make it happen." I was so close. Soon, I'd be free. And then I could do what I wanted. I just hoped my brother cooperated with me. Because like it or not, in two months one of us was going to be prince, and one of us was going to be nobody.

17

SEBASTIAN ...

Fuck. I was nervous. I'd never been nervous in my life. But this was different. I needed this badly. And there was a part of me that no longer wanted to be alone. I no longer wanted to bear the brunt of all that pressure. I needed the guy and needing someone made you vulnerable.

Whatever. Even if I wasn't used to the feeling, I could deal. After all, I was already here.

I pushed the doors to the diner open and saw Lucas sitting in a booth at the back. I made my way through the throngs of people, nodding at the hostess that I was meeting someone. When I reached the table, Lucas didn't smile.

Okay, not exactly a friendly reception. That was all right. I had a plan. Not exactly the best of plans, but still, it was a semblance of a plan. "Thanks for meeting me."

"Well, considering I haven't been able to think about anything else since we talked, it's not like I really had a choice."

And it all came down to choice, didn't it? "Look, sorry to ambush your life man. But I thought you should know."

The corner of Lucas's lips tipped into a wry smile. "The thing is I was ready to believe that you were a complete wacko. And then I looked you up. The Winston Isles, your name. You're a fucking prince, goddamned royalty."

I slid my gaze around. "Please, keep your voice down."

My brother leaned forward. "And that's just the thing. I've been seeing all these reports of you in Mallorca, or Ibiza, or Fiji. Partying it up, causing international incidents wherever you go. But then here you are, sitting in a diner with me. It doesn't track."

I was glad Lucas had done his due diligence. I didn't want someone gullible sitting on the throne. To manage politics in a monarchy, he needed to be shrewd. "Did you come to any determinations?"

Lucas sat back. "Well, I went back and had a look at the photos of you with your parents. With *our* father. And there are a couple of close-ups. For example." Lucas indicated his own chin, rubbing the backs of his fingertips against it. "For example, the Crown Prince of Winston Isles has a scar right here. Supposedly he fell off a horse playing polo."

I nodded. Not bad. So far no one else had looked that close.

Lucas shrugged. "I checked out those doubles. Neither one of those guys in Mallorca (or wherever the fuck) had any close-up shots. But you, sitting right in front of me, have that very same scar. Which leads me to believe those guys are doubles. Which leads me to believe you set that up to so that the world would think that you were doing things that princes do. All the while you're here. And I want to know why."

Okay. So my brother was better than shrewd. Sharp as a tack actually, which would make things a lot easier. "I didn't know anything about you up until about six months ago. My father, *our* father, is trying to push through a change to the Constitution where you and our supposed sister would be in line for the throne."

"So what? You're here to make sure that I don't challenge your birthright?"

I shook my head. "Nope. The exact opposite. I want that vote to go through."

Lucas's brow furrowed. "But why? That makes no sense. If he establishes me as a prince, won't that be a danger to you? Couldn't I just, like, kill you off or whatever and then become king?"

I grinned. "I would hope for a less bloody method to make you king, but yes in theory."

Lucas stared me. Lucas worked his teeth over his bottom lip. "I spoke to my mother. She had a fascinating story to tell me."

And here it was. The part I had been waiting for. Lucas was starting to believe. And it was exactly what I needed.

"Italy. I guess she always wanted to go. She managed to win a study abroad scholarship. You see, unlike you, my family didn't grow up with a silver spoon. So Mom goes to Europe and does all the things that girls studying abroad do, including sleeping with some guy she thinks is hot. And having some crazy mini affair. He had to leave and they made all the promises to keep in touch. Which he doesn't."

He cleared his throat and shifted his gaze to the cracked linoleum of the table. "What she doesn't recognize until a couple of months later when she's safely back at home is that she's pregnant. With *me*. She tries to get in touch with that guy. But she doesn't have his full name, at least not his real one. She has no one to contact, no one to let know that he's going to be a father. A couple of years later, she's hooked up with Darren the Douche con man, and Study Abroad guy appears and wants to be part of my life. She's pissed, so she kicks him to the curb." Lucas took a sip of his coffee. "She must have really loved him."

"How do you know?"

"Because she didn't fleece him. Or go to the press."

I nodded. "In the pieces I have from our father, he talked about how he met your mother and how he had to return to the Winston Isles. He said he wasn't allowed to give her his real name. And in his own way, he was doing his own get-away-from-his-life thing. But unlike her, he tracked her until her found her. When he turned up in her life, she wanted nothing to do with him and wouldn't accept any support for you."

"Probably a good call. Darren would have blown the cash at the track."

I shrugged. "All I know is that he's trying to push this vote through to make sure that you get what you deserve. There's no reason for him to do that, unless he really does want to claim you."

Lucas gave a harsh chuckle. "No reason besides guilt. You're okay with this?"

I nodded. "I am."

Lucas frowned. "I still think you're insane, but fill in the holes for me."

"Okay. We're going to need more coffee for this."

Penny ...

TODAY WAS A NEW DAY. Today would not include fantasizing about the crown prince. Today would not include fantasizing then masturbating about the prince.

This was my new mantra. Especially the parts about how I would *not* fantasize about Sebastian. What the hell was wrong with me?

Nope. I would not spiral downward. Not going happen. Last night's dream happened. *Fine.* People dreamed all the time. I was not going to take this one too seriously. Besides, it wasn't entirely my fault.

He'd been all sexy and stuff. His Royal Fucking Majesty lifted heavy things for me. It was *biology*. Biology made me click the ol' O-getter button repeatedly. *Biology.*

It wasn't your fault. That was my story and I was sticking to it.

In my dream, he'd leaned in and kissed *me* with his whole I'm-going-to-rock-your-world look. I couldn't be held accountable for finding the man attractive. The guy was hot. The abs. Hell, just the face alone. When Dream Me grabbed onto his shirt, I'd found soft cotton had been laid over a hard-as-granite six-pack. It was not my fault that my body responded. *Liar*.

I hopped out of the shower, more resolute than ever to do a good job. Nothing was going to get in my way. I just had to prove to myself that I could do this and that I was meant to do this job. So what if my father didn't believe in me?

Who cared? Ariel thought I could do anything. Okay, also to be fair, Ariel was my best friend. But more importantly, she thought I could do this. And I was going to. I was going to take the bull by the balls. All I had to do was find a way to get close but remain detached. Maybe it was time to suggest a hang out. So far I'd managed the random bumping-into, but I needed to speed this along. We'd had one personal conversation, so I just needed to build on that. I could do that. I *had* to do that.

Besides, I wasn't dumb enough to think that he cared about me. I knew enough about the prince. He was hell on women. Besides, he loved himself some socialites. He wouldn't look twice at a wannabe artist and subpar Royal Guard. Not going to happen.

Those stories where the low-born girl somehow caught the attention of the prince and managed to marry him? Those were called fairy tales for a reason. Because just like fairies, they didn't exist.

I pulled out my phone and cursed under my breath, running back to the bathroom. The curses rained from my lips. "Fuck. Shit. Bugger." There were several alerts that he was on the move. And this morning was my shift.

I'd lost him. I checked my laptop monitor quickly, only to confirm he wasn't in his apartment. And while I'd managed to bug his place, I still hadn't managed to tag his phone. The guy was already gone. *Damn*. I was so totally screwed. If I were a prince, where would I go?

With legs still slicked wet from the shower, I tried to tug on a pair of jeans hastily as Ariel called. I answered on the first ring. "Yep, Ariel, I know. I can't talk. I lost the fucking prince."

On the other end of the line, I could hear something dropping. "What the fuck do you mean you *lost* him?"

"Calamity Penny is back. I didn't get to tag his damn phone. That's what I was supposed to do when he helped me, but he never even pulled the damn thing out of his pocket."

"Shit, where do you think he is?"

"No clue. Where would you go if you were him?"

"Honey, I don't know. Maybe an appointment? He loves photography. Maybe he'd catch the early morning light?"

"Yeah, sure. Except that leaves an awful lot of places." I pinched the bridge of my nose. "Think. Think. Think. Think. Okay, listen. I'll head out, maybe down toward the bar. There are some cafés near there. I will call you later." Then I hung up with my best friend and hoped I hadn't ruined my future already.

Shit. Shit. Shit. I had been so busy patting myself on the back I hadn't kept my eye on the prize. I still needed to clone his damn phone. But now, I'd lost the damn prince.

I shoved my feet into my combat boots, not caring that I had on leggings with holes in them and a graphic T-shirt with paint all over it. It was fine. It was a look. I was going with that. The most important thing right now was to find the prince. And possibly save my job. *Yes, but is it even a job that I want?* Oh hell no. I was not having that whole career-crisis situation right now.

I had no idea where the hell he was. And since when did he leave the house before ten o'clock? I was going to have to get on a different schedule if I wanted to keep ahead of him. *Think. Think. If you were the crown prince of the Winston Isles, where would you go at the ass crack of dawn?* The only place I could think of was maybe the bar. Maybe he left something at the bar?

Okay, that was my first stop. If he wasn't there, I was fucked. But I wasn't going to think about that. I just had to get my ass to the bar, and I'd figure it out from there.

I hustled the three blocks in the direction of the bar where he worked before my phone rang. I didn't even bother to look at the caller ID before answering. "Yeah?"

"Penelope?"

I froze. I knew that voice. "King Cassius?" I choked out.

There was a little chuckle. "Were you expecting someone else?"

I froze like a cockroach in daylight. Holy shit balls. "Shit. Oh my God, Your Majesty. I'm so sorry." Shit. I'd sworn at the King. What was wrong with me? Damn. "I was just working on Sebastian. Oh bugger. I don't mean like *working* on him. I swear. Not in a sexual manner." Oh my God. I needed to stop. "Or any manner. Shit. Oh dammit. I just did it again." *Shut up. Just stop talking. As a matter of fact, you should never talk again.*

I stopped running too. Maybe my brain would start to function if it wasn't so worried about hauling ass to the bar.

This time the King's laugh was a low rumble, and my skin flushed. Great. Now I could probably get a job as the court jester. Well, at least I would have a job. "This is probably the most I've laughed in several weeks."

"Always glad to be of service to the crown. What can I do for you, Your Majesty?"

"I'm just calling for an update. Are things going well with Sebastian?"

"Yes sir. We've met, and I've established myself as the neighbor. I also set up surveillance just yesterday in his apartment." I left out the part where I'd had a sexy dream of Sebastian kissing me and that I'd thought about doing some really inappropriate things with the crown prince.

"Good. Good. He doesn't suspect you?"

"No. Not that I know of. But sir, this might all be made easier if I didn't need to lie. Maybe if I was just—"

"No. I know Sebastian well. If he finds out that you're Royal Guard, he will never trust me again. As it is, whatever you're doing made him engage with me for the first time in six months. He called home. So no, I need you to keep this quiet."

Great. I would just go ahead and keep lying. That was *if* I found the prince again. And just as my brain was scrambling to find something to say, something I could offer as a better status update, I glanced across the street to Joe's Cafe. And there he was, with Lucas. "Oh, thank fuck."

"Excuse me?"

Shit. I'd said that out loud? "So sorry, Your Majesty. I was saying thank God. I think keeping him in the dark is the best idea. He'll disclose more to me. Keep me closer. And I can keep him protected."

This was treason. I'd just lied to my king. *Because like a moron, you're starting to feel things you have no business feeling.*

Well, I was going to have to get over it, because that was not part of the job.

"Very well then. I'll call again in a few days to check in."

"Your Majesty, would you rather I call and give you regular updates? Maybe once a week?"

"I prefer to call you on a blocked number. That way if he should check your phone, he won't find anything amiss."

Would he be checking my phone? "I'll make sure he's not suspicious of me."

"I think that's a good idea. And Penelope ... "

"Yes, Your Majesty?"

"Thank you. I've slept better knowing that you have Sebastian's best interests at heart."

I hung up with the king, unsure if that was entirely true.

18

SEBASTIAN ...

I WASN'T sure what made me look up. Maybe it was a trick of the light, or maybe it was a waitress walking by with coffee for the table by the window. Whatever it was, I looked up at just the right moment to see Len on her phone just across the street. What I should have done was sit my ass right there. Lucas and I were getting to know each other, which was exactly what I wanted. But there was that part of me that couldn't quite stay away from her, the sick, masochistic part of me. That part of me that was becoming a damn pain in the ass.

"Listen, you mind company for breakfast? I see Len over there."

Lucas glanced out the window then chuckled. "She's cute. I didn't exactly picture you as the bohemian-artist type. But hey, I don't judge. She is definitely hot."

I narrowed my gaze. "It's not like that. And do me a favor and don't hit on her."

Lucas grinned and shrugged. "Look man, if she's digging the vibe I put out, I might not be able to help myself. Can you keep her from flirting with me?"

I had the sudden, irrational urge to wipe that smug grin off my brother's face by any means necessary. Jealousy? Why was I jealous?

The girl had a boyfriend. I couldn't have her anyway.

Because you want her.

No. I did not want her. Never mind that I kept thinking about how soft the skin at the nape of her neck was, or that little strip of skin just between her tank top and the top of her jeans. Never mind that I desperately wanted to kiss her there.

Nope. Not part of the plan. I had just made that pact with myself. Or rather *remade* it. But before I knew it, I scooted out of the booth, out the door of Joe's, and went jogging across the street.

She saw me as she was finishing up her phone call. I didn't like the stress lines around her mouth. Though even when she was frowning, she was gorgeous. Her hazel green eyes were both fiery and bleak, and as she hung up, she plastered a fake smile on her face. "Oh, hey."

"Hey, yourself." I cocked my head. "You following me?"

Her eyes went wide. "Why would you say that?"

I frowned. Something was up with her. "Relax. I'm teasing. No painting this morning?"

"I wanted to grab a cup of coffee and get some air. Maybe it'll inspire me."

I inclined my head toward the café. "Want to join us?"

She smiled up at me. "Wow, a double-team date. Kinky." A flush lit her face and her hands flew up to cover those pretty cheeks. "Shit, that came out wrong."

Two things happened simultaneously. I laughed, and my dick twitched. *Back away slowly. She's trouble.* "No." Though I wasn't sure if the no was for her or my dick. Damn thing seemed to have a mind of its own. "More like, you need to eat, and I'm trying to say thank you for the good advice."

She shook her head. "No thanks needed. Besides, I think I owed you."

I shoved my hands into my pockets and rolled back onto my heels. Why were things so hard with her? Or so easy? Because even though this was an awkward conversation and I should be desperate to get away from her, it was easy to be in her presence.

I had zero urge to run. I just wanted to be closer. "Right. Now that we have that reestablished, come have breakfast. Come on. I won't bite."

"That's disappointing," she murmured under her breath.

My dick swelled. Mother of fucking God. I was pretty sure the damn thing was never going down.

She rolled her shoulders back. "Sure. I need to eat."

The relief flooded my veins.

"Come on. I'm buying."

"You just said the magic words."

She trailed behind me into the restaurant. And I could see that even though she was agreeing to join me, her sour mood hadn't dissipated. Something on the call had bothered her. "You okay? You seem a little upset."

"Fine. Just an unexpected phone call."

"I had one of those last week. Your parents?"

She shook her head. "Worse."

When she didn't elaborate, I let it go for the time being. I wanted to smack her twat of a boyfriend. I led the way to the table where I'd left Lucas, who stood immediately. "Len, you remember Lucas?"

She treated him to a sweet smile that had me holding back a growl. "Nice to see you again, Lucas."

Lucas turned on the charm, and I wanted to hit him. "Pleasure is all mine. Here, sit next to me." He shifted to allow her into the booth.

Len stuttered. "Oh, thank you. That's sweet."

"This way I can get to know Sebastian's friend better."

Oh hell no. I took her elbow and guided her into the booth next to me. I was not letting Lucas poach this one.

It's not poaching when you say you don't want to be with someone. Never mind all that.

Len's brows furrowed. She didn't say anything. And Lucas,

well, my brother just laughed. It should have felt like the most awkward thing ever. Having a conversation with a brother I never knew I had, with a girl next to me I wasn't sure I wanted. But it felt like the most natural thing in the world. I was the most comfortable I'd been in months.

Penny ...

"So, Lucas, do you live in the city?"

Lucas nodded. "Yeah, I go to NYU."

He, like Sebastian, was a stunner. Like a jaw-on-the-floor, lick-some-abs kind of stunner. The two of them partying around town would become a problem if the media ever caught wind that Sebastian was the prince.

Lucas grinned at me. "Sebastian tells me you're an artist. Isn't that handy? He's kind of an artist. A photographer. Seems like you two are a match made in heaven." He grinned.

Next to me, Sebastian stiffened. "Lucas, please try and behave."

It was weird. When Lucas grinned, there was something familiar about him. It was in the jaw.

"I am behaving. I'm just trying to see what's up with you two crazy kids."

I glanced between him and Sebastian. "Uhm, we're just friends," I mumbled. "Neighbors, really."

From the corner of my eye, I could see Sebastian's jaw tense. "She's right. Friends. Len has a boyfriend."

Lucas clutched a hand over his heart. "My heart is broken. But that doesn't mean I'm not going to give it a try."

I couldn't help but laugh. "Are you always this outrageous?"

He winked. "You better believe it."

Sebastian shook his head. "Ignore him. He's dicking with you, but mostly me."

Lucas laughed. "It's true. I am fucking with him. Honestly, if you do chuck your boyfriend don't fall for Sebastian. You could do better. Like me. I'm not seeing anyone. I happen to like bohemian artists."

I turned my attention to focus on Lucas for a moment. "So Lucas," I said as I tried to diffuse the dick swinging, "what's your story? Why are you sitting here hitting on me and not out running around with some fabulous NYU coed?"

He shrugged. "Why would I? You're the most beautiful girl in the world."

Sebastian ran his hand through his hair. "You just won't quit, will you?"

Lucas shook his head. "Nope." He winked at me. "Are you buying it?"

"Only as a hook to a song. I think you're flirting with me because you think it will make Sebastian crazy. It won't. Because we're just friends." I sat back and deliberately picked up Lucas's coffee. "So, why don't you tell me about why you're a commitmentphobe?"

Next to me Sebastian laughed. "Oh, this should be interesting."

Penny ...

ONCE LUCAS HEADED off to class, Sebastian offered to walk me home.

"Actually, I was going to check out a studio nearby if you want to come." For a moment, he looked like he might say no. But he surprised me.

"Sure. Why not? I don't have to be at the bar to do inventory for another few hours."

"Oh, okay." I hadn't anticipated him saying yes. I'd already texted Ariel to take the handoff, but I had to be flexible. I'd let her know once we got to the studio.

I found the studio easily enough. It was in a little hidden alcove in the East Village where you'd be just as likely to find artists who lived in their trendy lofts or former warehouse spaces as you would be to find actors and students and vintage shops.

I found the tiny studio that offered short-term rental space and knew it would be perfect if I wanted to lend some credence to my cover. And also, if I actually wanted to paint, which I did. More and more each day.

"This place is great. Awesome light. You can people watch."

I nodded. "Yeah. It's not too expensive either."

"You know, I've never actually painted anything before."

I turned to face Sebastian. "How is that even possible? You pick a paint brush and put something on canvas."

He shrugged. "I guess when I went to school there were some options to take some drawing classes but never painting. Besides, I preferred the camera."

"We have to fix this immediately." I went over to the reception desk hidden in the corner and paid for some studio time. The supplies in the studio were free to use for anyone who paid for the time, though most would bring their own. It would be handy in case you forgot something.

"We're all set. Grab a smock in the corner and the canvas and we'll get started."

He laughed. "You serious?"

"Yep. I paid for an hour."

"You? Paid?" He frowned.

I nodded. "Well, I was going to check out the space anyway and see how I liked it. You just happened to be with me. You can choose to paint, or you can watch, or you can go do whatever you have to go do."

I prayed his choice would be the former. I wanted him to stay. Despite what I said earlier about staying friends, despite knowing that was the better course of action, I still wanted him close. *And not because you're supposed to be keeping an eye on him.*

For the second time in thirty minutes, he surprised me. He

pulled up a stool and sat right next to me. "Okay, so what do I do? What do I paint?"

I laughed. "What do you *feel* like painting?"

He laughed. "Is this the part where I request a nude model?" He winked at me.

I giggled. "I think we're going to start you off with more basic subjects first." I pointed at the bowl of fruit sitting on the table against the far wall. "Why not start with that? And *then* you can move on to the naked model and shadowing."

He leaned over to me. "Are you sure? Because it looks like I might have a model right here."

I flushed. *No, you idiot. It's not real flirting. You cannot take him seriously.* "Not on your life."

He shrugged. "Can't hold it against me for trying," he laughed. "So am I getting this painting lesson so you can get a photography lesson?"

"Actually, that may not be a bad idea. I have a camera that I haven't busted open but once. It's doing nothing in a drawer." And that part was the truth. I'd brought the camera that I'd gotten as a gift to myself. I hadn't started any long-range surveillance of him yet. I'd planned to bust that one out if he was dating and I couldn't get close, but he mostly kept to himself.

He worked on his photos, worked at the bar, and worked out. He didn't seem to have anyone significant in his life. No one except for Lucas. Speaking of which, I made a mental note to start tracking Lucas's whereabouts. Ariel and I would need to start double duty or ask Noah Blake for more help. If he was getting close to Sebastian, he could put Sebastian in danger. He was also a wildcard, and wildcards always had to be watched closely.

For the next hour, we painted. I got paint all over myself, but that was par for the course. The best part was Sebastian got paint all over *himself*. And he didn't do a half bad bowl of fruit either. It was easy talking to him. Laughing. When the hour was up, he carried our canvases to hang them on the wall. We'd retrieve them when they were dry tomorrow. "So where to?" Sebastian asked.

"I don't know. I guess I hadn't really planned anything past checking the place out."

"If you have time, want to get your camera? We can tool around the city a little bit before I have to go to work."

"You sure there isn't something else you'd rather be doing?"

His gaze fixed on mine. "Actually, no. Not really."

"Then by all means. Show me the ways of a world-class photographer."

"Well, not world-class yet. I like it. And if I could, I'd pursue it full-time."

"Why don't you?"

"For the same reasons that you're just now pursuing becoming an artist: too many obligations, too much pressure to do the 'other thing.'"

"But you know what? It's terrifying. It absolutely is. I'm not going to lie to you. But something about you seems brave to me. You could absolutely do this if you wanted."

He was a prince. While his father was alive, he could do as he pleased ... for the most part. He still had to do state-required things, but he had freedom. Didn't he?

19

SEBASTIAN ...

THINGS HAD GONE BETTER with Lucas than I'd expected. It had been a couple of days since breakfast. I'd had two shifts at the bar, and so far, Lucas hadn't called, or come by. I thought it had gone well. Had I played this wrong? There was no manual for, "Hey, I'm your long-lost brother. I want you to come to my island and take my place."

And to make things worse, Len was distracting the hell out of me. It was like I couldn't turn a corner without seeing her or thinking about her. *Well she does live next door.*

I hadn't been avoiding her exactly. Every time I walked to work, like tonight, I passed directly in front of her apartment. And sure enough, she always had the French doors open, and I could see inside.

Usually she was wearing some short-shorts and some top that left little to the imagination as to just how ample her assets were. The funny thing was, the old me could have been all over her. But I couldn't afford that distraction right now because if I wanted to be free, truly free without the weight of responsibility, the need to focus on the Lucas thing.

It was only after I left Len back at her place a couple of days ago that it occurred to me that the morning in the studio had pretty much been our first date. Well sort-of date, anyway.

You're pathetic.

Every dating experience I'd ever had, even when I was in the wild rebellious phase, someone else had always been there. King's Guard, some kind of chaperone, or rooms full of people.

Today had also been the first time that I'd been able to just hang out with a girl with zero expectations. And these last six months had been the first time I'd actually ever been on my own. I was so used to everyone treating me like a royal and bending over backwards to cater to me.

And women, they were a-whole-nother fish. Every single woman I'd ever met always envisioned herself a princess. I wasn't an idiot. I understood that I breathed a certain rarefied air. Because of who I was, I had unfettered access to the whole world. I had access to the kind of places, money, and women most people could only dream of. And of course, I wasn't complaining. I recognized I was lucky. I wasn't that self-involved.

But I still wanted Len to like me because of me. And my whole life I'd had real doubts if that had ever happened. But not with Len. She had no idea who I was. There was something about her that drew me to her. There was a certain vulnerability mixed with an iron-core strength that I found so sexy. And she didn't even know it.

And she was awkward and hilarious and funny and sweet. Jesus, I sounded crazy. I didn't even know this girl. *Don't you? You recognize her as a mirror to yourself.*

My phone rang as I walked the several blocks to the bar. Blocked number. My father, of course. "Hi, Dad."

"Sebastian. Tell me you're well."

"Of course I am, Dad." The guilt ate at me. I recognized that my parents might be worried about me. I had no Prince's Guard. Roone still hadn't answered a single one of my emails. He was probably pissed as hell.

For as long as I could remember, I'd never gone without bodyguards somewhere nearby. While it was liberating for me, it was probably frightening for my parents. "I know you're worried. But I'll be back soon. In time for the vote."

My father sighed. "You really think I worry about the vote? You think that's why I want you home?"

How had the two of us grown so far apart? I used to idolize my father. He was my hero—my everything. *And then you got a different dream.* There'd been a time I wanted to be king just like him. And now, we were on two different planets, on everything. "I didn't mean it like that."

"Sebastian, I'm only worried about your safety. I'm worried because you won't talk to me. I'm worried that my son has grown so far apart from me I won't recognize him when I see him again."

"I'm still me. Just different." And because I didn't know what else to say, I added, "I saw him a couple days ago."

"What's he like?" I could almost hear the emotion in his voice.

I wasn't sure how to answer. But then I decided to be honest. "He's shrewd. Cunning in a way. Also, a total troublemaker." I chuckled to myself. "He's also smart. Loyal. Believes in justice. Fights for those who can't fight for themselves."

"I still can't believe you found him. I looked for ages."

"That's the part that took the longest. Obviously, I didn't want to use your men. So I found a few less-than-scrupulous guys who didn't have to go through legal channels to track people. It took all this time. His life has been so *different* from mine."

My father's voice was shaky. "Did he … ask about me? Want to know anything?"

I'd never heard my father like this before. He sounded … unsure. "Oh, he wanted to know everything. I told him what I could. What I knew. But I don't think that could possibly satisfy him. He has questions. Because despite the circumstances, regardless of whether or not you knew or didn't know, he didn't have you in his life. And he feels that loss."

Another silence. And finally, when my father started talking, it was as I expected. "I didn't fall in love with your mother until several years after she had you. I married her because that was the arrangement. She was young, beautiful, kind, as far as I could tell. But our interactions were so formal, so stilted. It wasn't like now. We weren't allowed freedom to move about how we wanted. Even our dates weren't free roaming, and I was always hyper-aware that we had snipers and Prince's Guard who were following close. This event here. This charity function there. I liked her. I thought she was bright. But it wasn't the same as marrying someone you love."

"If you didn't love her, then why marry her?"

"Duty. I knew what was expected. What was needed. It was what my father wanted and what the monarchy required."

"What about what you needed? If you didn't love her, you didn't think about what that would do to her? What that would do to the children that you eventually would have, sensing something was off with their parents?"

"Son, I'm sorry about that. I knew what I had to do, but like you, I wanted my freedom. I just didn't know how to go about getting it. Once I married your mother and she was immediately pregnant with you, I was crawling out of my skin from the level of responsibility. Your grandfather had stepped aside, and I was the new king with a new wife and a new son on the way. And I had no idea how to do any of my jobs: monarch, husband, or father.

"It was terrifying. I barely knew your mother. We couldn't really talk. Before we got married, all we'd ever had were surface conversations. Neither one of us really knew how to work at it."

I frowned. That was not the family I remembered. My earliest memories were of my parents dancing in the ballroom, just the two of them. I must've been five, six? I'd found them in the grand ballroom. My mother was wearing slippers, and she was dressed for some luncheon. Her makeup was still only half done. Her hair hadn't been styled yet. My father had been dressed in his military uniform.

He'd twirled her around and around the dance floor. I snuck

away from my tutors and watched them as they laughed and talked and kissed. I remembered thinking that part was gross, but it felt like love. "I don't understand. I remember you two loving each other. Or at least acting like it."

"We do. We *did*. But that happened gradually. Not until you were six or so. Before then, we were fine together, but we were strangers. I traveled as often as possible for state business. That's when I went to Italy and met Lucas's mother. She was alive in a way that I didn't know I could be. Not with your mother. Not with anyone. When I left, I didn't know she was pregnant. I'd spent a total of two weeks with her. That was it. It was a bout of nostalgia that had me calling her to check on her after I left. Only then did I find out that she had a child. And I immediately wanted to bring her here and raise Lucas, if not as a prince then as a member of the royal court. I knew the scandal would kill your mother, but I was willing to face the consequences."

"What happened?"

"Your grandfather happened. And, Lucas's mother. She didn't want him raised here. Your grandfather was adamant that I was single-handedly bringing down the monarchy. We had a terrible row. I will always regret the decision to let him stay with his mother."

"What about my sister?"

My father's voice shook when he spoke. "I wasn't able to confirm your sister's paternity until ten years ago. You were about four or five when I met her mother. I was more discreet this time, but, I thought I'd found love. What we had was private, secret. I met her in the States. Your mother and I were contemplating divorce at the time. Again, another scandal, but the pressures of being monarchs were eating at us. We couldn't cope. Or maybe I wanted to escape."

I could hear the audible swallow over the line. "That relationship was the first time I'd felt anything akin to love, but that time I wasn't the only one who was married. We didn't mean to start an affair. It's one of those things that just happened. It was my first taste of maybe falling in love.

"And when she got pregnant, there was no telling who the father was. And because she got pregnant, she insisted she needed to stay and work on her marriage. So that was that. Again, I was robbed of the opportunity to take care my potential child. And that one more than hurt. It nearly broke me."

I stopped on the corner, leaning against the wall of the library. I was almost at the bar, and I deliberately slowed my progress so I could hear the rest of what my father had to say.

"I was angry, broken. When I returned home, your mother could see it. And I don't know what possessed me, but I told her everything. About Lucas, your sister, all of it. It was funny. The honesty was the thing that made us fall in love."

"She's accepted what you had done?"

"Your mother is an amazing woman. It seems she'd fallen in love too. Just not with me. With someone else before me. And she hadn't been allowed to marry him. So she'd closed off as well and that night I returned home was the first time we had any kind of real conversation. The first time I'd ever been vulnerable. It was like this threshold had been crossed. I could see how hard she'd been working too. So we decided that from that moment forward, we were in this together. And then I realized that love was a *choice*. Marriage was a choice. You wake up every day, choose your partner, and go through life together. Regardless of what's going on. That was the day I grew up. I got to know my wife. It was ten years later that your sister's mother passed away. Once again I reached out, and her stepfather made an attempt to determine paternity."

"You've met her?"

"No. I haven't. She knows nothing about me. Or the relationship I had with her mother."

"Are you so sure she's my sister?"

"Your mother encouraged me to put a team on her. With a little digging we found out that her father needed a kidney transplant. She wasn't a match, obviously. At first none of the doctors thought anything of it, but after a series of blood tests were done, they found out that he wasn't her father at all."

I cursed under my breath. "So he kept her from you on purpose."

"It would seem that way. I would have forced the issue. But he had a point. She'd grown up completely unaware of this world. She hadn't been influenced or tainted. So I did the same thing I'd done for Lucas: set up a trust. The trust would keep tabs on her to make sure that she had what she needed. So at least in some way I could provide for her. I was waiting till she got older to approach her and let her know who I was."

"How old is she?"

"She just turned nineteen."

"I guess I'll find her next."

"Sebastian. I don't need you to find her. I know where she is. After the vote, I'm going to go see her myself."

I froze. "You are?"

"Of course. I wanted to give her her birthright."

Somewhere inside, the man I knew was there, and he had been trying to do the best thing, the *right* thing.

I cleared my throat as I stopped in front of the bar. "Dad, I have to go."

"I'll talk to you soon, Sebastian. I love you."

I frowned. I couldn't remember the last time he'd been so demonstrative with his affection. "I love you too, Dad."

When I opened the door to the bar, I saw the one person I was too raw to see. *Len.*

Penny ...

SEBASTIAN WAS LATE. I'd gotten the text from the cute Blake Security guy that he'd left his apartment and was en route. It only took ten minutes to get here, so where the hell was he?

Should I backtrack? But that put me at risk of missing him. Five more minutes, then I'd go looking. Ariel was off tonight. I was just about to dial Ryan, when I spotted Sebastian in my peripheral vision.

It was also about the time I noticed the guy to my right sitting far too close.

Were those his hands on my ass? I glanced down at the guy next to me and to where his hands had wandered. "Hey, excuse me. Do you mind not touching my ass?"

He leaned in closer, his hot alcohol stench hitting me directly in my olfactory glands. "Don't act like you don't like it. You're sitting here looking all sexy, just waiting for me to hit on you. I'm finally doing you the favor."

I gritted my teeth. "Seriously, it's a really good idea to get your hands off of me right now."

He swayed a little to the left. "God, I was just being friendly. No need to be such a bitch."

Friendly, right. Ashton had a habit of being friendly too. Good thing I'd learned a long time ago how to deal with overly friendly guys. All I had to do was be my normally klutzy self.

I acted like I was setting my drink back on the bar and then deliberately tripped over my feet, kicking out my right leg which caught him in the knee. And then I swung back around, my hands raised as if to say 'oh my gosh, I'm so sorry.' But then I added the 'accidental' backhand to his face, with a direct hit to his nose.

He grabbed his nose and howled.

"Oh my God I'm so sorry." I leaned forward with enough force to bring my forehead in direct contact with his nose too. And sure enough, he leaned backward cursing some more.

Then I delivered the piece-de-resistance. I lifted my foot, raising my knee and leaning my hips forward. The move delivered an elegant knee to the guy's groin, making it all look accidental.

When he crumpled to the floor, I leaned over. "Oh my God. I really am sorry. I don't know how that happened."

Behind me, several patrons howled with laughter.

Sebastian caught the ruckus and came over. "Is there a problem?"

I shook my head. "No. This guy just didn't seem to understand my disinterest in him. And when I put my drink down, I accidentally kneed him in the balls."

Sebastian's eyebrows rose. "You *accidentally* kneed him in the balls?"

The guy was still moaning on his knees.

"Yeah, I didn't *mean* to do it." I blinked my eyes as innocently as I could. Then the unthinkable happened. Sebastian's arm went around me, and his voice went low and deadly as he addressed the guy on the floor still howling and holding the family jewels. "Listen to me. She's a friend of mine. If I see you near her again, I'll make your life very difficult. What she did to you on accident will seem like a walk in the park."

When he pulled me closer, I tipped my head up to glance at him, eyes wide. I was unprepared for what happened next. Sebastian squeezed me tightly, and I could see the muscle in his jaw twitching. He leaned over and brushed his lips against mine.

Oh God.

Holy. Shitballs. On. A. Cracker. *Pussy down. Pussy down!*

The kiss was electric, hot, and quick. And then it was over so soon I couldn't be sure it had happened. His electric blue gaze bore into mine before he whispered, "Like I said. She's mine."

He let go of me then, and I had to work hard to fight the feeling of emptiness.

Yeah, that's right dumbass, you're not actually his.

Sebastian ...

WHAT THE FUCK was she doing here? *Moreover, why did you kiss her?* My mind had still been on my conversation with my father. Then I saw that guy messing with her.

I really wasn't mentally prepared for my neighbor wedging herself into my life. But she was here. At the bar. Drinking. Though better here than somewhere I couldn't look after her.

Is that what that kiss was? Looking after her? Yes. No. I had wanted the asshole with the grabby hands to get the message not to fuck with her. But she'd taken care of him all on her own. I was starting to think she wasn't nearly as helpless as she looked.

"Fancy seeing you here."

She grinned up at me. "Yeah, I figured I'd check out the local hot spot."

I leaned toward her. "And somehow you managed to cause trouble?"

Her mouth fell open, making her even cuter than usual. "What? How was that my fault? I was just minding my own business and that twat waffle thought it would be a good idea to mess with me."

I shook my head. "Do I even want to know what a twat waffle is?"

"Nah, it'll take too long to explain. Tell you what, though. How about you make me a drink and I'll school you in all the things twat-wafflery."

And that's how my sexy neighbor ended up sitting at the bar hanging out for the majority of my shift. I'd been covering a half shift for one of the guys, Jacob. His girlfriend had her opening in an off-Broadway play.

As soon as he showed up though, I dragged her out of there and took her home.

I took her keys out of her hands, and all the while she grumbled behind me. "I can open my own damn door you know."

"Oh, can you? Maybe next time don't do so many shots at once."

"How was I supposed to know they had that much alcohol in them? They were so sweet."

"That should have been your first clue."

"Okay. Got it." She swayed a little on her feet, and I put an arm around her to steady her. There it was: the electric charge between us. I immediately steadied her and backed away, lest I sniffed her again. Fuck, she smelled so good. But yeah, I wasn't going to sniff her again.

"So you're good now?"

She smiled happily up at me. "Perfect." Except that with her next step, she tumbled right onto her butt. "Oh, my God."

I ran and kneeled in front of her. "You okay, princess?"

"I don't know. I don't know anything right now. One thing I do know is that I'm not a princess."

I took her hand and helped her to her feet. And then gently took her to the couch. "You need to be careful." Pretty soon, she was going to call me Prince Charming for real. When I turned, my breath caught.

The painting she'd been doing on the balcony the other day was now hanging on the wall. The red was the skirt of a flamenco dancer flared out as she danced for the world to see.

There was something regal in the woman's expression—haughty even, like she was untouchable until you watched her dance and then she'd show you everything. It was astonishing. "That's the one you were doing the other night?"

She nodded. "To be fair, I've been sketching her in my mind for years. I don't even know what it means. But in art school it was my favorite relaxation project."

"Relaxation project?"

She shrugged. "You know, that thing that you work on to get your mind off of whatever is bugging you. And then when you come back, you've somehow miraculously solved the problem. She's that for me."

"What problem resolution made you decide to paint her?"

"Oh, you know ... the question about who I'm supposed to be."

I walked over to the canvas next to it. She'd been painting something like a beach scape. It could've been easily the shoreline of the Winston Isles. The blue was a perfect match.

Melancholia hit me hard. I was homesick. I cleared my throat before turning back around. "These are really good. Better than good."

"Thanks. You don't have to say that. I know being here, moving without any support, is a risky move. I get it. But I figured if I was gonna do it, I needed to *do* it. You know?"

I chuckled. "I know exactly that feeling."

"I haven't done anything with my art until now because my parents didn't really believe it was a viable option. You know, going to art school was meant to be the thing that I did to close out my childhood and then finally grow up. The problem is I loved every minute of it. I know what that says. I'll probably never grow up. But the idea of being locked in an office, following someone else's directions all day, every day, is stifling."

I studied her closely. "They put a lot of pressure on you?"

She gave a snort of laughter, and I had to smile. "They want me to be practical. You know, go home. Follow in the family business. Toe the line."

I took another glance at the flamenco dancer. "I don't know. I mean, I'm just some guy who lives next door, and I really don't know anything about it. But I know if I had talent like yours, I'd follow it. You're amazing." My chest tightened as the emotions clogged inside. What the hell was wrong with me? "Whatever they said to you about your talent or being unable to follow your dreams, in this case don't listen to them. They're wrong. I know enough about parents who don't get you."

She gave him a weak smile. "What do you know about it?"

"Enough." Pain twisted in my chest. "I know what it's like to not be good enough. Thinking nothing I do will ever be good enough in my dad's eyes." I shook my head. "So I learned to build my own barometer."

"As a way of saying fuck you?"

"Maybe a little. I get all this pressure from my parents because I'm not living up to their expectations. But they're human, you know. They make mistakes. But they expect me to be perfect. So I just chose not to be that guy. And of course—"

"It usually backfires on you?" She finished the sentence for me.

"Seems like you know the song and dance." I turned back. "How much for the painting?"

Her brows lifted. "Are you serious right now?" she asked with a laugh. "I can't sell you that. It's just something I was doing in my spare time. Putting off the inevitable. I can't in good conscience sell it to you."

"Name your price. I want to frame it and hang it."

"But why? I mean, it's just a painting."

When I turned back and met her gaze, the tension crackled between us. "You and I both know that's more than just a painting. Now, go on. Name your price. I'm not leaving here without it."

20

PENNY ...

HE WAS HITTING TOO close to home. Like he knew exactly how I felt. Like no matter what I did, I was never going to be good enough. That no matter how hard I tried, I would always be the screwup. *Because you're trying to fit a round peg into a square hole.* I shook that thought. The difference was he was a prince, and he could make the world what he wanted. If he wanted to have all the time in the world to go paint or to write a book, or to chase women, then he could find the time, *make the time*, and do that. Sure, the king was disappointed. But he would eventually become king and do those great things. He had more freedom.

"You can't have that painting. It's not for sale. It reminds me of a place I once visited."

"Well, it reminds me of home."

I glanced up at him with a smile. "Where's home?" Of course, I knew the answer to that. But given I was doing the whole under-cover thing, I was supposed to ask.

"Florida. Key West, actually."

I vaguely remembered a trip to Key West the royal family had taken. I'd been six, so that meant he'd been almost eleven at the time. My father had gone along as King's Guard.

He'd managed to arrange for his family to come as well. Not

that Sebastian would remember that. "Oh. I've never been," I lied smoothly. "It's just a little painting. It's not anything special."

"And that's where you're wrong. You need to believe it's special in order for someone else to believe it too." He stepped closer. "I have to insist that you sell it to me. Name your price."

I shifted on my feet. "I couldn't charge you." How had this night gone from drunken intel gathering to him trying to buy my art?

He stepped even closer, and I fought both the urge to flee and to lean in and start climbing him like a tall tree.

"I am going to have to insist. I want that painting, and I would like it to be a fair exchange. So you give me something I want, and I give you something you want. Usually it's money."

He was standing so close I could feel his warm breath on my cheeks. I swallowed hard. "I'm telling you. It's not for sale. I'll just give it to you for free. For services rendered toward helping me move in or something."

Sebastian shook his head. "It's worth something to me. And I want to show you that."

"Why are you insisting?" My voice came out as a whisper. *Get it together, Penny.*

"Because I think it's special. And I think you need to acknowledge that you have a great gift. So how much?"

He wasn't going to let up. "Okay then, the price is a dollar."

He pursed his lips. "Make that a thousand."

My eyes went wide and my mouth hung open. "Are you insane? That's too much. And besides, you work at a bar. How do you have a thousand dollars?" Yeah, okay.

"I'm good for it."

"That's crazy."

His lips tipped up and a smirk. "How do you know I don't own the bar? Or the property it's on, or all the property surrounding it? I just like working at the bar so I can meet people."

I frowned. "Do you own the bar?"

He shrugged. "I'm not telling you until you sell me that painting."

I threw up my hands. "But it's just a painting. I can paint six others just like it right now."

He shook his head. "Somehow I doubt that. Somehow, I think you saw this exact image in your head, and you wanted to paint it. And because of that, and because it reminds me of home, I want to buy it. Because it's beautiful. So just let me."

"Okay, fine. If you want to buy it, it's all yours."

He grinned at me. "Now was that so hard?"

"Yes, if you really must know it—"

I didn't get to finish. Sebastian closed the distance between us and then his mouth whispered over mine in the hint of a kiss.

"Jesus, woman, do you ever stop talking?"

Too stunned to speak, all I could do was shake my head. And for a moment we stood frozen in our embrace, him with his hand on my face, fingertips tickling the hair at the nape of my neck, and me trying desperately to figure out just what was happening here.

Then his fingers gently pressed into my neck, and I didn't care anymore. All I wanted was his lips on mine for real and to hell with the consequences.

Sebastian slid his lips over mine, licking into my mouth. Giving me these drugging kisses. It was all I could do to hold on. My hands clutched his shirt, my head swam, and my knees threatened to buckle. Good lord, Prince Sebastian could fucking kiss.

Someone was making a mewling, desperate sound. Where was that coming from?

Oh yeah, that was me as I tried to get closer.

My only consolation was that he seemed just as desperate. As he dragged my body to his, his hand latched into my hair and he angled my head in place so that he could deepen the kiss. With every stroke of his tongue over mine, I melted. With every lick, it became more apparent to me that I was dealing with a bona fide kissing expert.

Against my belly, his erection throbbed. *Jesus lord*. His erection was thick, insistent, and I could feel the searing heat of his length as he pulsed against me. My knees wobbled as I rocked my hips into him, seeking more contact. With a low groan, he slid a hand down my back and over my ass and tucked me tighter against him.

But then suddenly, as quickly as he'd begun kissing me, he released me and stumbled backwards.

It took me a moment to drag my eyelids open and fix my gaze on his. He panted shallow breaths in and out, whereas I couldn't breathe at all. My lungs had ceased working along with my brain. I might pass out any second from oxygen deprivation.

What the hell had just happened?

Sebastian shook his head. "Shit, I—I'm sorry. I shouldn't have done that." And then he frowned slightly as if not sure where he was or why he was just kissing me. "I—I'm going to go. I was serious about that painting though. I'll be getting that check to you tomorrow."

"Sebastian, I—"

I didn't get to finish. He had the last word as he stormed out of my apartment.

Well hell.

Sebastian …

WHAT THE HELL WAS THAT? I hadn't meant to kiss her. That hadn't even been on my mind. And given the state she was in at the bar, there was no way I'd ever intended on kissing her. So then what the hell happened?

All I knew was that I was standing there, trying to do her a favor, and she was telling me no. It pissed me off. It also intrigued me, but mostly it pissed me off. Then I just wanted her to be quiet and stop trying to tell me her work wasn't good. She'd been going on and on, and the only thing I could think to do to shut her up was to kiss her.

You wanted to kiss her.

No. I didn't.

Len was all wrong. She was sloppy, she always had paint on her somewhere, and she talked a mile a minute. And, she really, really, got under my skin. Someone like that would drive me up a fucking wall. But shit, I couldn't get her out of my head. And now that I'd tasted her, I couldn't stop thinking about how she smelled, how she tasted, and God help me, the sounds she made.

You can't always have what you want, Sebastian. Her words clanged around in my head.

Both she and Lucas seemed able to tell me no with no problem. I wasn't sure I liked it. So I'd gone all caveman and kissed her. There was something seriously wrong with me. Len was different. *Len is trouble.* I tended to date refined socialites.

And maybe that is part of the problem.

Maybe that was why I was so bored with that part of my life.

Desperately trying to sleep, I fluffed the pillow, tucked it under my neck, and then when that didn't work and I couldn't get comfortable, I flopped facedown onto the pillow. The problem was in that position my dick was throbbing and hurting. And it was going to get more than uncomfortable. I returned to my side, resolutely ignored my throbbing cock. But every time I closed my eyes, I could feel her lips against mine. Feel her soft, satiny skin.

Hell.

My damn dick wasn't going to be ignored. Now that I'd tasted Len, it seemed I couldn't keep my shit together.

I'd sworn to myself that I could do this. Sworn that I could keep my head straight. But next thing I knew, there I was making out with her. Okay, that wasn't exactly making out. It had been just a kiss. A perfectly innocent kiss. Yeah innocent. That was one hell of a story I was trying to spin to myself. Kissing her had been like strapping a rocket to my dick. And worse, I wanted to do it again.

With a curse, I rolled onto my back, and my dick made a nuisance of itself by tenting my boxers. The damn thing wasn't going to go away until I did something about it, even though I'd sworn I wouldn't.

With a frustrated growl, I slid my hands into my boxers. And of course, my dick twitched. Damn thing was hard as steel. Just because of one stupid kiss? "Okay, I hear you. She tasted good. But we can't have her. I'm going to take care of this, and then we're not going to do this again. This stops now. This is not why we're here."

Then I closed my eyes and took my cock in my hand while images of Len danced in my head.

PENNY ...

A DAY OFF ... I really shouldn't be taking days off as I didn't have much time. But Ariel and Dylan from Blake Security had Sebastian covered. And honestly, I needed some separation.

I was getting too close. I knew it. Ariel probably knew it. Everyone knew it. But still, there I was, playing with fire. And kissing a prince.

This was one of the few times I'd been alone since leaving home. In my apartment, yes, I was alone. But I was always well aware that Sebastian was next door. I was always aware of his movements, of who was watching him, and the timing of when I'd have to be on again. This morning I was grateful for some time out. Sebastian was safe for now. He was being tailed as he took pictures around the city, and I could focus on getting my head straight.

As I crawled on my blanket in the middle of Bryant Park, I grabbed my book and lay back. I tried not to think of Sebastian, which honestly, at this point was impossible. Was this what it was like to actually be with him, to have every single solitary thought focused entirely on him? I wasn't sure I wanted that.

Good for you because you can't have that. He's not yours.

Yes, the ever-present truth. Playing with fire was indeed playing with fire. I was playing with my future. I was playing with the respect that I was so desperate to own. And if I was being honest, I was playing with his life. I knew I could do a good job. And I knew I was going to, but getting too close to him would blur the lines. It would make me cloudy. And maybe I would miss something. Hell, maybe I was missing something now. The king had been adamant that the prince's life was in danger. So far, outside of the club and Lucas as an unknown, I wasn't exactly sure what the danger was. I hadn't yet seen anything to prove that he *was* in danger.

So you doubt your king?

God, I was such a mess. I scrubbed a hand over my face. *Get your shit together, Penny. You have a job. Just do it. In a matter of weeks, you'll be back home and this won't be a problem anymore.* Inside my bag, my phone rang. For the briefest of seconds I considered not answering it. Ariel knew I was taking a day for myself, but if it was a Sebastian emergency, I needed to deal with it. With a groan, I rolled over, grabbed my purse, and pulled out my phone. Instead of some kind of Royal Highness emergency, it was more of a *Home Alone* situation.

"Hi, Mom."

"Hello, daughter. You're still alive? I wanted to confirm myself by hearing your voice, because as you know, all I've gotten is a series of vague emails from you."

Ah, the guilt. "Mom, you know I can't go into detail, so stop sulking. You know where I am. What I'm doing. I can't tell you the day-to-day detail."

I could almost see my mother rolling her eyes. "But I'm your mother. I'm also a member of the Royal Guard. I know *things*. Besides what can possibly be happening that I can't know?"

Lord have mercy. "Yeah, Mom, I know you know *things*. It's just not particularly interesting. Do you really want to hear which route I took to follow the prince last Friday?"

My mother groaned. "Fine, but at least tell me you're alive."

I laughed. "The sound of my voice isn't enough confirmation?"

"You know it's fine, but a video would be better."

I hit the FaceTime button on my phone and waited several seconds for her to connect. When her beautiful face lit the screen, my heart squeezed. *Mommy.* I missed her. I missed having someone to talk to who understood me. Ariel was amazing and she always backed me up, but she wasn't quite the same as my Mom. "Hey, you."

"Hey, baby face. You look tired. Are you tired? Are you not sleeping?"

Maybe a video wasn't such a good idea. "I haven't been sleeping great, but I'm fine. I had the day off today, so I'm in the park with a book. I'm just going to relax for a minute."

"Why aren't you painting?"

And this was why I loved my mother, because she understood me. She knew that at my core, art was my passion. It was what I loved, an expression of who I was. And without knowing my daily routine, she just assumed that painting was going to be part of it. "I have been, actually. But today I just needed to get out of the apartment, and I didn't want to be stuck in the studio all day. It's the end of October and it's blazing hot still. So I figured I would try and catch a cool breeze in the park."

"Ah, I wish I was there with you."

"Me too. Maybe when I get home we can actually take a trip together. Come back to America and go on some kind of wild city group tour."

My mother laughed. "Yes! We're going to Vegas."

I covered my eyes. "Mom, Vegas is probably the last place I want to go with my mother."

She waved me off with a hand. "Whatever. I'm a cool mom. I'm gonna get you a boyfriend." I must have winced because her brow lifted. "Let me guess: you're officially done with the one you had before?"

How should I answer this? "Yeah, you were right all along.

Besides, having him and holding on to him is keeping me from doing what I needed to do."

She pursed her lips and lifted a perfectly arched brow. "Is that it? It has nothing to do with the whole 'he had no idea how to treat you' thing? Now that you're not with him anymore, you and I can have some hard-truth conversations about your ex-boyfriend."

Oh shit. What did she know? What did she suspect? "Key-word: ex. And do we really need to? Honestly, he didn't take it well. He actually told me no."

Mom laughed. Her peals of laughter made my lips twitch. It was hard not to smile when my mother was laughing like that and throwing her whole body into it. "I mean honestly, how are you going to say no when someone breaks up with you?"

"That's what I said to Ariel. I mean, I was like, 'Hey, we're done,' and he was all, 'Nope.' As if I was just going to heed his directive. It was crazy considering what he did to me—" I cut myself off. *Shit.* "Um, I just mean why was I so insistent about holding on to our relationship?"

Mom shook her head. "Look sweetheart, you don't have to tell me exactly what happened. Just knowing that he hurt you is enough for me to give him the hairy eyeball. I don't need to know all the details. And you don't need to feel like you can't talk to me."

"I know I can talk to you. I just don't want to go into all the details, you know?"

"I get it. I just want you to know that I am here if you want to talk."

Was it safe to tell her? What if I didn't give her any specific details and just talked in a general sense? Besides, I was dying to talk to someone who wouldn't judge me. "The thing is, I sort of think I have a thing for someone else."

Mom's brows lifted and she grinned, leaning forward toward the camera. "Oh, do tell. I want all the juicy details."

It was funny how in some ways my mother acted like she

was my best friend. I hoped I could be as good a mother as she was one day. "It's just this guy. It's a really complicated situation. Um ... " How can I say this exactly? "He's emotionally unavailable. We're sort of friends now, I guess. But it feels like something, and it's confusing because I just got off the thing with Robert, and he is clearly not open or available for anything. But then he kissed me the other night and—" I could feel the flush creeping up my neck. "I don't think I've ever been kissed like that before."

My mother clapped her hands. "Oh my gosh. You look like you're falling in love."

And there she was being too enthusiastic. "Mom, it's not love. It's just that for the first time, I felt *different*. You know, like I've been making too many safe choices. I can't have him, but this feels ... good. I feel different when I'm around him, you know?"

"Penny, I know. It's how I felt when I met your father."

"Oh God, please don't go into too much detail. But I do love it when you talk about how you guys fell in love back then."

Mom shook her head. "You're such a stubborn girl. Listen, baby, I have just one question."

"No, Mom, he's not married. It's just a complicated situation. He's got a lot on his plate, and he isn't looking for anything right now." Somehow I got the impression things would be better if he was married.

"Well, sweetheart, in my experience, when a man says he's not looking for something, he's usually running scared. It may either be from his past, from responsibility, or from pain. You just keep being you, and he won't have any choice but to fall in love."

If her advice was right, then we would both be entering a world of hurt. "A part of me hopes it could be that simple, Mom. But I don't know."

After another half hour of talking to my mom, and the rest of the morning spent at the park enjoying the sunshine, I headed home. I wanted to grab a shower and change into my painting clothes for my shift with Sebastian. The plan was to be on the balcony painting when he returned home. That way, maybe he'd be compelled to come over and talk to me.

As always, I avoided the elevator and took the stairs up the three flights to my floor. When I unlocked my front door, the hairs at the back of my neck stood at attention. Immediately, I reached for the baton that I kept tucked inside my backpack.

Weapon in hand, feet in fight stance and hands up, I prepared to fight the intruder.

―――――

Penny…

"THERE'S no need to fight me, Penelope." The voice was smooth, low, and familiar. "I'm not here to hurt you."

I reached out and flipped on the light switch. "Damn it, Michael, what the fuck are you doing here? You can't be seen here."

He folded his arms. "What? I'm going to interfere with your secret mission to bring in the prince?"

My eyes went wide. "How did you know about that?"

My brother threw up his hands and started to pace. "I swear to God. You pay zero attention to what I do. I work in the *intelligence* department, right under Dad. From the moment that you called Robert and he said you were in New York, I reverse engineered that. The crown prince went to university at Columbia. He used his mother's maiden name to buy him some anonymity. And lo and behold, when I did a search on that name, it turned up in this apartment building which he owns and a bar a few blocks down the street. It really wasn't that difficult. Once I knew the job, he was easy to find. And that made you even easier to find. What the hell are you doing here, Penny? Do you understand that we have a whole division of men dedicated to finding the prince and bringing him home? And somehow you stumbled upon his location and you think that you're going to become some kind of conquering hero being out here by yourself, to what, fuck him into coming home?"

I stared at my brother. The rage monster inside my head jumped to her feet and flipped on the ass-whooping switch as I extended the baton. "You have no idea what the fuck you're talking about. You need to get out. If he sees you, he'll bolt."

"I'm better than that. No one saw me come in here, and no one will see me leave."

"You're such a pompous asshole. You think you are so goddamn perfect that you can stroll in to my apartment and tell me what to do?"

"Someone needs to. You're lucky I didn't take this to Dad. He gives you some bullshit assignment and you ditch it to come after the prince? He's going to kill you. But I'll cover for you. You need to pack up your shit and come home. As soon as you do and you're out of here, I'll call in a guard to come and babysit the prince."

There had been many times I'd been jealous of my brother, many times I wished he was kinder to me. There was only one time that I'd felt betrayed by him, and only once, in this moment, did I hate him. "Did it ever occur to you that maybe I'm *not* the town idiot?"

He shook his head. "Not for a moment."

I spread my arms and then started to walk toward him, the baton still extended. He narrowed his gaze at my weapon, and then his brows furrowed for a moment as if he wasn't sure if I would get physical with him. "You think I magically happened upon the prince? You think it was luck I got an apartment right next to his?"

"Yep, pure luck. And it's no secret Ariel is a wizard with a computer. If she accessed classified files to deduce where he might be, she's in a lot of trouble. But you can protect her. All you have to do is pack up and go home."

"Oh, sure. I'll just pack up. I'll just abandon the work I've been doing here for the last month. I'll just stop and go home and let you call in a guard and take the credit."

"You think that's what this is about? I'm trying to keep you safe. I'm trying to protect your reputation. Can you imagine what this would do to your career when everyone finds out that you're boning the guy?"

I couldn't help it. I feinted to my left so he would think I was going that way, and then I delivered a straight right jab, hitting him directly in the nose. His yowl of pain gave me a kind of satisfaction I hadn't ever felt.

"You fucking hit me!"

I held on to my baton. "And I *will* do it again. If you ever insult me like that again, I swear to God, I will maim that pretty face of yours. Never mind that you look just like my father, I will end you."

He glowered at me as he shifted onto the balls of his feet. "You got off a lucky hit, little sister. You won't catch me off my guard again."

"You know what? I've been feeling bad for you for *weeks* now. I was wondering what it was like to walk around with a secret like yours. It's the only reason I didn't tell Mom and Dad, because I was worried about you. I was protecting you. *You* betray *me*, and *I'm* worried about *you* ... like an idiot. There's something seriously wrong with me. But then you show up here and suggest that somehow I'm here *playing* at Royal Guard. Did you for once think that Dad knows exactly where I am?"

He frowned at that. "There's no way anyone in their right mind would have sent you after His Royal Highness. You're the worst at this job."

"You know, for years I've laughed it off when people poked fun at me. But you know what? I'm actually pretty good at this." *Now all you have to do is keep believing that.* "I was assigned this job, you shit. I'm not playing. I'm *protecting* the prince. And here's the kicker, asshole: I wasn't assigned by Dad."

He glowered at me and still held his pose. "What? You're suggesting the king himself sent you here?"

I didn't respond. I just squared my shoulders and glared. "You can get out now. Go back to your boyfriend. Leave me the fuck alone. I'm not leaving this assignment unless King Cassius himself calls me off. You can feel free to attempt to call a Royal Guard, but I know for a fact that it has to go through Dad. You will *not* be the one taking credit for finding Sebastian. Your career will not propel for it. This has *nothing* to do with you. It's your turn to go home." I turned from him, walked toward the door, and opened it. "Now get out. Oh, and if you ever suggest that I'm sleeping my way through doing my job, I really will fuck up that pretty face."

He looked like he maybe didn't want to leave. His brows furrowed in confusion. When he stepped by me, his scowl remained in place. "You're playing with fire here. You don't have what it takes, and you're going to get hurt. I'm trying to prevent that from happening. Why can't you see that?"

"The only person who has hurt me in the last several months was you. Go."

My brother stalked out of my apartment. Childishly, I slammed the door behind him and then sank to the floor, letting the tears flow freely.

SEBASTIAN ...

SHE'D BEEN QUIET TODAY. I didn't know what had prompted me to ask Len to come over for a photography lesson, but when I found her on her balcony yesterday, she looked sad. Distraught.

Something was bugging her, and I couldn't help trying to fix it.

I knew better than to develop feelings for this girl. I *knew* better. Once the press got a hold of this—whatever it was—it would be over. "Pussy got your tongue?"

She started coughing on the gulp of water she'd taken from her water bottle. "Oh my God, did you really say that to me?"

I grinned. At least she was acting more like herself now. "What? Pussy means cat."

She rolled her eyes. "More like pussies got your tongue."

Oh God, I really wished she hadn't said that, because now I kept picturing what my tongue might do to her.

Get a grip man.

"That's not even a fair assessment. You've never even seen me around many girls. I live a quiet life. I work, I take pictures, and that's about it."

She slid me a sidelong glance as if she knew better than that, as if she had knowledge of what I'd been like before. "Something tells me that this quiet existence of yours is relatively new. Besides, I saw you at the club with Lucas. I got the impression that women hang all over you a lot. I also got the impression that you were used to that."

She wasn't wrong. "Yeah, okay. So maybe the assessment is a little accurate, but I haven't really been like that for a while. You know, I just have a different focus."

She turned to me as we set up the lighting. "Why is that? Why did you stop ... playing the field, so to speak?"

"About six months or so ago, I had some major family drama. I think I told you about it. Basically, my family didn't really understand me and they were trying to control me. I wasn't really down for letting that happen. I was pissed off for a while, but part of me understood where they were coming from, you know? I hadn't really given them an opportunity to see something different about me." He shrugged. "I hadn't really given myself the opportunity either, and I had other things to focus on. So I kinda focused on work and stepped back from the women."

"Wow. I didn't even think guys as good looking as you bothered to do the introspection thing."

I put a hand over my heart. "Ouch." I could see the light dancing in her eyes. That was how I knew she was kidding. Or maybe I just *hoped* she was kidding. "You wound me right here."

"But hey, I said you were good-looking."

I flashed her a grin. "I do have a mirror."

"So humble." Then she was laughing.

God I loved that sound. *That shit is making you crazy.* I needed to change the subject.

"So how are things going with your boyfriend anyway?"

Her brow furrowed. "Um, actually, we broke up."

Those simple words hammered against the confines of my chest.

They'd broken up. Why? How? When? The *when* was extremely important. "Oh, you didn't say anything."

She shrugged. "It's new. I'm not really sure how I feel about the whole thing."

"You didn't want to break up?"

"Oh, I did, especially after I caught him cheating. But I guess in my head I kept thinking that he was really the only guy in the world who would want to go out with Calamity Jane here."

"Well, I find you endearing."

"Yeah, but can you believe it? I broke up with him, and he said no."

I frowned. "What did he mean no?"

"I don't know, honestly. I told him we needed to stop seeing each other, and he was all, 'No.'" She shrugged. "I was really clear and firm that I didn't just need time away from him. I didn't just need to figure myself out, but rather I just didn't want to see him anymore. A large part is the fact he cheated, and then he gave me some bullshit excuse for that. I can't believe I've wasted so much time with him."

"How long were you together?" I prayed for her to say weeks —months even. It was easier to get over shorter term relationships.

"Just a little over a year. And even through that whole year, I knew he wasn't the right guy. But I kept going out with him anyway because he looked good on paper. Honestly, the whole thing was my fault."

"Somehow I doubt that."

She changed the subject quickly. "Okay, photography instructor, show me all the things. I want to learn about studio lighting and studio shots."

"Well, the best thing about a studio shot is they can be honest. There's not a lot of extra stuff going on. There's no interference. You control the environment."

"Control the environment. I like the sound of that.

"Okay, so the first lesson is don't be afraid of the camera." Sebastian handed me the beautiful Hasselblad camera. He was right. I was afraid of it. "It's a really nice camera." I had no idea how much it cost, but it looked expensive.

He shrugged. "Yeah, it is. But it's a tool. So as long as you're careful and don't juggle it, we'll be okay."

I sucked in a deep breath. "Okay, handle the camera with care."

He gave me a wide grin that was just a hint on the side of dirty. "You know, like a guy's balls. You don't squeeze too hard. Be gentle. Nice even."

My mouth unhinged and I stared at him.

His laugh was booming and echoed off the walls. "You should see your face."

"Are you always this outrageous?"

"Sometimes. I know it makes you crazy, so that helps. Well, come on over here. I'll be your subject. All you have to do is shoot me."

He moved over some blank canvas background that was pulled down. It was stark white. He pulled a stool over and planted himself in the middle of it. Then I realized with startling fear, I had no idea what to do. If he was a model and I had my paints, I would capture the shadow, the light ... I would know exactly what to do. This was not my medium. I flushed. "Um, I don't really know what to do right now."

"That little button over there, click it and point the camera in my general direction. Easy. Then, you look at the photo you've taken. Make your adjustments for focus, light, and the subject." He winked.

I could do this. I was just going to shoot the crown prince. Simple. It's not hard at all. I snapped a shot. I looked down. No. That was fuzzy. I adjusted the camera, and focused it tighter on his face. I clicked again. Much better. Then I moved a little, adjusting the light, kind of like I would move my easel to cater to what I needed. I started to get the hang of it the more photos I took. He was a good subject and teacher all at once.

"Just like with your models, you want to make yourself comfortable. Relax. People tend to get real tense when they know they are being photographed. Even though they think they're relaxed, there's always something that gives them away, something that takes away from it being candid. That is why a lot of photographers use music or tell models to bring a friend who will talk to them, make them laugh, so you can capture real moments of who they are."

"Okay, so why don't you talk to me so you'll be more relaxed?"

"I am relaxed."

I laughed. "Are you sure about that?"

"You got any ideas on how to relax me?" His voice was low, warm ... suggestive.

Holy shit. "I, uh, I don't know. With you, there seems to be a part of you that's always holding back I guess?"

That made it worse. He stiffened. "No. What you see is what you get."

I giggled and clicked again. Then I turned the display over so he could see it. "You tell me. Do you look relaxed?"

He chuckled. "Okay, I guess not. Let me turn on some music." He turned on the speaker and a woman sang, "I am an endangered species." The sound clearly had African elements, and blues, and a little bit of a rock 'n roll feel. It was awesome. It made me certainly feel a lot looser. As she sang about not singing a victim's song, I snapped photos of Sebastian who danced a little on the stool. He gave me genuine smiles and flirty winks.

This is not real. I tried to tell myself all the things that would remind me not to fall for him, but they weren't working. The more he talked to me, the more he pulled me in. He talked mostly about photography, capturing just the right shot, how it felt, and his excitement about his opening. It was easy. So easy.

"I've been talking for a while now. Aren't you supposed to tell me about yourself?"

I shook my head. "No, I am not the subject. You are the subject."

He laughed. "Fair enough. Isn't this the part where you, as the photographer, are supposed to tell me to make love to the camera?"

I coughed a little as I imagined saying the words 'make love' anywhere near Sebastian. Yeah, that wasn't a good idea because then I would just go ahead and remember the other night. My hand slipping into my panties, touching myself, thinking about him, pretending my fingers were his. A flush crept up my neck. Not okay. "You wish."

He shrugged. "Fair enough. Then I'm going to make you talk. Why don't you tell me about your boyfriend?"

I lowered the camera for an instant. "What do you want to know?"

"It shouldn't be this hard for you to talk about your boyfriend. I mean, you had to have met him somewhere. I'm sure there's some sappy girl reason as to why you fell for him?"

"Nope. All I can think about is how he cheated on me with someone close to me. I walked in on it." At least that much was the truth.

His brow creased. "Wait, this was recent?"

I nodded. "It happened before I moved, really. I thought distance and all that would help ... give me some clarity. All it did was make me realize that I shouldn't be holding on to someone who treats me like shit."

He nodded. "Amen. I'm sorry he hurt you. And I'm sorry this friend of yours hurt you too. That's fucked up."

"Yeah, it is fucked up. I'm still pretty angry about it. It's not even really about the guy because, at the end of the day, I think deep down I knew he wasn't right for me."

"How did you know that?"

Somehow this conversation felt too intimate. It was the closest to who I really was that I'd shown him. It was hard to be that raw. "I don't know. It was easy, I guess. He knew my family. I knew his family. It felt like on paper, we were supposed to be together, right?"

He nodded. "I could see that."

"Except I don't even think he really ever liked me. He would never actually put me down or anything. It was more that I always felt like maybe I was a consolation prize or he liked me *despite* who I was. It's intangible. I can't really put my finger on it. But he never put me first. And I think that maybe I liked his family a lot more than I liked him."

He shook his head. "You should be with someone who wants to put you on a pedestal."

I snapped another shot. He was natural now. Loose. Relaxed. He watched me intensely, eyes slightly narrowing, as if waiting, watching to see my response and how I was reacting to this conversation.

"He must have had one hell of a family."

"He does. They're lovely. But I can't date someone's family. I can't stay with someone for that."

"No, you sure can't. So what now? Am I going to find you on Tinder or something?"

A giggle escaped. "Um, I think I'm going to leave the guys alone for a while. After this last time, perhaps I'm a little gun-shy."

"You shouldn't let that asshole stop you from living your life. Not all guys are assholes. Not all guys lie to you."

"Yeah. This is the part where I should say 'I know,' but I don't actually believe you."

His lips tipped into a smirk. "That's okay. You'll believe me one day."

His voice dropped an octave. It was low, rumbly, and made me want to cuddle up to his side. But I didn't do that. Instead, I snapped another shot. He checked my every movement across the section of his apartment that we'd set up for the studio shoot.

The tension swirled around us as if trying to concentrate. Somehow this felt intimate. I felt vulnerable. Naked. "You're watching me. It's making me nervous."

"You shouldn't be. I'm sure you're doing a great job." The

music changed again to some upbeat song by the latest pop princess, but it was low ... sexual in a way.

"You make a really good model. I'm sure dozens of artists have volunteered to paint you before."

He shook his head. "Not that I can recall. Why, are you offering?"

I grinned. "I usually do nudes." Why did I say that? It wasn't true. *Because you're hoping he'll volunteer as tribute.*

He shrugged then reached behind his back and pulled his shirt up, tugged it free, and tossed it aside. "How is this for nude?"

Fuck. Me. I stared for a moment, mouth open and looking like an idiot. Then, well, I snapped a picture. Okay fine, I snapped several. "Uh, that's a start."

He ran a hand through his hair and tousled it, so I snapped several of that. These were romance-cover gold. Getting into it, he started posing for me, making silly faces. I got closer to him, snapping more close-ups of his face. That incredible face.

Then suddenly he went deadly serious again, the intensity in his eyes going harder somehow, sharper. Like a razor. "You look nervous. I thought you said you were used to nudes."

I swallowed around the lump in my throat. "Yeah, at school whenever we had a model, they were always nude. I got used to it."

He narrowed his gaze. "Are you sure about that?"

Shit. He could tell. "Yeah, I am. It's just a human form. Male. Female. No big deal."

His lopsided grin flashed, and my stomach flipped. Stupid traitorous body ... and damn him for being so damn good-looking. I tried to keep the lens centered on his face, but I had to get several of his abs, for you know ... research.

But when his hand rubbed over his stomach and then slid to the button on his jeans, I gasped, "What are you doing?"

"Well, you said you were used to doing nudes. Will that make you more comfortable as a photographer?"

I swallowed again, unable to answer, wanting to know what he was doing. How far he would go. And how far would I go?

The button popped, and I swallowed the sawdust in my mouth. I snapped a picture of his hands.

Well yeah, and his abs. So sue me. He popped a button, giving me a hint of the forbidden thing I couldn't have. I kept snapping away. We were locked in this odd, intimate game of chicken. I swung the lens up to capture his face. His gaze was slightly hooded. His lips parted ... Turned on. I stepped back a step to capture all of him. His jeans loose, his feet bare. Sitting on the stool, leaning back slightly and giving me the sex face, because that's what it was—God's honest truth—the sex face. And I was a total goner.

"You're not taking pictures, Len." His voice was barely above a whisper.

"Oh, sorry." I snapped several in succession. Full body shots, face shots, torso shots. There were several torso shots. I wanted to fully capture what was happening.

He unbuttoned another button, taunting me, tantalizing me. Then he reached into his jeans, and my gaze snapped to meet his. I wanted to say something. Intervene in some way ... help maybe ... ask him what he was doing. But I couldn't. We were locked in a game that I couldn't break free from. Now I wanted more. I wanted to know just how far he would go.

Would he go nude? Or would he stay in this half-undressed state, teasing me, tempting me to do the thing that I shouldn't do?

I snapped more photos, but this time I was close. I was looking down on him with the camera, angling so I could see his perfectly sculpted abs as they flexed. His hand was inside his jeans. From the bulge, I knew he was touching himself. And then I snapped my gaze up to his face.

Sebastian licked his lip, and I captured the moment that tongue met flesh.

Heat flooded my body, and I pressed my thighs together to

abate the ache. At that point, I was just snapping photos, completely in the zone, wanting to see what he might do next.

"Len … "

"Sebastian." My voice was so breathy I could barely get it past my lips.

"Do you want to come closer?"

"I—I think maybe I'm close enough?"

His teeth grazed his bottom lip. "Are you sure about that? I have another question for you."

I snapped several more images, ranging from face shots to shoulders, to torso. Yeah, I also went back to the hand-around-his-dick thing because … Wow. "Yeah? Go ahead."

"Why didn't you tell me about your boyfriend 'til now?"

Oh shit. "I—I'm not sure. I didn't think it mattered. It sort of feels like we're supposed to be friends." *Lies, all lies.*

He stood, his big body crowding me. "Yeah, friends … "

I swallowed hard. I couldn't bloody think with him so close. His scent assaulted me, sandalwood and something that was pure Sebastian wrapped around me, making me weak. Making me tingle as I inhaled his scent. Heat throbbed between my thighs, even as my knees went weak. "Sebastian, wh—what are you doing?"

"Proving to you that we're not friends. Will you let me?"

He was asking my permission. I knew what I wanted to say. I understood what was at stake. But then he raised his hand and traced his knuckles over my cheek, and a whimper escaped.

His voice went softer, so low when he spoke that his words were more like a rumble than anything intelligible. "Is that you telling me to stop?"

Seriously, there were supposed to be words. There were. But somehow I couldn't manage them, so like an idiot I shook my head.

His hand slid into my curls as he gently angled my head. When he leaned down, his lips a whisper from mine, he whispered, "This is all I've been thinking about."

With a deep inhale, his lips crashed down to mine, and my world swam. His lips were soft but demanding. His tongue sure. His hands first gentle, then rough as he changed the angle. Our last kisses had been intense but not like this.

The first had been a surprise. The second had been an explosion. This one was a searing brand. One hand furled and unfurled in my hair. The other slid into the back pockets of my jeans, squeezing gently before aggressively tugging me close to his hard body.

Sebastian moaned low, then grunted before releasing my curls and picking me up. The next thing I knew I was on the side table and he was stepping between my legs.

The moment the hard, throbbing length of him pressed against my center, minuscule eruptions of pleasure exploded over my skin.

Holy hell.

His hands roamed, one tucking under my T-shirt, his fingers teasing my skin. The other, tucked into my jeans, grabbing my ass, kneading the flesh.

He wasn't the only one who was getting handsy. I'd been so starved for physical contact for so long and hell, I really wanted to lick, er, touch his abs.

My hands shook as my fingers played over his abs. When he hissed, I pulled back quickly. "Sorry."

"No, don't stop. I need you to fucking touch me so bad. It feels too good."

I blinked up at him. "You like it?" Tentatively, I trailed my fingertips my hands back over his golden skin.

He held perfectly still, groaning low as I let myself play. The man was seriously carved out of stone. With every pass of my fingertips, his muscles jumped. "Fuck yes. Can't you tell?"

I could feel the pulse of his dick insistently pressing against me. I closed my eyes and I could literally feel his heartbeat through the length of him. I rotated my hips trying to get closer to him to feel the delicious press of his dick against me.

"Fuck, Len—" He growled low, before crashing his lips back to mine. His tongue stroked over mine over and over again. I stroked back, desperate to have more of him. Desperate to have any part of him that I could. Desperate to have the part of him I had no business wanting: his heart.

I kept rocking my hips into him. It felt so good. So right. So wrong. Heat pulsed between my thighs, and tingles started in the base of my spine. I wanted him in a way I'd never wanted anyone before. His hands trailed sparks of electricity over my skin. His thumb traced under my breast and I shivered. *Please, please, please. Higher. Just. A. Little. Bit. Higher.*

He broke the kiss then lifted his gaze to meet mine. "After that, are you sure *friends* is the right word?"

Before I could tell him to shut up and kiss me, there was a sharp rapping at the door. It broke the spell. Sebastian cursed and removed his hand from my skin. "Just a second."

I took that as my cue. I eased off the sideboard. "I'm going to go."

"Len, no, don't—" The sharp rap came again.

I headed for the balcony. "I'm gonna go this way."

His gaze narrowed. "Are you running?"

I considered lying. "Yep. Sure am. Thank you for the lesson. I'll catch you for our next session."

I skipped onto the balcony, fully aware that I'd narrowly missed making a grievous error. I'd have my shit together by the next time I saw him. I'd lock down all the vajayjay feels.

Sure you will.

Sᴇʙᴀꜱᴛɪᴀɴ ...

I wasn't even sure if we were still going to be on. I didn't think she'd show. It turned out she was braver than I thought.

I left the bar after finishing up the inventory and setting up for the next shift. Sure enough, there she was outside, leaning against the light post with her camera. "Hey."

I stopped short. "Hey yourself."

"Is it still a good day to do this?" She shifted slightly on her feet.

"Yeah. I pretty much always have my camera. I just didn't know if you'd still want to."

I wasn't sure what her response was going to be after what had happened with us. That shit in my apartment ... I could still feel the imprint of her lips against mine. I could still fucking taste her. It had been two days with no goddamn sleep, thanks to her. I hadn't really seen her much. I'd kind of been avoiding her. The push and pull dynamic between us was driving me fucking insane. I needed her. I wanted her more than I should. It terrified me. And here she was, acting normal.

"Not sure why I wouldn't. We had a date, right?"

The D word hung between us, and she started walking in the wrong direction. Then, classic Len, she started talking a mile a minute. About her day in the studio, what she'd painted, pretty much anything but that kiss. The one where I'd slid my hand up her ribs, the one where I'd traced a thumb over her nipple and made her moan my name. Yeah, apparently she wasn't talking about it, which was fine by me in a way but also annoying. But if she could be cool, then so could I. It was fine.

"Right. Yeah, let's head down to Battery Park. The light is good. And it's almost the golden hour. We'll get some gorgeous sunset shots, if you want."

She nodded. "That works."

I stopped. It took her another thirty steps or so before she turned around. "What are you doing?"

I inclined my head in the other direction. "It's that way."

"Right." She trotted up to meet me. "I knew that."

I couldn't help but chuckle. She had a way of making every-thing fine. Normal. Easy. *That's because you like her*. Or maybe it was because she made my body hum and feel good. I felt happy when I was with her, which was concerning because I couldn't have her. But I wasn't going to think about that today. No, today I was going to show her my Manhattan.

As we walked, we took pictures of West Village. Then we hopped a train down to Wall Street and took photos on the subway and of the buskers along the way. I was desperate to ask her about the kiss.

The itch was like this gnawing, persistent little tingle that I couldn't quite get at. I wanted to just scratch it and get it out of the way to soothe the twitchiness, but I couldn't. With every step we took and every subway car we sat in, she was right there, right next to me. I could smell her perfume and could practically touch her, but I think I knew better. It was safer if I didn't touch her ... Better for everyone. *Who says?*

Finally, as she was shooting a couple of kids climbing on the Wall Street Bull, I couldn't help it anymore. "So are we gonna talk about it?"

She froze and then turned her head up and raised a hand over her brow to shield her eyes from the sun. "Talk about what?"

"So now we're pretending it didn't happen?"

"Well ... " She stood and turned to face me while shoving her hand inside her pocket. Her camera hung between her breasts and I tried not to let my gaze flicker down. "The thing is I ran out of there like my hair was on fire but you didn't pursue me. So I guess we're both a little emotionally unavailable. And well, to be honest, I just broke up with Robert, and it was one of those things that just happened. So I'm not gonna dwell on it, I guess."

Fuck that answer. "So we're going to pretend it didn't happen."

"I'm not sure what to do. I wish I knew. It all happened so fast. I don't know. I just—" She looked down and shifted her feet again. "I like spending time with you, and I wanted another photography lesson. You know, one that was outside that didn't involve any clothes being taken off. So here we are."

I nodded slowly. "Yeah, that was ... intense."

"Yeah, I'll say."

I slid my gaze to her. "So what does that mean now?"

"I don't know."

"I don't kiss my friends like that. I'll just be really fucking clear. I want you. But there are a number of reasons why this is a really bad idea. So maybe we will just be friends." It killed me to say that. I wanted her. I wanted her under me. I wanted her over me. I wanted to possess her. I wanted to share my secrets with her … But she wasn't mine to keep.

She blinked up at me. "So, friend, what's next on the agenda?"

"More pictures."

Penny …

FRIENDS.

The word clanked around in my head the rest of the afternoon. Considering the way he'd kissed me, it didn't feel like friendship. But, like I'd already told myself, I couldn't have him. So we were going to be friends because I still needed to stick to him like glue. As we headed down toward our building, my stomach started to grumble. He laughed and turned to me.

"Let me guess, time to feed the beast?"

"I can't help that I get hungry. Besides, it is dinner time."

Still laughing, we took a right toward the Thai place near our apartments. "Okay, let's feed the beast. Come on." In my peripheral vision, a motorcycle passed on the left. Its blaring engine warning us not to cross the street yet.

"I'm not sure I want Thai. Maybe that Italian place down the street?"

He shrugged. "I'm easy. I'm not the one who has an active tapeworm."

"I just have a healthy appetite, that's all."

"No, it's impressive. I'm a fan."

I heard the grumbling whine of a sport motorcycle and I frowned. That was the same sound as two minutes ago. I turned and looked around, and the same bike was heading down the street. Cars were parked along the way. Not a single spot was available. There were a few pedestrians coming but not many. I squinted my eyes, but I knew from just a glance that it was indeed the same bike. I always made it a habit of staying on Sebastian's side toward the street no matter where we were walking.

The bike's engine roared nearer to us. Then I heard the quick *pop* and a scatter of rocks pebbling, and time slowed. I don't know what prompted it—instinct, fear, pure fight or flight, or if it was my training finally kicking in. Either way, I immediately turned and shoved Sebastian into the bags of garbage by the dumpster, deliberately tripping over my feet and landing on top of him. It wasn't much for cover, but it would have to do in a pinch. More rocks scattered above us, and one of the steel railings holding the awning from the restaurant we were next to fell off of its mounting and clattered around us.

I didn't look up until I heard the engine sound decrease. When I did, Sebastian stared at me. We'd narrowly avoided being hit by one of the metal poles holding up the awning and green fabric billowed over us.

I'd narrowly avoided getting him hurt. Hell, I'd narrowly avoided having him killed on my watch.

"Are you okay?"

"Yeah." He rubbed his head. "What happened? It was like you tripped over your feet and sent us both flying."

What the hell was I going to say? I couldn't have these things that kept looking like accidents around him. "Oh my God, I'm really sorry. It's just that motorcycle … it sort of looked like Robert's, and I just didn't want to see him right now. So I took the coward's way out and hid."

At first he stared at me, and I was pretty sure he wouldn't believe that. Then he let his head fall back and a crack of laughter fell from his lips. "Oh my God, you must have the worst luck known to mankind. We narrowly avoided being killed by this stupid awning just because you were hiding from your boyfriend?"

I pushed myself to standing and then helped him up. Jesus, he was heavy. "It wasn't my fault, okay? I just didn't want to see him and then have to deal with the whole I-broke-up-with-him thing and that I was with you. I panicked."

He laughed. "Are you sure you're okay though? No bumps or scrapes?"

"I'm fine. Are you okay? You could have hit your head all because I panicked."

He laughed. "It's okay. I'll just call it my adventure for the day. There's never a dull moment around you, Len."

I eyed the passage along the street. The restaurant owner came out screaming apologies and asking about our well-being. He thought it was an accident. I knew better. That motorcycle rider must have had a silencer. His first shot had gone wide, just over my shoulder, and hit the wall. While the owner talked to us, I took out my phone and held it casually. We talked to him and assured him that we were fine. I snapped as many wide-angle shots as I could, trying to get the exact location of the bullet holes.

I'd heard the crackling of the brick wall when the shots hit, and that's when I'd known something was wrong. Sebastian could have been hit. My guard had been down, all because I was in happy la-la land with him.

I had to remember why I was here. I had to do my job.

I left Sebastian at his apartment and unlocked the door to mine, ready to call Ariel to debrief, but I found her on my couch looking concerned.

"What the hell happened?"

"I don't know. All I know is that someone took shots at us. We were just down the street, Ariel."

"The prince is fine?"

I nodded. "Yeah, he's fine. I shoved him into a pile of garbage and nearly brought an awning down on top of us, but he's okay."

My bestie searched my gaze. "And you? Are you sure you're okay?"

"Yeah, but shit Ariel, that was really close. I was distracted and not paying attention."

Ariel dragged her hands over her face. "I knew I should have gone with you."

"No, it's better you didn't. There wasn't anything you could have done about it. Besides, it's my fault. I was distracted and … I don't know—enjoying the moment or something. God, I was so stupid. I saw him go by the first time, and something told me to pay attention but I just didn't. I was—"

Ariel stood and grabbed my hands. "Relax. It's fine. You're doing what you're supposed to do by getting close to him and trying to get him to come home. And you did save his life. So everything went right. You're fine."

I shook my head. "I'm *not* fine, Ariel. I'm getting *too* close to him. This whole time, I was busy daydreaming. I was thinking about having dinner with him, like a fool. I almost got him killed. Maybe Michael was right."

Ariel just wrapped her tiny body around me and held me tight. "You're just spinning out. It was traumatic, but you're okay. He. Is. Okay. That is the important thing. And you saved him. Imagine if he'd just been coming home from the bar, and we were only tracking him. Imagine how horrible that would have been. You did your job."

"What I did was get lucky."

"This isn't on you." She pulled back and smoothed my hair. "You saved his life. That is what matters." She licked her lips as she studied me. "You're not too close to him. You're doing your job."

I didn't care what she said. I knew the truth. I *was* getting too close to him. If I wasn't more careful, I was going to get him killed.

23

PENNY ...

"PENNY, WHAT HAPPENED?"

"I'm fine, Dad. And Sebastian is fine. I managed to protect him, and he didn't notice anything was amiss."

"But what the hell happened?"

"There was somebody on a motorcycle that came out of nowhere. Both shots missed. If they'd been on target, they would have hit me and then taken Sebastian out. It's all on my report, Dad."

"Your report? This is getting too dangerous. I knew the king sent you there to protect Sebastian as Royal Guard because he was worried about any potential enemies, but this is something else. We know where Sebastian is. We'll bring enough guards so that we can force his hand and make him come home."

"No, Dad. I can do this. Give me the chance."

"Penny, at this point you're endangering yourself for a mission."

"Isn't that what you do every day? Don't you send Michael on missions? Don't you put him in danger? Isn't that the whole point of being Royal Guard?"

He started to speak but paused before finally saying, "This is different."

"Why is this different? My whole life all I have heard is that this was the job, to protect the royal family. I'm doing that. I did it today." Ariel's words kept coming back to me. I *had* saved Sebastian's life. Granted, I'd also been distracted in happy land like an idiot, but I wasn't telling my father that. And I certainly left that bit of info out of my report.

"But you're my daughter."

"And Michael is your son. There's no difference between us. Isn't that what you and Mom always say?"

"Penny, you don't have children yet. So you don't understand what it's like to read a report that someone shot at your daughter."

I tried to remain calm and inhaled deeply. "I'm sorry you read it in a report, but I needed to file it. I would have called after, but you didn't give me the chance."

My words were met with silence.

"Dad, just answer one question. Would you be this angry if Michael had been shot at?"

"I would be just as worried, yes."

"Fair enough, but would you demand that he come home? Would you demand that he walk away from his post? All you've ever talked about is the pride being a Royal Guard gives you. I've never felt that before. I've never had the opportunity because, let's face it, up until today I was quite bad at it. But the one time I did my job well, you want me to cut tail and run? I don't think so. That's not how this goes. That's not how it works. I have a job to do."

"Look, Penny, I understand, but this is getting dangerous. You need to get Sebastian to come home, or I'm sending the guard there. I'll talk to King Cassius. We'll get—"

"You will do no such thing. Did you send Michael after me?"

"What are you talking about?"

"Last week my big brother came to New York to tell me to stop playing toy soldier. To be the little woman and come back home where it was safe."

"I didn't send him, Penny. He had leave. How did he know you were in New York?"

"Oh, I'm pretty sure you have Robert to thank for that. I'd spoken to him earlier. I didn't tell him where I was, but I think he deduced it from something he heard in the background."

"Why the hell wouldn't he bring that information to me?"

"Well, my guess is the two of them thought that they'd get the credit for finding Sebastian and bringing him back. My darling big brother told me to slink away and leave and he'd stay behind to protect Sebastian and call the guards as back up. So since you are now suggesting the same thing, I assume you're on his side."

"Penny, that's not fair. I didn't know your brother came to see you. He didn't tell me, and he should have. I'll address that with him."

"Don't bother. If I see any Royal Guard, I'll tell Sebastian myself."

"Penelope."

"I have my mission direct from the king. Until I hear otherwise, I'll assume that's *still* my mission, but I'll need to hear it from him directly. Otherwise, don't bother trying to interfere."

"Penny, I'm just trying to keep you safe."

"And I would be fine with that if you could tell me that you would do the same thing for Michael. But you can't, so I suggest you leave me alone and let me do my job." Then I hung up. I've never hung up on my father before. Never once in my life had I even considered something like that. My hands were shaking. I couldn't quite breathe. Just this once, I expected my father to have my back.

24

PENNY ...

MAYBE MICHAEL and my father were right. Maybe I was a fool thinking I could do this.

The problem was I couldn't help it. I *liked* him. And that was going to be a problem for me because I couldn't have the prince.

In the last week since the shooting happened, I reminded myself of that fact every day. I was performing a job function. Nothing more. But that didn't stop me from running out the door toward the bar to meet him like a woman who didn't know she was going to get hurt.

Since the shooting I'd been extra paranoid. I hadn't been able to force myself to leave his side. And what's more, he seemed to enjoy my company and we'd been spending more and more time together. It was a good thing because I was running out of time. Three weeks.

You want to get close.

I did. But I could do my job and get him home where it was safe. I could separate my feelings. Couldn't I?

He didn't make it easy though. Because every time I was with him, he kept looking at me like he wanted to cross the line of friendship, and it made me want to cross it too.

Besides seeing me, he spent a fair amount of time with Lucas.

When he was out with Lucas, Ariel and I had to work double duty with Blake Security. We had to keep from being seen *and* keep them both from doing something idiotic. Usually Lucas.

Since last week though, Sebastian had started inviting me out with them. That made things a lot easier. And thankfully, Ariel was damn good at disguises, so if she was on follow duty even I had a hard time recognizing her.

I yanked open the door of the bar, and the place was empty. Sebastian was behind the bar stocking bottles. He looked up with an easy smile. "I was wondering if you'd show up."

I shrugged and held up my laptop. "About the pictures that we took ... I figured I could edit them. I had an idea for taking these and turning them into canvas prints with paint, so we'll see how it works."

He grinned at me. "Perfect. Can't wait to see what our progeny look like." I froze. He didn't seem to realize what he'd said.

I was an idiot. He clearly didn't mean my children with him. What was wrong with me? I was getting all caught up in believing the hype. Just because we were friends here didn't mean we were *actually* friends.

It certainly didn't mean he wanted me. Although the way he kissed me last week said otherwise. To him I was just a walk on the wild commoner side. If we were at home, this wouldn't stick.

No. I'd promised myself I was going to forget that kiss.

The problem was I liked him ... a lot. Whether or not that was entirely appropriate was the question.

"Yeah, open it up. I'll show you how to do some shading and messing around in Photoshop. We'll change the make-up of the images, and you can use them to make whatever art and painting you want to."

"That would be awesome. Thank you. Once I saw some of the pictures I had an idea, and I can't seem to let it go."

He continued stocking. "We'll take a look. Just give me a few minutes to finish up."

I took my usual seat. But even as I opened the laptop, I

couldn't help but watch him. "Actually, there's something else I'd like to learn."

He laughed. "Oh boy. Does this particular skill require me to hide or sneak in anywhere?"

"No. And that was not my fault. I did not know it was a private affair. I just saw the event listed and figured we go." There'd been a gallery opening I wanted to attend. How was I supposed to know it was a closed event?

"You know what? At least life with you is never dull." He planted his arms on the bar, and my gaze was immediately drawn to his strong, tanned forearms. "So, what do you want to learn?"

"Can you teach me how to bartend?"

His brow furrowed. "You want to learn how to make drinks?"

"I've never done it. I've never even waited tables or anything like that."

"Seriously?"

"Nope. I've always just worked for my parents. You know, as an … uh, intern. File this. Answer that call. Fetch me coffee. This looks far more fun."

"What the lady wants, the lady gets! Come on around. I can show you how to do a couple things. What do you want to learn how to make?"

The words were out of my mouth before I could even think to recall them. "Teach me how to do a blow job."

His gaze immediately dropped to my lips. Suddenly I felt too hot, my skin too tight.

His voice went low and husky. "Are you sure you want to start with that? If you want we could start easy. Those can get a little complicated."

I shook my head. "Nope. That's where I want to start. They were so delicious."

Sebastian threw his head back and let out a roar of laughter. It was only then that I realized exactly what I'd asked him to help me make, and the innuendo that followed after.

My face flamed. "Shit. That's not what I meant."

SEBASTIAN ...

Oh shit. I tried to shove my mind away from the automatic place it went. Somewhere very dirty, somewhere damn near euphoric. The idea of teaching her how to do a blow job just the way I liked it. Jesus Christ. I stared at her blankly for a moment. Thinking, willing my brain to come on line. And when it finally did, I shook my head a little bit. "The shot. Right. The girly drink from the other night."

She nodded. Of course. "It kind of tasted like chocolate. And as an added bonus, it was on fire. So of course, I'd like to make that."

Right. I'd teach her how to make that. Because teaching her how to *give* a blow job was not on the appropriate list of what friends to do. And I was the one who'd made that distinction after I kissed her at my apartment. I wanted to make sure that she understood that I didn't have time for a relationship. *We* didn't have time for any of this. Except now, with her standing in front of me with her cocky, sassy smile, all I wanted to do was kiss her again and touch her and teach her how to give blow jobs. *Make.* I meant how to *make* blow jobs. Fuck. "Sure. I'll just go get more Kahlua."

"But isn't there some—"

I disappeared behind the bar and went into the back hallway. Yes. There was plenty of Kahlua out there. But I needed a fucking minute. She was standing there all soft and warm and sexy, and fuck she smelled amazing. I didn't know what it was but it reminded me of home, and all I wanted to do was kiss her again. I really wanted to do a fuck lot more than just kiss her.

But I wasn't going to because that's not why I was here. I had another couple of weeks at best before my little excursion would be called off and I'd be forced to go back home. But I wasn't going without Lucas. They needed Lucas. Because once the vote was done and my father had enough support to officially make Lucas royalty, then I would be free.

Properly free. Not this bullshit rendition where I always saw myself somehow being dragged or forced back. And that's what I had to focus on. Not Len. Not my memory of her lips, or the way she parted them on a gasp, or how she tasted like sweet spice, injecting my veins with pure lust and adrenaline.

No. A girl like that needed permanence. As the prince, I couldn't be what she needed. Someone who understood duty and honor. According to law in the Winston Isles, I couldn't even have her if I wanted to because she had no royal blood. Like my father, some kind of suitable wife from some noble family would be chosen for me.

And I was not looking for complicated. I was looking for the ultimate freedom … from the crown, from *everything*. Where I could just chase the sunlight and the perfect shots and that was all that mattered. Beholden to no one.

I knew she understood. She was an artist. Of course, she understood the need to not be encumbered, the need to not be forced into a rigid box. Wasn't that why she had left her family?

"Hey, you? I was trying to tell you there was plenty of Kahlua out there."

In the dimness of the storeroom, the soft light danced and lit her skin, making it look luminescent. "I must not have seen it. Let's get back to the bar, and I'll teach you how to make that drink."

She put the bottle down on the counter and followed me, crossing her arms. "What gives? You're acting weird. Weirder than normal."

"How do you know I'm acting weird?" I swallowed hard. "You barely know me. For all you know, this is completely normal behavior."

"Sure. I'll buy it. It's like you're trying to avoid me, and I don't know why. Did I do something? Did I say something? Or you heard of my terrible bartending skills and you refuse to teach me?"

I shook my head. I had to get out of this small, confined space with her. "No. Let's go. Let's get back out there and make the drink."

She shook her head. "No. Tell me what's going on. A minute ago, you were fine. Next thing I know, you're running from me and hiding in here."

The words were out before I could stop them. "Because I am fucking dying to kiss you. Because I'm literally dying to teach you how to do a blow job. Just not the kind you're thinking."

I pushed away from the opposite counter and advanced toward her. "Ever since that night with the mouse in your place, it's all I've been thinking about. Then there was that kiss in my apartment. I know you feel it too. The pull into each other's orbit. And then of course, I've already seen that ridiculous body you have hiding under those clothes. It should be illegal for you to wear clothes. And you're distracting me from what I'm supposed to be doing. I can *still* fucking feel the imprint of your body against mine."

She stared at me, lips parted, eyes wide, every part the innocent ingénue. She had no idea what she was doing to me. "But I—"

"Jesus. You don't even know how sexy you are, do you? And there's something so fucking familiar about you. Like every time I talk to you I'm coming home. And I can't seem to stop that feeling. And it's the last fucking thing I need right now."

She squared her shoulders. "Then why even hang out with me? I've been minding my own business."

I threw up my hands with each word, my voice rising. "Minding your own business? First, there was your ass sticking in the air, taunting me, tempting me. Next time I see you, you're half naked from the shower. Then you're at the club, saving me from overzealous women and I break a little and fucking sniff you. What is that even? I have never done that before in my life. You're everywhere. Under my fucking skin. I can't escape you even when I try, for fuck's sake."

She blinked rapidly. "I—"

"The first time I kissed you, you had a boyfriend. I knew it. Trust me. I *fucking* knew. I just didn't give a shit. It didn't stop me from wanting you. Needing to fucking be around you like some kind of needy asshole."

"Sebastian, wait—"

"So you've been driving me insane. And I can't help but think you're doing it on purpose. I do not have time for this. I do not have time for *you*. I do not have time for feeling like I always need to be around you or wondering what the hell you're doing when you're not with me, or for imagining what painting you're working on. I do not have time for this shit."

She blinked her wide, hazel eyes at me, and her bottom lip started to quiver. *Shit.* She was going to cry. But no, instead of crying she whipped around and started to storm out. And I don't know why I did it. But I reached a hand out and grasped her upper arm before she could make her escape.

"Let me go. You don't want to be friends. I hear you loud and clear."

Her skin was so soft in my grasp, and I had to be careful not to hurt her. "Don't you fucking get it? No! I don't want to be friends. I want to be a lot fucking more than that."

Kissing her that first time in the bar had been spontaneous and surprising. Kissing her in my apartment had been getting carried away. It was a taste I couldn't forget. Kissing her now, when we were all alone with no one to stop us, was a *choice*. One that I couldn't come back from. But that knowledge didn't stop me.

I slid my lips over hers, even as I wrapped my arms around her to pull her close. At first she held still, refusing to kiss me back. But then with a low moan in the back of her throat, she melted against me, her lips parting, allowing me entry. And then I slipped inside.

There wasn't much thinking on my part after that. More like

registering of feelings. Softness. Need. Longing. Desire. Lust. All of it. I felt it all. As much as I tried to keep that shit at bay, there she was insisting, demanding that I feel. Demanding that I pay attention to her. Demanding that I touch her.

I slid my tongue over hers, relishing her flavor and her taste. She was so small compared to me that it was easier just to pick her up and place her on the counter.

Hell yes. So much better because I could step between her legs and press the tip of my dick against her sweet center. All I wanted was more. I needed to be closer, needed more from her. She rocked her hips into me, and my damn eyes crossed. *Fuck.*

She moaned as I slid my hand up under her T-shirt and ran my thumb over her ribs. So goddamn soft. I wanted more. Would she let me drag her T-shirt off her head and palm her perfect tits? Would she let me bury my face between them, lick them, suck them? Would she let me fuck them? They were so full. That would work, wouldn't it?

My dick was rock hard and ready to cut steel, and she kept making those tiny little rotations with her hips as if begging me to strip down her leggings and slide home deep. I could do that. Who gave a fuck about consequences? I knew she would be tight. I knew she would squeeze around me.

"Sebastian, please—"

I cut her off with another kiss. I couldn't stop touching her. When I eased my hand up to slide over the soft, silky fabric of her bra, she gasped into my mouth. I felt the sound and moaned in return as the delicate little bud peaked under my thumb. Shit, she was responsive. And I could feel her heat pulsing at me through her soft leggings.

Too impatient to wait, I slid my hand up her back and managed to unhook her bra with a single click. And then her breasts were spilling forth into my hand and ... fuck yes. Soft and full and ... God. I squeezed gently, kneading, plucking the tight peaks into even sharper points.

"Oh my God. Jesus."

I dipped my head, bending down to taste her. I told myself it would be just for second and then I would put her bra back on, set her on her feet, finish the goddamn inventory, and get the fuck out of there. Take her home, lay her across my bed, spread her wide and sink home deep.

I was *not* fucking her in the storage room. Any second now I would stop. Any second now I would stop torturing myself and her. I couldn't have her.

But God help me, I *couldn't* stop.

Her hands were in my hair, dragging me closer. I relished every minute of it.

The way her nails scored my scalp, the sounds that she made, the way she licked into my mouth, each shuddering breath she drew … I wanted more of that, more of her unabashed response to me.

I released one nipple with a slight pop and kissed across the other. Licking over her with my tongue, using my teeth to gently graze. *Yes.* Damn, she tasted so fucking good.

The more she rocked her hips up, begging for attention, the more I wanted to put my mouth on her clit and fuck her with my tongue. And I didn't plan on stopping until she nearly cut off my air with her lean legs.

"Oh, God. Sebastian … " Her words trailed off on a moan.

I couldn't think. I couldn't process. Everything was lost in a blur of sensation and heat. I dragged my lips off of hers, kissing along the column of her neck, down past the hollow of her throat.

Her hands were in my hair pulling me close, holding me tight. She grasped at my T-shirt and tugged it off.

I trailed hot kisses between her breasts, skipping over two of my favorite parts because I had a better target. I'd been twisted up for weeks wondering what she tasted like.

I kissed past her belly button, hitching my hands behind her thighs and widening them. When I lowered myself, she tossed her head back on a low chuckle. "What are we doing?"

She had a point. What the fuck were we doing? Why did she twist me up like this?

Fuck, does it matter? No. It didn't. Because I was making her mine.

My mouth hovered over the soft cotton of her leggings, and my heart thudded so loud I would swear it could be heard in Brooklyn. Just as I was about to press my lips to her cotton-clad heat, a deep voice called out from the bar.

"Seb? Are you in there? I know you're here. Bar's open. Hello?"

"Fuck." My dick throbbed in protest.

Len blinked in surprise. "Lucas?"

I stood slowly. Holding her to me. "Fucking Lucas."

"What's he doing here?"

"I forgot. He mentioned he'd stop by. I figured you and I would just be hanging out; I didn't think—I mean, I didn't know we'd ... " My voice trailed.

She blinked at me as if trying to put the pieces together. Gently, I reclasped her bra and readjusted her top. Then I grabbed my T-shirt off the floor and shoved it on more hastily.

She still sat perfectly still, looking shell-shocked, so I ran my hand over her curls. "You okay? I didn't mean to get so carried—"

Her gaze snapped to mine and she interrupted me. "I'm fine. I'm just horny."

I couldn't help it, and the laugh escaped before I could call it back. "That makes two of us." I kissed her lips gently again before I called back to Lucas, "Back here."

I readjusted myself, trying to make some room for my dick in my jeans, and took a steadying step away from Len. When I picked her up and put her back on her feet, she moaned. Her eyes were still half-lidded, her lips bruised and swollen, and all I wanted was to kiss her again.

But Lucas opened the door and a cocky smirk flashed. "There you guys are. I've been calling for you. What were you two crazy kids up to?"

Len flushed and slid a glance at me. "Uh—"

"Getting more Kahlua to make a drink. I didn't realize you were coming so soon. I thought you were going to call."

Lucas shrugged. "Figured I'd just come see you. I didn't know I'd be interrupting anything."

I cleared my throat. "You weren't."

Lucas laughed. "Done so soon, bro?" He leaned over to Len. "I promise you, I last *a lot* longer. Want to take a spin? I promise to satisfy you a lot better than Sebastian can."

I couldn't help it. I smacked him upside the head. "This one's mine. Get your own." I grabbed the Kahlua and showed them both the way out.

Past the main office, Len gasped. "Is that my painting?"

Busted. I flushed as I turned around. "Yeah. I got the owners to agree to put that in the VIP area. Looks good there, doesn't it?"

She stared at me and then started rapidly blinking her glazed eyes. "It does. Thank you."

The warmth spread throughout my chest. "It's beautiful. And it deserves to be seen. Just like you."

Lucas immediately broke up the tension. "Jesus, if you two are done eye fucking each other, I need a drink."

25

PENNY ...

THIS WAS INSANE.

What was I doing? *Holding hands with the crown prince of the Winston Isles.* And it seemed like the most natural thing in the world.

"You're quiet. This okay? The thing back there in the bar ... " His voice trailed.

Yeah, if by 'thing' he meant hot-as-hell make-out session that still had heat flooding my veins even hours later. "Fine. Completely, totally fine."

"Okay. It's my general experience that when a woman says she's *fine* she's not actually fine. She's pissed off, or in this case, freaking out."

I nudged him with my shoulder. "Or I'm just thinking. It seems like you're having some kind of fight with yourself. Like maybe you don't want to do this." It killed me to say it. Because hello, I was still horny and I didn't think BOB was going to get the job done tonight.

He squeezed my hand tighter, his warmth enveloping me. "I want to. Believe me. I am so desperate to be inside you right now. I've pretty much been only half-listening to Lucas because it's all that I'm thinking about."

"What's the problem?"

I watched as he swallowed hard. "I don't impress you. You want nothing from me, and it freaks me out. My whole life I've been trying to avoid being controlled, but without even trying you have me completely twisted up. You are in control here and it scares the shit out of me."

I blinked up at him. "How the hell am I in control? I think it's pretty clear I'm in control of nothing." I shook my head.

"I want you so much. But this is a really bad idea."

I understood what he was saying, but I knew he didn't have all the information. I knew what his stakes were here, but he knew none of mine and he couldn't.

What my brain was saying: *You're an idiot. He is a job.*

What my pussy was saying: *Why aren't you naked?*

What my heart was saying: *We're toast. I'm in love.*

What the hell was wrong with me? Walking away was best for the both of us. I knew what I needed to do, but it wasn't what I wanted. *Because you're the moron who's falling for him.*

Sebastian's voice was low. "I wish I could explain. I can't. But I've already crossed a line, and fuck, I want to cross it again and figure out the rest later."

As he spoke, electricity skipped over my senses. I really, really wanted us to cross that line. Screw consequences. What were those? *You are stupid.* I was blurring the lines of my job. This wasn't just about keeping him safe anymore. This was about so much more now.

But when Sebastian squeezed my hand reassuringly in the elevator, I realized for the first time since I could remember that the confined space didn't bother me so much. I was too focused on him and the charge of electricity between us.

And then came the long walk down to our doors. He stood in front of mine first and waited until I opened the door. "I'll see you tomorrow morning."

I nodded slowly. "Yes. Cameras at the ready. Early light is the best light. Good for painting too."

He rocked back on his heels and shoved his hands in his pockets. "Deal. You get a little bit better with your camera, and then we can switch back to my painting lessons."

I nodded. "Okay. So this is it tonight. We'll just see each other tomorrow." Why was my voice high-pitched? And loud ... so loud. The whole building was conspiring against me and being completely silent, straining to hear what we might say to each other.

Sebastian nodded, his voice so low. "Yep. Tomorrow. Bright and early."

He turned to leave, and my disappointment warred with confusion and loneliness. I didn't call out to him. I knew I couldn't, so I watched him silently walk to his door. This was all kinds of fucked-up in all kinds of ways.

But he turned around as if he'd heard my internal call. And then he strode right up to me. "Fuck it. This is impossible on so many levels, but I just don't care."

And then there was kissing. His tongue slid onto mine, licking into my mouth. His hands were in my hair, angling my head, directing my positioning. And his body was pressed into mine, pressing me back up against the door.

He made a low, growling noise as his hips rocked into me. I couldn't think, couldn't breathe. I could only feel and I wanted to feel ... *everything*. Screw the consequences.

All I cared about were his hands in my hair. All I dreamed about was his body pressed into mine. All that mattered to me at that moment was Sebastian touching me. I didn't care about consequences for these actions or what would happen to me after.

Because there would be an *after*. *After* this false, blissful existence. *After* he made me feel. *After* he helped me see who I could be. There would be a moment when he found out who I was, when I revealed I knew who he was, and when we both had to go home.

It would be one hell of a painful punch to the heart when he went back to his life and he might occasionally see me. *Will you even go home?* I didn't know, but in that moment, I didn't care.

I didn't care because Sebastian was touching me. I didn't care because Sebastian was kissing me and his teeth nipped at my bottom lip. His hand, gently tugged on my curls. His body pressed into me, making me want things that I didn't think were possible and that I'd never felt before. And it didn't matter because Sebastian Winston, the crown prince of the Winston Isles, wanted *me*.

The nobody screwup.

The one that no one saw coming. He wanted *me*.

And for once in my life I wanted to take the brass ring. I wanted the one thing that could never be mine. Even if it was temporary.

Sebastian ...

I tried to remember to take deep, even breaths. I did not want to screw this up. I knew I couldn't keep her, and the last thing I wanted to do was hurt her. I just wanted her too much to walk away.

Selfish prick. Didn't I know it.

For that moment in time, I just wanted one thing that was mine because of me and not because I was the prince.

I dragged my lips from hers. "Inside. Now," I growled.

Stop being a caveman, asshole. Shit. I needed to get it together. My hands were shaking and I couldn't fucking get my breathing under control. I couldn't pull some caveman shit on her. She deserved better. I wasn't fucking her in the wardrobe of some royal function. She wasn't sneaking me blow jobs under my desk when I was supposed to be taking an audience with my ministers. She wasn't one of the girls that wanted a piece of the prince.

She *mattered*. And I needed to treat her like it.

She led the way into her apartment, and my hand reached out

to stop her before she could flip on the lights. She shifted in my arms, causing her ass to rub against my dick, and I about crashed off the road to good intentions.

"You smell incredible, you know that? Something lime and mint."

"It's my shampoo."

I nodded absently as I turned her around. The gasp that slipped through her lips was quickly muffled by my tongue sliding on hers, coaxing hers to play.

Fuck.

I groaned deep even as her body molded to mine. My hands tightened on her hips automatically, and I angled my head to deepen the kiss. Len's arms looped around my neck, her fingers teasing the hair at my nape, pulling me down to her.

The pulsing heat in my veins controlled me now. All I registered was that I needed more heat. More lust. *More. Of. This.*

Our tongues fused and slid over each other again and again. Each of her low moans made the blood rush in my ears. I let my hands slide down her back to her ass and cupped the generous curves, bringing her hips into contact with my steel hard dick.

She automatically rocked into me, and I dragged my lips away from hers, panting and desperate for more. She whimpered and I bit back a smile as I dragged my lips over her cheekbones to her neck then sucked on the soft spot behind her ear that made her fingers tighten in my hair.

"Sebastian," Len breathed.

"You're so beautiful," I murmured into her skin as I dragged my lips over her softness. Gently, I nipped on her ear, drawing another whimper from her as my hands slid up to cup her breasts.

Her sharp inhale was quick even as her body bucked against me.

Hell. Yes.

I ran a thumb over her nipple through her shirt, loving the way she arched into the caress. I needed more. If I could only have her this one time, I wanted to make it count. Needed to make it count. I needed to see her. To taste her. Just thinking about it nearly sent me over the edge.

Her hips tucked against mine and she cried out, moaning loudly as I ground my cock against her. So hot. I could feel the bite of her nails even as I devoured her lips, sliding my tongue over hers, desperate to possess her.

Gently, I backed us up and trapped her against the counter in her kitchen. When she shifted in my arms, I lifted her legs up and wrapped them around my waist, making room for my bigger body.

Frustrated and needing more skin, I grabbed the hem of her shirt, and tugged it up over those perfect tits before tossing it on the floor.

Oh hell. I drank her in as her breasts threatened to spill from her bra. The black lace framed everything just how I liked. High and proud and ... mine. Every breath she took looked like an invitation to lick, to suck, and to fuck.

My damn hands shook with the need to touch.

Reaching behind her, I fumbled with the clasp of her bra, bringing the black straps down and running my thumbs all over the tops of her soft breasts. When I reached her nipples, I gently caressed them.

"Sebastian?" she breathed.

"Yeah?" I asked as I dipped my head and blew a breath over one.

She sucked in a breath. She shuddered beneath me, her fingers weaving into my hair, scoring my scalp and tugging me closer as she wrapped her legs around me tighter. I drew a nipple into my mouth. She tasted sweet, so sweet.

As I gently teased her nipple with my teeth, Len lifted her hips up, grinding her heated core against me. Her soft moans filled the silence when I flicked my tongue over a distended peak. Why did she taste so damn good?

I pressed a kiss on the valley between her breasts, licking and nipping along the path before I took the other nipple into my mouth, and sucked harder.

Len arched her back and writhed. Her hips rolled into mine as I cupped her fullness, teasing one peak with my thumb as I grazed the other with my teeth.

"Yeah, Len … "

"Oh. My. God."

I shook my head as I nuzzled her soft flesh. "Nope," I teased. "Name's Sebastian, remember?" I placed her on top of the counter.

She laughed and made a strangled whimpering sound as I gripped and parted her thighs further. Her fingernails clutched at my hair, and a shudder racked my body.

"Sebastian, please … "

"We're really going to have to work on your patience," I muttered.

I kissed down her belly, nipping along the way, taking my time to explore her body. I dipped my tongue into her naval, exploring that little button before moving on.

With every kiss, Len arched her back and pulled me close. Her body tight, coiled, ready for me. She tugged at my T-shirt and I helped her out by yanking it off. I shivered when she ran delicate fingertips over my skin.

I picked her up and set her down, then tugged her leggings down her long legs, leaving them in a pile on the kitchen floor as I grabbed the waistband of her lace panties.

My eyes never leaving hers, I yanked the flimsy fabric down with one tug and grinned when the fabric tore. I'd buy her new ones.

I licked my lips as I watched her. *So pretty.* Then I picked her back up and set her on the counter again. "I want to see you, Len."

She swallowed hard and tried to close her legs, but I gently held them apart. "I think you're beautiful. Will you let me?" If she wanted me to beg, I'd beg. At that moment, I'd give her anything she asked.

Her tongue peeked out and moistened her bottom lip, but she nodded slowly. "Okay."

I wanted to growl my satisfaction but remembered to curb the caveman bullshit. Sliding my fingers over her slick flesh, I stared down at her soft, pink lips. They were so pretty. In the dim light, I could almost see the dewy slickness. I'm not sure I'd ever wanted to taste anything so much.

Sinking down to my knees, I kissed her slick folds gently.

"Oh ... My ... G—"

Her words cut off when I parted her tender flesh with my thumbs and ran my tongue over her slit. Just like I thought, she melted like sugar on my tongue.

Working my tongue over her, I tightened my hold on her hips. I didn't want her to come until I'd had my fill.

I only teased her clit, never applying direct pressure as I drove her crazy, just to the brink, and pulled her back again. Her loud moans echoed around the room as I slid my tongue into her, gently fucking her.

Her hand slid into my hair again, and she held me to her as she rolled her hips onto my tongue. I wanted her so blissed-out she couldn't move. I wanted her so delirious she couldn't think about anything else but me and how I was making her feel.

I slid my hands up over her belly to palm her full breasts then pinched her tight nipples as I tasted her.

Blood rushed in my skin and my cock throbbed, begging for release. I wanted to be inside her. I wanted to know if the buzzing electricity was going to consume me. I was so keyed up, I thought I would lose it right there.

"Sebastian ... Sebastian ... Sebastian ... "

Her murmured chants warned me of the impending climax. When her body tightened, her legs clamped tight, holding me in position.

"Oh no you don't. I'm not done with you yet."

I withdrew from her and carried her through the living room and into her bedroom.

"What are you doing?"

"Hush. Prince Charming at your service."

I laid her on the bed and stripped the rest of my clothes off in record time. I could feel the heat of her gaze on me as my fingers moved quickly and efficiently. I sent buttons flying, not giving a fuck where anything landed as I ran my gaze all over her body. The delicious taste of her on my tongue urged me on.

When I was naked, I held my breath and ran my hand over my length, pumping once, twice before fisting more tightly to stop myself from coming.

I shook my head. Damn, I needed to get my shit under control. I gritted my teeth and blew out a slow breath. I wanted to be inside her when I lost my control. I felt like I'd been waiting for this moment for so long that I didn't want to blow it. With patience running thin, I grabbed my wallet and fished out a condom.

I returned to her, using my knee to spread her legs further. Taking the tip of my cock in my hand, I aligned the tip to her slick entrance. My gaze locked on hers, and she wrapped her legs tightly around my waist as I sank in, inch by inch.

Oh my God.

I wasn't ready. How could I not be ready? I'd done this hundreds of times. Maybe thousands. I'd screwed around so much in my life. So many women. How was it possible that not one of them had ever made me feel like this?

Nervous and worried, and desperate and triumphant.

Because none of them mattered before this one.

I cursed as the heat of her warmth wrapped around me. My cock jerked, and the pure electricity set me on edge. "Shit, Len." My words sounded distant and feral to my own ears. Almost like a growl.

Fuck. I needed this. I needed her. I was fooling myself if I thought this was a one-time thing. I was a fool if I thought I could walk away from her unscathed.

Feeling her heat around me raised the stakes for me. She was against the rules. Being with her was against the rules. But I might have to change those rules.

My hands tightened on her hips, and I drove myself deep, sheathing my cock in her velvet grip. I heard her chanting my name. But it was like she was talking through a tunnel.

All I could focus on was how hot she was, how slick, how tight. I wanted to go slow. That was my intention, but I needed her too much.

She was mine. With every roll of her hips, she branded me. I dug my fingers into her hips and held on, thrusting into her silken warmth as I threw my head back.

Her tight muscles clenched around my cock. With sweat slick on our flesh and our breathing ragged, she came, and her inner muscles milked my dick. I was so close, but I didn't want to come yet. I needed to feel her walls pulsing around me again before I let the fire racing up my spine take me to oblivion.

Reaching between us, I sought out her clit. Her eyes went wide as I made butterfly strokes over the tiny button.

Fuck, that did the trick. She cried out as another wave hit her and her body began convulsing around me.

"Fuck!" I growled and picked up the pace, making the bed shake. And Len's cries only made me drive harder. I tucked my head against her chest, taking a nipple into my mouth.

"Faster, harder!" she pleaded.

I cursed low and did as she told me. "So fucking tight … Could fuck you forever … " The fragments of speech tripped out on my ragged breaths as we came together.

Sebastian …

CHRIST, I wanted to keep her. The rational part of my brain tried to perk up and quash that little hope that I could, but my heart refused to let that go.

She doesn't know anything about you. Which was beyond fucked up. Would she look at me differently when she found out? *Of course you idiot, because you're lying.* If I told her the truth, would she still care about me? Or would she only see the prince?

I wanted to believe the answer was yes, that I could do what I needed to do at home and come back.

For what? For something real? It surprised me how badly I wanted that. A world where I was someone normal and could just fall in love. Shit. That word. Where the hell had it come from?

She was a mystery. And yes, I wanted to peel her like an onion. And photograph all her smiles. The quirky ones, the fun ones, the sly ones, the mischievous one. I wanted to capture them all and hold onto them forever.

I wanted to know why it was that kissing her felt like going home. Something familiar danced on the edge of my consciousness, but I couldn't quite grasp onto it or figure it out. It was like trying to catch a rainbow.

All I knew was how I felt when I was with her. A little on edge. A lot confused. The antithesis of everything I'd ever been told. Everything I'd ever needed. She was fun, and quirky, and not at all royal material. And I adored it. She was real. Honest. Intangible.

Every woman my family paraded in front of me was like this glossy facsimile of a real person. All their interests aligned to mine. The women loved to watch polo. A few of them actually even liked to ride, or so they were programed to believe. Lila had been like that. She would have been miserable with me. That still didn't excuse what she did.

Len was different. Bright, and too honest, and wide-eyed.

She painted. And her mouth ran a mile a minute. When she laughed, she threw her whole body into the act, sometimes falling off of the stool because she was laughing too hard.

For the first time, I wanted to know everything about a woman. I wanted to know what caused her brow to furrow like that. Who it was that called her that made her so sad and angry. I wanted to know why she knew the color of azure blue so well. As if she'd spent a lifetime staring at that water herself. I wanted to know the full story of why she was terrified of being in confined spaces and why every time she laughed, she quickly apologized for being too loud. It was a shame, because I would pay a prince's ransom to see her laugh like that every day.

She rolled over in my arms, and her lashes fluttered against her cheeks before she smiled up at me. "You're staring."

I shrugged. "You're beautiful. Am I not supposed to admire the beauty in front of me?"

She wrinkled her nose. "And I have a feeling you say that to all the girls."

I frowned. Yeah, okay. I might say that to a lot of women. I went for something more original. The truth. "Okay. Then, how's this? I was just thinking about how I don't want to let you go."

The smile touched one corner of her mouth first before spreading. "You do have a way with words, Sebastian."

I kissed her forehead, ignoring the sudden rush of blood to my dick. For now, I was content to hold her. Okay, yes, I wanted her again. And before the night was over, I would be sliding into her again and again. Because with her, I was a starving man. But for a second, I wanted just to hold her.

She murmured against my skin, "You know, I don't even know that much about you."

I pulled back a little and cocked my head. How much could I tell her? Just enough of the truth? There would come a point when I would either have to tell her, or leave her. And I didn't look forward to that moment. I didn't want to lie either. I'd just have to tell her what I could. "What do you want to know?"

"What makes you happy? What makes you frustrated? Where did you grow up? Do you have siblings? What's your favorite breakfast? Tea or coffee? And also, where did you learn that thing with your tongue where you—" She shook her head. "Never mind. I don't want to know. I think that answer will only irritate me."

I grinned. "I see you have a lot of questions."

She nodded just before brushing her lips over my nipple. I shivered, and my dick throbbed against her thigh. Shit. I adjusted myself so that I could actually think. Because with her soft skin touching my dick, all I could think about was getting back inside her and feeling her slick smoothness against me.

I just wanted to bury myself inside her and never come up for air. I wanted nothing between us as I made love to her. I wanted to feel her bare.

What?

No. I couldn't do that. No way. I was not my father. But still, the idea of it … feeling her wet heat surrounding me, clamping around me. The thought of it made me harder than steel, and I had to count backward from ten to try and cool off.

News flash: It didn't work.

"Earth to Sebastian. What's wrong?"

I cleared my throat. "Nothing. I'm trying hard as hell to focus on being with you and answering your questions, and not on sliding back into you. You know, I figured we do the talking thing and not just the screw-your-brains-out-thing."

She giggled. "Well, I still have a few brains left. How about we talk for a minute, and then you do that thing with your tongue again?"

I laughed. "See, you keep asking for that and I will pretty much keep you in the bed forever, pleasing you until you can't get up and walk away from me."

"You know, I may not be opposed to that."

"*Fiend.* Okay. Let me answer your questions in order. What makes me happy? The perfect lighting, usually that mere moment just after dawn. When it's quiet and nothing's moving, that's my happy place. What makes me frustrated? Having to conform. Follow rules. Where did I grow up? Close to the water." I'd already lied once and told her Key West, but I wasn't going to lie to her now.

"Did you love it?" she asked.

"Growing up was kind of idyllic. Who is that painter? Rockwell? Not quite so WASPy, upper crust, but I spent a lot of time with my cousins and a friend. You remind me of her actually. She was always giggling." I frowned. I'd always wondered what had happened to Penny.

Not enough to ever ask? I just assumed she'd headed off to uni. *But you never asked.* I forced myself to focus. "You know, we ran around barefoot all the time. I was always dirty, getting into stuff. And for the most part, I had free reign to do as I wanted. It's kind of like that when you live on an island. So I used drag my friends and cousins into adventures."

She whispered, "You look happy when you talk about it. How come you don't go home?"

My jaw tensed. *Tell her the truth.* "Obligated. And I haven't been that carefree kid in a long time. I hit eleven and I was at boarding school. I didn't spend much time at home after that. But I miss it." I cleared my throat, but I couldn't seem to choke the words out to tell her I was hurting her.

"That's really sad considering how happy it makes you. I can see it in your face."

"I know." Determined to change the pace of the conversation, I went back to her questions. "I just found out I have a brother and a sister I knew nothing about. It's why I'm here in New York—to get to know my brother. When I find my sister, we're going to go meet her." My heart hammered like the thumping foot of a rabbit. I was on shaky territory here. I had just given her a secret that would rock my kingdom.

But she has no idea who you are.

That was true. And somehow it made me feel so much worse.

Her wide hazel eyes blinked up at me for a moment as she stared. Finally, she shook her head and asked quietly, "Lucas?"

I nodded. "Yeah, Lucas."

"I can't believe I didn't see it before. You guys look a lot alike."

I rubbed my jaw as I contemplated this. "I guess so. The jaw probably. The mouth. The nose. My eyes, though, are my mother's."

Her smile was soft. "I've grown partial to those eyes." Her next question hit straight in my heart. "Are you close to your parents?"

"I wish. My father and I used to be extremely close."

"What happened?"

"I found out he wasn't the man I thought he was." I cleared my throat. "He only just told me about Lucas and our sister."

Her eyes went wide for a moment then she chewed her lip. "If you never knew before, I'm sure *he* had a good reason for keeping it to himself. I think we all find that our parents are only human eventually."

"This goes way beyond human. It felt like betrayal when I found out. But I guess I didn't have the whole story. It's complicated."

"I don't know. It almost always is, I suppose. With my parents, I try to look back on the good things that they gave me. And I realize that it's probably strange for them that I don't follow what they say like a little puppet. I'm theirs, but I'm also my own person, coming into my own and making my own decisions. It frustrates them when I don't make the choices they want. Just like I want them to be perfect, but they're just human. They're not in charge of my life. I am. I'll make mistakes. Hell, I might make the same mistakes they have for the right reasons."

How did my beautiful dreaming artist tap into her logic like that? "How did you get so smart?"

"It's all the paint fumes," she laughed.

"You may have a point there. It's like I looked up to my father all these years. He was exactly who I wanted to be. But the older I got, the less I wanted to be exactly like him and the more I wanted to be my own person. And then I found out he's flawed. He makes mistakes. And it's like that person I looked up to all those years didn't even exist."

She sighed. "He *did* exist. Because of him you turned out to be a good man. Kind. Someone who will help a random stranger move into her place and save the same stranger from a mouse. He did a good job. You're just now seeing him with different eyes. He's not any different."

I hadn't thought of that. Could it be that he was the same man that he always was but now I have to look at him differently? "I guess in some ways I always saw him as trying to control me. And I've always fought against it. But I guess that's part of who he is."

"He's only human."

And after the time I had spent with Lucas and Len, I was starting to see things in a different light. I was still disappointed and hurt by the old man, but most of the anger had dissipated since all of a sudden I wanted to stay, wanted to get to know my brother better. All of a sudden, I wanted to hold onto this girl that was like a ray of moonlight. The urge to run, to free myself of those shackles—it wasn't as strong. And I wasn't sure if I could trust the emotion.

26

PENNY ...

I REALLY SHOULD'VE KNOWN that trying to probe into Sebastian's mind would earn me some uncomfortable questions of my own. I just hadn't been able to resist the lure of finding out more about him. The private things. And as I'd already crossed the line, there really was no going back. Too late to consider the consequences now.

"Your turn. What about you? Any siblings?"

I told the truth. "Yep. One. He's in the family business and the pride of my father's eyes."

He frowned. "I'm sure your father is proud of you too."

"You've been listening, right? He's not. But it's okay. I don't think I want him proud of me for doing something I don't really want to do, you know?"

He nodded. "Do I ever." He bit his bottom lip and seemed to consider for a moment. "Favorite breakfast?"

I grinned. These questions I could answer. "Pancakes."

"Can you tell me the circumstances around the elevator situation? Why would he do something like that?"

I stiffened in his arms. But he held me close and kissed my forehead.

"You don't have to tell me. I was just wondering something about you."

"Who the hell knows. My, uh, cousin … Like I said, he locked me in a closet when I was little and wouldn't let me out for hours. At first I thought maybe it was a joke, but I realized he really just hated me. My parents were frantic. Then at the end of it, he acted like it was just a game."

"That sociopathic asshole. I have a cousin like that who did similar things. And of course he got away with it all the time."

I nodded. Of course there'd be similarity. I was talking about *his* cousin. *But he doesn't know that.* Because I was lying to him.

I shoved that aside. I would deal with that later. I was just grateful we were at my place. At least there were no bugs in here so Ariel hadn't heard that little bomb drop about Lucas. I would tell her because it would inform what we were doing here, but shit. The real question was whether I should tell King Cassius that I knew.

Lucas was his fucking brother. And he had a sister. Hell. I'd deal with that later. *Much later.* But for the moment, we were in a cocoon, a safe cocoon of just the two of us and the hot sex. And some questions. Shit, I had all the questions.

"So how long has Lucas known about you?"

"We just connected."

"Where did he grow up? Are you going to take him to see your parents? I can't imagine what it must be like."

He went quiet for a moment, and I shut my mouth. "Sorry. I'm curious. I don't mean to pry with all the questions."

He shook his head. "It's fine. On one hand, it's great. But there's a part of me that's, I don't know, annoyed, I guess. My father sounded so happy when I told him I'd found Lucas. I'm not used to feeling like I have competition—for anything. I don't think I like it."

"Of course you don't like it. No one does." I laughed. "I mean look at you. It's a wonder women across the globe don't drop their panties."

His gaze met mine. "*You* didn't."

"Yeah, well. You were a bit of a dick."

He chuckled. "And you unsettled the hell out of me. I was merely defending myself from an unforeseen assault on the senses."

"No. You were being a prick."

"I swear to God, I thought I would have to beg for mercy the day you were using my shower. Hell, I almost did beg."

I slid my fingers down his pectoral muscles and his abs, heading for my new happy place. "I bet I can make you beg now."

Sebastian squeezed his eyes shut and groaned, but then he gently restrained my hands. "Trust me, I'm going to be buried inside you again soon enough. I'm going to suck on your pretty nipples … again. Tease you a little bit but never give you what you want until you beg." His fingers skimmed just under my breasts. "Then I'm going to use my mouth on you. I'm going to lick and suck on your perfect pussy. Spread those gorgeous lips apart and go to town on your clit."

Oh. Holy. Fuck. Me. "Sebastian … " With his words, he slowly teased me, as if he had nothing but time.

"Shhh, sweetheart, I'm still talking. I'm going to slide my fingers inside you, adding one, then another while I suck on that perfect, sweet button. And then after that, I'm going to fuck you. I might want to start with you riding me. I think I might like the show of your perfect tits on display."

Holy shit. I squirmed, and my core pulled tight. I liked what he was saying. I liked *how* he was saying it, his voice low and full of promise. Warming me from the inside out.

"No matter what else we do, I'll want you on your hands and knees last. First, because it will give me the most perfect view of your ass. But also because I think I'll be able to go deep. I want to see if you clutch the sheets. I also want to feel the way you squeeze my dick as though you'll never let me go."

"Sebastian, *please*."

I was not above begging. I was wet, horny, and ached deep in my core. His skill for dirty talk was killing me.

He licked his lips as his large hand cupped my breast. "While I want nothing more than to make all of that happen right now, I still want to talk to you first. So for now, you're going to answer some more questions." His thumb brushed over my nipple and I shivered.

"Sebastian, that's not playing fair."

"Who said anything about fair?"

He continued asking me every random thing he could think of. From my favorite color, to whether I preferred socks or tights. And even though he cataloged each of my responses, I knew it wasn't about that. He wanted the time with me. Just like I wanted the time with him.

We were both working on a borrowed chunk of it. We both knew we would eventually have to return home, and when we did, neither one of us could have the other. He was the crown prince, and I was his guard. Except he didn't know that, but when he discovered it, he wouldn't *want* to be with me anymore.

The knowledge made my heart squeeze. And even though he was hiding who he was too, I knew that mine was a far greater betrayal. I needed to tell him, but I couldn't. His life was in danger and I'd already seen evidence of that twice. The girl at the bar. The gunman. I didn't know who was trying to hurt him, but I knew that they were serious about it.

So I needed to do my job, and I could only do that if he didn't know the truth. And despite how I felt about him, I could do my job well without letting any of that get in the way. Because I might not be the best King's Guard, but I might be exactly what he needed in a Prince's Guard. I understood him and knew exactly what he needed. I understood what he was trying to run away from, trying to escape. And if I could help him tap into some of that in a safe, controlled environment, I might be able to keep him safe for now.

PENNY ...

"You're supposed to be relaxing. Why aren't you relaxing?"

Ariel and I had headed uptown earlier that morning for some shopping and lunch in the park. Blake Security had three men on Sebastian today, so we had the rare day off, but somehow I was still tense. Like I was waiting for the other shoe to drop. So far, after that little brush with death, there had been no other attempts on him. After a conversation with the King, we rotated in more Blake Security men. We had good coverage on the prince so why was I so tense?

You know why you're tense.

I had to tell her. I couldn't keep it to myself anymore. I'd screwed up and I needed my friend. "I need to tell you something."

Ariel took a sip of her blueberry lemonade concoction, and then she set it down and sat back. "You mean about you and Sebastian sleeping together?"

My mouth fell open.

Ariel shrugged. "Honey, I'd have to be blind not to notice. You guys are into each other. You have been from the start. Trying to pretend otherwise is sort of futile."

"But, b—but it just happened."

Ariel nodded. "That much I can see, or rather I can guess from your glowing look. We don't have listening devices in your apartment, thank God, but it's written all over you. And thank you for not making me listen to that shit by boning him in his apartment. Because I love you, but ... Eww! I feel like I shouldn't know what your 'O' sounds are."

I let my head drop into my palms. "I don't know how it happened. At first I was trying to get close to him to be able to do my job, you know? Keep him safe. Convince him to go home. I thought it was working. We were friends, sort of. And then ... I don't know what happened. It was just ... We were getting closer and ... God, I am such a fool."

Ariel shook her head. "No honey, you're a woman. He is gorgeous, and from the sounds of it, sweet. He's into you. It's not like you're chasing after some guy. He wants you, and you want him. It's kind of inevitable."

"You make it sound so simple."

"Isn't it? This is the part where you ride off into the sunset."

I just stared at her. What happened to my calm, rational friend? She was the one being romantic all of a sudden. "You've forgotten the tiny little detail about the fact that I'm lying to him. Oh and the fact that I'm a commoner. I have no royal blood. We can't be together, at least not as the law stands. And that's a little cart-before-horse since he doesn't even know my real name."

Ariel scrunched her nose. "Yeah. I mean technically, it's more of an omission than a lie because you really do want to be an artist. You don't want to be a Royal Guard. So that's the truth. Plus, you're being truthful in your interactions with him. Len is really just a version of Penelope. It's what your family used to call you when you were little. It's all the truth."

"I think you're splitting hairs. What happened to my cool, calculating, rational friend?"

Ariel shrugged. "You forget I also love cheesy romantic Christmas movies. I'm a woman. I'm complicated. I can be more than one thing."

"So what do I do? I mean, the king needs us back in a matter of weeks. That's my deadline. I promised I'd have him home. So do I tell Sebastian the truth now and have him leave, keep lying and try to convince him to go home, or worse yet, call in the Guard who will force him to go home? The King only said to convince him to come. Maybe I have a loose definition of *convince*."

For once, Ariel didn't have a snappy comeback. She chewed her bottom lip. "Okay, as tempting as it is to try and force his hand to go home, I think calling the Guard in is a mistake."

"Well, you would be in the minority because Dad and Michael seemed to think it's a fantastic idea."

Ariel raised her brow. "Yes, but for two very different reasons. I have to say I'm very disappointed in my future husband's take on this whole thing. He wanted you out of the way so he could take credit, and that doesn't sound like Michael at all."

I smirked. That actually sounded exactly like Michael. "Yeah well, that's not going to happen. If I do call the Guard, I'll be staying. He won't get the credit and take this from me. At the same time, how could I do that to Sebastian?"

"Honey, you would never do that. That's not even a real option. There's no way you would call in theGuard, because you know that would hurt him. And that's not you."

I wish that was true. "Apparently it *is* me because no matter what happens now I *am* going to hurt him."

Ariel pondered this some more. "Okay, well your father is trying to protect you. As misguided as that is, it's sort of sweet. Maybe your dad could come to get him. He wouldn't need all the guards. He's head of security, and Sebastian respects him. Maybe he'd go with him."

The more I thought about this, the more I didn't like this idea. "No. None of these are working for me. I feel like I just need to tell him the truth. The idea of failing kills me, but his safety is more important. Maybe if I just tell him that his life is in danger and that his father sent me to keep him safe, that would be fine. And things will work out."

Ariel sipped on her drink. "So you're going to tell him the truth. You think that's going to fly?"

I sighed. "I have no idea. Honestly, I don't know what I'm doing. It wasn't supposed to feel like this. I didn't think that we'd get this close. I thought I'd be his spunky neighbor and we'd grow close over hijinks like an old '80s' sitcom. This whole job has me so confused. On the one hand, I feel alive and like I'm doing the right thing, and I'm finally coming into my own as a Royal Guard. On the other hand, I'm getting to explore my art and a part of me that I have loved for so long. But then, like an idiot, I went and fell in love with the person I was supposed to be protecting. Gosh, how stupid was that?"

Ariel leaned forward and took my hand. "Honey, it's not stupid. He listens to you. He understands you. That's a damn sight better than Robert ever did. Sebastian spends time with you and treats you like you deserve. He's not someone who constantly runs out on you, one who is never there when you need him, or who does everything to avoid being alone with you."

I couldn't help it. My eyes stung with fresh tears. But I blinked them away. She was right. Sebastian was there for me in a way that Robert had never been but also in a way that my father had never been. He didn't think any of my ideas were silly. He saw who I wanted to be, and he accepted it. "I'm so screwed. It's not like we can be together. As soon as we return to the Winston Isles, this is over."

Ariel sat back and crossed her arms. "He's the prince. He can push for a vote allowing royal marriage to commoners. But wait … Is that even a law? I mean, I know it's a *custom,* and I know that the stupid Regents Council would have to vote on it. But this is insane."

I gaped at her. "Oh my God. He doesn't want to marry me. That's not even a possibility. Like I said earlier, there's that tiny detail about him not even knowing who I am."

Ariel was right though. He could do all those things to be with me. But that wasn't even what this was about. He had a very specific life to live, one that I couldn't be a part of and that I would be shut out of as soon as he knew who I was.

I was the one who'd fallen in love with him. *I* was the one who would have to walk away in the end, no matter how badly it hurt.

Sebastian …

THIS WAS the wrong time for this conversation. I was distracted. My mind was on Len. But I needed to get Lucas on board. The problem with learning not to be a prick was that it made me feel bad about shoving that kind of responsibility onto Lucas's shoulders.

But if you can go through with it, maybe it would be possible to keep Len.

The idea of giving her up twisted my gut.

"It's not always so complicated. I swear though: you'll love the islands."

Lucas leaned forward, propping his elbows on his knees. "I've actually been thinking about it … what you said about going to meet him, my father."

My heart started to jackknife. *Easy does it. Don't look too desperate.* "Oh yeah? What were you thinking?"

Lucas met my gaze. "I think I want to do it. Go *home* or whatever. Meet him. Look, I know it's not easy being the firstborn, and I know that you've had a lot of pressure on you. I know that you're looking for me to possibly step into your place, but I don't know about all that yet. I figure I should go see the place you're from first, and at the very least, I'd like to meet him and see what it is you love about the islands."

Relief washed through me. I could see the light at the end of the tunnel. If everything went right and all the stars aligned, I could just become a normal person. It could be possible. I could be with her.

———

SEBASTIAN ...

Later that night, my fingertips trailed up Len's nude back. She was sound asleep, lying across my chest. I'd never been more comfortable in my life. I could be here forever. On her night stand, my phone buzzed. I lifted my head up to take a quick look at who was calling.

International number. *Shit.* It was my father.

I hated to leave the bed, but I needed to tell him that Lucas was coming home. I had managed it. And now all he had to do was make Lucas love it. That was his job. The island would do the rest.

I silently shifted Len slightly. She grumbled low in her sleep, but when I substituted a pillow for my warm chest, she wrapped herself around it halfway. She shifted some, revealing the curve of her naked ass, and I considered not answering my phone. But for once I did the calm, rational thing and covered her up again. I took my phone and headed to the balcony. "Hello?"

"Sebastian."

"Sorry, Dad, give me a second." I headed across her balcony toward my apartment and closed the door so I could talk more freely. Somehow that conversation with Lucas the other night had only exacerbated the fact that I was lying to her. It was gnawing at me all the time.

I'd nearly told her six or seven times as it was. I'd nearly blurted out, "Hey, I'm the crown prince of the Winston Isles. How do you feel about living on the islands?" But I hadn't had the courage to do so.

"You sound tired. Were you sleeping?"

I was not going to tell him what I had been doing. "No, I was just leaving. Is everything okay?"

"Yeah, I just wanted to hear your voice. I miss you, son."

"I miss you too." I missed it all: being home, the people, and the island. "I've actually got some news for you."

My father was silent for a beat. "You do?"

"Yeah. I'll uh … I'll be home in time for the vote."

Another beat of silence. "You're sure?"

I nodded, even though he couldn't see me. "I've been gone long enough. And I'll be bringing Lucas with me."

"He's coming?"

"Yeah, we've been talking about the Winston Isles and he wants to see it. So I'm gonna bring him with me in another couple of weeks. He has exams to take first, but then, yeah, we'll head out in time for my birthday."

"Wow. I don't even know what to say. Suddenly I'm nervous."

"You're the king. You're not supposed to be nervous."

My father's laugh was low and reminded me of when I was a child and the way my father had laughed so easily. That sound came less and less as I'd gotten older. "Is that how it seems to you? I'm nervous a lot. Part of the job is to not show it though."

"Well, I'm pretty sure Lucas is nervous too, but I made that happen."

"Yes, you did." They both went quiet for a moment, the silence stretching between them. "Listen Sebastian, I wanted to apologize for the way things have gone with us. I don't know how the distance between us grew to be so vast, but I'd like to change it if you would."

Something in my heart twisted. Would he feel the same way if he found out that I planned to abdicate? I would just have to make him understand that it was no rejection of him. I just wasn't cut out to be monarch. "Thanks for the apology, but it's not necessary. I'm pretty sure I've been kind of a pain in the ass, so—"

"Yes, you have. But you've been chasing your dream with the tenacity that I would expect from a Winston. That's all. And because of who you are, you've been denied the possibility of doing that freely, and I am sorry about that. I'm also sorry that I pushed you to do things that you haven't been ready for or were that interested in."

"Dad, you don't have to apologize for any of that. Don't forget about all the great parts of being a prince. It comes with some responsibility. I see that now."

"I'm glad. And honestly, I can't thank you enough. It will be good to have you home."

"It'll be good to be home."

SEBASTIAN ...

I PULLED Len tighter to my side. This was starting to be a problem. Because what I wanted was Len at my side *all* the time. And the way Lucas was flirting with her outrageously was starting to tick me off.

My brother flashed her a grin. "Seriously though. I'll take you salsa dancing. It's all in the hips. I can show you. I can even show you here."

I growled. What was wrong with me? Now that Lucas was on board, I'd be heading home in about a week, maybe less. I wanted her to come with me. I wanted to tell her the truth. I *needed* to.

There was no way in hell Dad was going to let her stand by my side. She was an American for starters and a bohemian artist. My father, like his father before him, would push for a better marriage. One with some blond socialite that aristocracy would accept. And that was even *if* I abdicated.

When, remember? *Fuck.* Yes. When. Not if.

There was enough snobbishness and classism on the island to tell me that no one would be happy about me marrying her. And then of course, there was the little matter of her own plans for her life. She'd wanted to strike out on her own. Could I really ask her to give that up? No. But I wanted to.

"Earth to Sebastian. What are you thinking about, dude?"

I slid my gaze up to meet Lucas's and shook my head. "Nothing. But maybe lay off the flirting."

Lucas grinned. "What's the matter, bro? You worried?"

Len rolled her eyes. This was nothing but an old-fashioned pissing contest. Lucas wasn't interested in her. He'd been eyeing half of the waitresses that walked by in the restaurant. He just liked getting my temper up. And I couldn't help but rise to the bait. Every. Damn. Time. The fucker was trying to prove a point.

Penny ...

ARIEL WAS in the back corner of the lounge, sipping on a drink, tapping away on her phone, pressing her earpiece. She was listening. I was going to have a lot of explaining to do.

"So Len. Where did you grow up?"

As it turned out, I had underestimated Lucas. So far every time I'd hung out with the two of them, it had been easy. Like a bar or lounge like this one, and conversation had been light. But ever since Sebastian had seemingly staked a claim on me, his brother had been eyeing me with an especially sharp focus. "I grew up in Portland. Not bad if you love hippies."

He nodded. "I've heard people say that. So what do your folks do?"

Sebastian jumped in before I could answer. "They own a security firm. What's with all questions, Lucas?"

Again, there was that carefree grin that I knew was far from genuine. "It's just a question, big bro. I'm pretty sure looking out for each other is part of the brotherly package."

I cast a glance between the two of them. "Yeah. What Sebastian said. The family business thing."

Lucas nodded. "So are you going to go into the same business?"

Maybe, if it meant I could be close to Sebastian. "No. I'm trying to be an artist."

Lucas nodded. "That painting. The one Sebastian snatched up and hung in the bar. It's really good. The colors you used remind me of one of the Caribbean islands I visited once for spring break."

I shook my head. "Never been," I lied smoothly. I could tell Lucas was up to something. Had I slipped up? Had I made a mistake somewhere?

"That's amazing. The colors were spot-on. Kind of like you have to have been there to capture it perfectly."

I shrugged. "I have an excellent imagination." The look I gave Lucas was dead-on. I wasn't going to blink or flinch.

He met my gaze levelly. "That's amazing talent, to capture the essence of something without ever being there. Not a lot of people can do that."

In my ear, Ariel cursed. "He's on to something."

My friend was right. "Maybe I'll get lucky enough to go one day." I hoped that was the end of it. But Lucas wasn't done with me.

"You said you went to Chicago Institute of Art, right? I have friends that went there. I wonder if you know any of them."

Shit. Shit. Shit. Chicago Institute of Art was a big school. It was conceivable that I wouldn't know them unless they happened to be in the arts department. In which case, I was fucked.

I shrugged, trying for nonchalance. "Maybe. It's a big school though. Even in the same department, if you're really digging in on your projects, you barely bring your head up. I studied graphic design you know. It made the parents happy for me to study something practical, and it also worked out for me because I got to take a lot of art classes."

He nodded. "It is a big school. It makes sense that she probably never met you. She's your age though. You would like Shelley."

I made it a point to repeat Shelley's name so that Ariel could quickly look her up and her department in case something was about to come back and bite me in the ass. I listened to Ariel mutter as she searched Lucas's social media for a Shelley that went to Chicago Institute of Art. When Ariel's voice whispered that Shelley Price didn't actually go to Chicago Institute of art, but rather University of Chicago and was actually an engineering major, I breathed a sigh of relief. "Yeah, what a really small world. What did she study?"

Lucas's gaze narrowed, as if he could somehow see through my question. "You know what? I guess I'm thinking of University of Chicago. She studied engineering." After that, he seemed to let it go, but I couldn't be sure so I stayed on alert.

The waitress brought us our next round of drinks and I switched to water. I'd need all my wits about me to deal with Lucas. On the one hand, he was looking out for his brother. On the other hand, he was going to blow my cover. Something caught my attention out of the corner of my eye and my heart started to hammer.

I would have sworn I'd seen someone familiar. But when I looked again, whatever it was had gone. In my earpiece I could hear Ariel. "Everything okay?"

I brushed one of my curls back, tucking it behind my non comm unit ear, then tapped it once, asking her the silent question, "Were we followed?"

All of a sudden she was all business. "Let me confirm with the sexy blond Viking." We'd taken to calling Oskar Mueller that. He'd been on our additional Blake Security detail more than once now and the guy, while seemingly serious, was a laugh riot. In seconds she was back. "No, you weren't followed. I checked the footage from the front too; no one is suspicious. You see something?"

Had I? Or was I being paranoid? I'd been on edge since the shooting. And thanks to my particular body guarding technique, I hadn't rotated out of my shift this morning like I should have. Instead, I'd been guarding his body with my vajayvay. So maybe I was tired and extra on edge. I silently massaged my left temple to let her know it was fine. Anything on the left side was meant to signal the all clear. Anything on the right side of my body was meant to signal trouble.

Besides, we had bigger fish to fry than imaginary shadows. Sebastian and Lucas kept alluding to a trip together. I could only assume it meant that Sebastian was taking Lucas home. To rightfully claim his part of the throne? I had no idea. And I was no closer to finding out who was trying to kill him.

We were running out of time. I needed to get some answers and quick because I had a feeling Sebastian would be no safer back home than he was here. And if he took his brother home with him, I could name at least a few royals who would be less than pleased by the discovery of another prince.

Sebastian toyed with the ends of my curls and I turned my gaze up at him, giving him a grin. When he grinned back, my heart squeezed. I wished I could tell him the truth. I wished I could tell him who I was. But I'd already woven the web of lies, and I knew I had to see it through.

Across the table, Lucas rolled his eyes. "Okay geez, stop with the googly eyes. Come on, Sebastian's girlfriend, let's see if you can dance."

I laughed. "Can *you* dance?"

"Don't let the pale skin fool you. Rhythm lives in my blood."

I went to scoot out of the booth, but Sebastian held me in place. "I think she's going to pass on that, Lucas."

I glanced back and forth between them. I didn't know what the hell was wrong with Sebastian. "You're acting weird. Did I do something?"

His jaw tensed. "No. Can't I want you with me?"

"Of course, but you look pissed off." I felt confident enough leaving his side for the moment because I knew Ariel was watching him. And Lucas was watching me, so I had no choice here.

It was unlikely someone would make a direct approach to him

in this crowd. But from the looks of it, he didn't want to let me go. Finally, he murmured, "Hurry back."

"Of course."

I let Lucas lead me away as I scanned the crowd. The hairs on the nape of my neck stood at attention. Something was off. I just couldn't put my finger on it. But maybe it was because I knew in that moment just how much it was going to hurt when I had to leave him.

Sebastian …

I KNEW I was being an asshole. Lucas knew it too. And sadly, so did Len. It irritated me to see the way Lucas looked at her. His casual flirting made me want to hit things. Namely, my brother.

Even as I watched them on the dance floor, I gritted my teeth.

You could stop being an asshole and get up and dance with her. Yeah I could. Because I sure as hell didn't like Lucas's hand on her waist. There was a respectable distance between them, but still. There was a word that kept reverberating in my head: *mine.*

Yeah, is she really? I was going to leave her soon.

Fuck.

That had me out of my seat in seconds. Striding right over to her, I tapped on her shoulder. "I think that's enough."

My brother laughed. "Oh come on. Relax, Sebastian. It's just a little dancing. Besides she deserves dancing and fun, not brooding."

She deserves someone who wants to be with her. She deserves someone who isn't lying to her. She deserves someone who could *be with her.* But that didn't stop me from wanting her. It didn't stop me from wanting to stake a claim on her to make sure everyone knew she was mine. That alone made me an asshole. I was well aware.

"Enough. I'm stepping in."

Lucas shook his head. "You can salsa with her later." He deliberately pulled her closer into him, even as she gently shoved against his chest.

"Oh my God. Would you two stop it? I'm going to the bathroom."

I watched as she ventured around the corner. Lucas laughed. "Did you tell her yet?"

I frowned at him. "Tell her what?"

"That you're in love with her? That I'm your brother? Anything that resembles the truth?"

"She knows you're my brother but not anything else." Because that's not what this was. I wanted her, yes. I wanted to keep her. *Yes*. But this wasn't love. I didn't fall in love. My understanding of the concept wasn't even real. "What the hell do you know about it?"

"I know enough to know that you're pissed as hell at me for flirting with her but you also haven't told her who you are, and it's eating you up inside. You don't know shit, man. I'm the con artist who has spent most of my life crafting lies, and even I can see the truth plain as day."

"That's bullshit."

"You keep telling yourself you don't care, that you're not in love with her. But if you don't tell her how you feel and tell her who you are, you're going to lose her. You're going to go home and she's going to stay here, and you won't see her again. Is that what you really want?"

"What I want is for you to stop flirting with her."

"Oh yeah? Like she's yours."

"She *is* mine."

My brother laughed. "Does *she* know that?"

It bothered me that Lucas was right. It bothered me that I had things to tell her that I hadn't told her yet. It bothered me that we had so little time together. I was going to have to tell her. I had to find a way.

When she came back, she pasted a smile on her face. "Are you boys going to behave now?"

Lucas put up his hands and winked at her. "I'm always well behaved ... until I'm not."

I didn't even bother to say anything. Instead I pulled her in close, and nuzzled her neck. The scent of her wrapped around me, intoxicating me. I skimmed my lips over her throat and was rewarded with a low moan. When I lifted my head and met her gaze, her pupils dilated. She wanted me. And that's how I wanted her to stay: always on the edge of needing me.

Because you love her.

Fuck. I dropped my forehead to hers and heard Lucas mumble, "Okay guys, I'm out. If you two are going to make out, I saw a blonde that will look awesome in my bed. See ya, man."

I barely acknowledged my brother leaving. My focus was entirely on Len. "I think I owe you a dance."

She nodded. "Sure thing. Just after you explain to me why you've been acting like an ass all night."

I was fucking this up. I knew it. I just had no way to fix it. For some reason, every single time I saw her with Lucas it triggered an emotion inside me I didn't understand. *Yes you do. It's jealousy.* Yes, I understood the notion. I wasn't used to feeling jealous. My whole life all the attention had been on me; all eyes had been on me. Deep down, I understood that Lucas wasn't flirting. I did.

Oh yeah, then why are your hands clinched into fists? I glanced down and immediately released my furled fingers.

This wasn't so much about Lucas as it was about her. Without my title, without my money, would she still choose me? The one thing I'd been trying to get rid of my whole life was the one thing I was afraid to live without.

What if, without all the trappings of being the prince, I wasn't enough? I was falling for this girl and her quirkiness, her penchant for random dance parties, and her mild awkwardness. I liked her.

Who are you kidding? You could love her. For the first time in my life I was falling for someone. And while she was choosing me for the time being, would she always make that choice? When I was just Sebastian, a photographer not a prince, would she still want me? When she found out, would I be enough?

Well, the promising thing was she liked me as a photographer and bartender. But the difference was how I felt about *myself*. With the confidence of a prince came the ability to get everything that I wanted. What happened when I wasn't that person anymore?

"You're not going to talk to me? Fine." Len turned from me and walked into the crowd.

I followed her, determined to talk to her. "Len, wait."

"No. I'm not waiting for you. You're acting like a crazy person and you won't tell me what's going on. Are you seriously worried about me with Lucas? What kind of person would that make me? I keep telling you Lucas is a hopeless flirt. He doesn't want me any more than I want him."

"Len, let me explain." But really, what was I going to say? 'I'm feeling insecure? I've been lying to you? This isn't who I am?' *Yes.* Would it be the end of the world to tell her?

She turned to face me. "Look. We need to talk."

My stomach fell. "That sounds ominous."

She licked her lips. And my eyes, of course, pinned to them. "And no, I'm not going to tell you that I've been harboring a secret crush on Lucas or something." She rocked back on her heels. "I swear sometimes you can be so daft, as you like to say. I'm falling for you, Sebastian. *You.* Not Lucas. *You.*"

Elation flooded my veins, making me feel like I was floating. "What can I say? I am pretty awesome. Oh yeah, and also, I'm falling for you too."

She shook her head and looked at her hand as she played with her nails. "*This* is not how I wanted to tell you. And there are things we need to talk about. Things I need to tell you."

Shit. There were certainly things I needed to tell her. "I need to tell you things too. There's a whole bunch of stuff we need to talk about."

She blinked up at me. "Sebastian, I don't know how you're going to react to any of this."

I shook my head. "As long as you want me, it doesn't matter what you tell me. We'll figure it out."

She searched my gaze. "Are you serious about that?"

"I don't even know how it happened, but I'm consumed with thoughts of you. I just want to be with you. You make me laugh. You make me think. I need *you*. Anything else we'll figure out."

I took her hand in an attempt to tug her to me. Her gaze flickered over my shoulder, then she wrapped her arms around me. "Let's get out of here."

"Not so fast." I pulled her close and dipped my head to tease my lips over hers. Her immediate, soft moan made my dick hard enough to cut steel. I didn't release her lips. Instead I licked into her mouth, savoring the taste of her.

She moaned into my mouth and hello, dick hard enough to cut steel. But then she was pulling back. Len shook her head. "Not here. Too many people. I feel self-conscious."

"Don't. I'm not." Automatically, I backed her into the shadows. "This better?" I mumbled against her lips before delving back in.

She tasted sweet, a little like that raspberry mojito she'd had. Mostly, she tasted of her. And that alone was enough to knock me on my ass. My fingers skimmed up underneath her top and traced over her soft skin. Shit, I could touch her forever. *Maybe you should talk first.* Tonight, we'd talk. Soon.

I kept backing her up until she hit a wall. And then I rocked my hips into her as I dipped my head down to get a better angle. She was so much smaller than I was.

Len dragged her lips from mine. "Sebastian. What are we doing? We can't do this here. We really should go."

Frustrated, I picked her up so that we could be more on one level. And I used my hips to bracket her against the wall. "I know. I'm just having a little taste right now." With my body notched against her core, I rotated my hips and she cried out.

Yes. This was how I wanted her: half crazy, begging. I wanted her this desperate. I wanted her feeling how I was feeling, needy and delirious.

"Sebastian. Please."

I rocked into her hips, my focus entirely on her, on making her block everything else out but me.

I gently palmed her breast, and she arched into the caress. Then I slowly rolled her nipple between my thumb and forefinger. I broke the kiss to watch her. I loved the look of ecstasy on her face. And I saw it: the blind need, the desperation, and I rocked my hips again, just where she needed me.

And then she was flying as she dropped her head back on a silent scream. I couldn't help the smug, satisfied grin that spread over my face. Yes. She was mine. Only I could make her do that. I was the only one to ever put that look on her face. I loved and relished every moment of it. "That's my girl." I kissed her softly, gently adjusting our position until her feet were safely on the ground. "Now we can go home."

SEBASTIAN ...

"I THOUGHT we were going to talk?"

And I planned to do that. I just needed her one last time first. I needed to show her how I felt. That way when she knew the truth, she could remember ... even if she didn't want anything to do with me.

Bullshit, I know, but that was how I was spinning it.

"Sure, we can talk. If that's what you want to do." I traced my thumbs under her top and around her belly button.

Her tongue peeked out and ran over her bottom lip. Immediately my dick stirred. He wanted some of that tongue action. "Are you telling me you brought me home under false pretenses?"

I swallowed hard. Now was the time to tell her. "No. I do want to talk to you." I pulled her to me. "I'm just afraid of what happens once I do. I don't want to lose you."

She reached up and caressed my face. "I need to tell you something too."

Something in her eyes told me I wasn't going to like what she had to say. Shit. Just one more night. One more night with her and then I would tell her the truth.

Her lashes fluttered and the dark depths of her eyes seemed to be boring right into my soul. "Sebastian, I don't know what's happening."

"Shh. Just kiss me. We'll talk when the sun comes up. But we have tonight." My hands gripped her hips. "I just—" What? What could I possibly say to her to that would cover how I felt? "You look beautiful." That wasn't what I wanted to say, but nothing I could say would be enough.

"I wish I could explain how you make me feel."

I just held her tighter. "Why don't you show me?"

A smile tipped her lips. "I think I can manage that." She took my hand and led me toward the bathroom in my place. "What do you say we shower together? It was sweaty and sticky in the bar."

Well fuck. I stared at her tight ass and tried for the life of me to remember what I'd been trying to say. "Hello? Earth to Sebastian?"

I dragged my gaze up, but I couldn't help a couple of downward glances. I pulled her back to me and kissed her shoulder before nipping. I knew her body well by now. "I like you hot and sweaty."

Instead of the bathroom, I led her into my bedroom. By now, I was a master at disappearing clothes and Len's were no exception. While she scooted back on the bed, I dragged my shirt off and made quick work of my jeans.

My heart squeezed as I looked down at her. I didn't want to give her up.

After I grabbed a condom I joined her on the bed. With a gentle slide of my fingers between her thighs, she was arching her back, her thighs splayed and ready to accommodate me.

I slid a finger inside her, making sure to tease her clit first. Once I slid home, her inner walls clamped around my finger.

I couldn't think with her doing that. "Len, that's not fair." At this rate, it would take no time to make me come.

"Who said anything about fair?" She laced her fingertips through my free hand and brought it to her breast. Gently, I plucked her nipple and she shivered. "I like that."

"I know. Two can play at this game. Turn over, baby."

When she complied, my cock slid against her ass. Her breath hitched and my cock slid between her cheeks again, this time grazing the pucker of her forbidden hole. But she didn't move away. Oh God, she was going to kill me.

She ran her ass over me once more, grazing the tip of my cock with her wet slit, and I groaned. When my cock nuzzled into her wet entrance, I shivered. Fuck. I wanted to make her scream my name. She easily coated me with her juices. With every slide of my cock over her entrance, she lifted her hips in invitation. "Please … "

"I know what you want. I'll give it to you, but you have to stop moving. Otherwise I'll come and we'll have all kinds of problems." She moved again and I cursed, the tip of my cock slipping inside. *Fuck. So tight. So damn soft.* With a little contraction, she pulled me inside to heaven and I stroked deeply. She pulsed around me and I squeezed my eyes shut. I never wanted to leave. I wanted to press my whole body against her and fuck her slow for hours.

But I knew better. I had to. With a low groan, I pulled back and tore open the foil packet. Once I sheathed myself, I reached into the bedside drawer for the little surprise I'd bought for her. When I settled over her, she wiggled her ass at me, taunting me.

"Little teases tempt fate you know."

She giggled before wiggling her ass at me again. "I'm not scared of you."

"That's good. I've lulled you into complacency."

I flipped the switch of the little red vibrator, and she stilled. "What is that?"

"It's a little gift I bought you."

I reached around and pressed it against her clit. Len screamed, coming apart in seconds. I held on and didn't move, didn't breathe as she writhed and screamed out my name. "Sebastian, oh my God. Please, please, please, God."

"There we go. Now that we've gotten the first one out of the way, I get to play." I pulled the vibrator back and pressed it against her ass. Turning up the speed, I held it in position with my thumb.

Len lost all coherent thought. "Oh—Sebastian—please. Oh yes."

When she lifted her hips up off the bed, I shifted into position. I held my cock with my free hand and lined up to her slick folds. With one stroke, I was home.

I fucked her slowly, pouring every bit of emotion into my strokes. Silently telling her how I felt. Silently sharing that things were different for me with her. I let go of the vibrator but it stayed in position as I pressed my chest against her back and entered her slowly again and again. She bucked beneath me and I whispered in her ear, "I love being inside you ... So tight ... So slick ... Never want to leave."

"Sebastian ...so good ... " Her fingers dug into the sheets and she made a low, keening sound.

Fuck, I just wanted to blurt everything out. Tell her how I was feeling. "Yes, it is good. You're different. All of this is different."

I held her tight as I nipped the nape of her neck. "Mine," I whispered before the darkness took over.

Sebastian ...

"WOMAN, WHERE ARE YOU GOING?"

Len giggled. "I need water. You know, the giver of life. That stuff that we die without. I need some." She began to slide out of the bed, taking one of the sheets with her, but I tugged it back. "You should never be covered. Your body is a thing of beauty."

"Says the photographer who wants to take naked pictures of me."

"Guilty as charged. But also—" I leaned up and kissed her lips briefly. "—it's true. Fine. Go get us this water you speak of. But I'm headed for the shower and if you're not there in five minutes,

I'm coming out here to drag you in with me. I have all sorts of things planned, dirty, debauched things. Things that might make you embarrassed to walk out in public again. Things that are illegal in several states."

She tossed her head back with a crack of laughter. And somehow, she managed to drag the top sheet off again and wrap it around herself. "Just how debauched are we talking here? After all, I have a reputation to maintain. The seductive artist. I feel like I'm going to need some details on exactly what you have planned."

It's not like I didn't know we needed to talk. I wanted to know what she was so scared of telling me, and I needed to tell her the truth. But maybe we could do a shower and breakfast first.

I hopped out of bed and her gaze immediately went to my abs. Then to my dick. I gave her a cocky grin even as I let her drink in the picture. At the very least, she couldn't resist me. I could tell that she'd tried. Even without the title, even without the money, she liked looking at me. That was check one in the bonus column. And what do you know? My dick liked her attention too.

Her eyes widened, and she shook her head. "Oh no. How is it possible you can be ready to go again?"

I stepped toward her even as she giggled and tried to scamper away. "It's you. All because of you. Every time I turn around and see you, he wants to play. Fuck that. He wants to be buried inside you and fuck you so hard you can't walk tomorrow. Or the next day. As a matter fact, let's just drop back into bed and he can slip inside you." *Bare.* It alarmed me how badly I wanted that.

"You know that sounds a lot like you want me to be your sex slave."

I caught her and whirled her around as I nuzzled her neck. "Now that you mention it that does not sound like a terrible arrangement. But if you prefer, I'll be your sex slave. You can tie me down and use me however you want. Just as long as he gets to be inside you." My dick merrily throbbed against her thigh, and I searched for a flat surface. *The counter.* The counter would do.

I picked her up as she squealed. I grabbed one of the glasses off the hanging rack above the sink, filled it with water, and handed it over. Len took a big gulp, and when she seemed like she'd had enough, I took the glass and set it back down.

Before she knew what was happening, I lifted the sheet and spread her legs until she was completely exposing herself. Then I dragged her to the edge of the countertop until my dick was lined up with her pussy. With one hand, I gripped the base of my dick then swiped it up over her clit, pressing.

Len tilted her head back. "Sebastian. We need condoms."

I nodded. Condoms, right. Because that was safe. But I knew I was clean, and she'd already told me she was on the pill. "Yeah. I know. I'm just playing. I just want to feel you. I'll grab the condoms from the bedroom in a minute."

Stroke. Slide. Press. My gaze pinned to the apex of her thighs where I stroked over her. The cinnamon brown of her lips giving way to petal pink softness.

Jesus. I could watch this all day. Her softness. The creamy silk as she became wetter and wetter for me. On the downstroke, the tip of my dick slotted just at her entrance, and I shuddered. Oh God. This felt good—so fucking good.

"Sebastian. God." And then she canted her hips, taking just the head of me inside.

"Oh, Jesus Christ. Len—" I knew this had to stop. There was a reason this wasn't supposed to happen. Jesus, no wonder just the tip never worked. It felt too damn good. Too damn amazing. Her inner walls constricted, and I knew I was no longer in control of the situation. Any second now, I'd be sinking into her, deep and bare.

She swallowed hard. "Well, I am on the pill. And I've never had sex without a condom."

I gritted my teeth. "I'm clean. I got tested six months ago. But I don't want to take any risks with you."

Jesus. It feels too good. I pulled back slightly and she moaned.

And then I slid in further. *Jesus.* I swore I could see star images in my vision. Why her? Why did this feel so good?

"Sebastian, stop teasing." She lifted her ass, trying to get closer.

That was all it took. I grabbed her ass with both hands, held her still, and slammed myself home. Len screamed. I grunted. But I couldn't stop.

The heat of her. The slide of her. The way she gripped me with her silken sheath. God, I was toast. Len lay back on the countertop and raised her arms until she gripped the opposite edge of the counter. She looked like a glorious virgin sent up for sacrifice. Yeah, that's right. She was mine. She *belonged* to me.

And now, I belonged to her. I searched for her clit and started to rub tight circles over it. Pressing hard, I set a quick pace for us. Because I was fucking her deep and fast, and I couldn't control myself right now. And I needed her to come. It seemed like her body was perfectly made for me, perfectly tuned to me. Jesus, it felt like heaven. Like this was where I belonged. Like I never needed to leave this place or her.

Eventually I pulled back, and Len groaned. "I'm just changing this up." I stepped back and helped lift her off the counter before turning her over. "Hold on, Len. I'm going deeper."

And I did.

Fuck me. When I sank back into her, I felt like I'd never been so far inside anyone before. Like I was discovering something new, *someplace* new. Someplace that I was going to fall into and never come back up.

I grabbed her ass, falling in deeper and deeper, losing myself.

My gaze traveled the length of her arched back. Over the shallow dimples above her ass, to the perfect ass I held in my hands, to the pucker. With my thumb, I gently stroked over it, and off she went again, her body clamping over me tight. She was still coming when she asked, "What are you —" and then she was coming again. And this time I couldn't stop. Tingles started in my spine then rocketed out, slashing through my body and robbing me of all thought, all will, all control. She owned me. And she always would.

So this was what it was like to fall in love.

I finally dropped over her back, cradling her, keeping her warm. "Fuck, Len. Are you okay?"

"I don't know. I've never—obviously—never experienced anything like that before."

"And for what it's worth, me neither." I kissed her shoulder.

I wanted this, wanted it to last. *But you have to tell her everything.*

And I would. I'd feed her, and tell her, and beg her to fucking keep me. Because I was headed home soon and I wanted her to come with me. Telling her now would give me plenty of time to apologize and to keep apologizing until she took me back. "I'm serious about the shower. After that I'll make you breakfast and we'll talk. I think we both have a few things to say."

She nodded as I kissed the nape of her neck. "Okay. That's a good plan."

I slowly disengaged from her body, and she hissed. She fell back over when she tried to stand on wobbly legs. "Oh my God, I think you broke me."

"God, I hope not, because I need to do that again. I have these things I want to try with you in the shower and see how they work out."

She shook her head. "Oh my God, you're a machine."

I chuckled, and there was a knock at the door. I frowned. Could it be Lucas? He had a knack for interrupting my good thing.

Annoyed, I dragged on the pair of jeans I'd tossed off hours before. "Get into the shower and warm it up. I'll be right there." I didn't bother with a shirt as I jogged to the door and swung it open.

Fuck.

In the doorway stood one member of the Royal Guard. *Robert.* I knew him because he'd been on my service detail before. His eyes were grave as he immediately sank down to one knee. "The King is dead. Long live the King."

No. No. No.

Not my father. Please, God, not my father.

Grief and horror roiled inside me to make a cocktail of pain and despair. My knees threatened to buckle as a wash of sickly heat took over my body. I was going to fucking pass out. Automatically, I sought out the one person who would steady me and drag me out of this nightmare. When I turned, she was right behind me, still wrapped in her sheet ... and also on one knee, bowed before me.

She knew.

She'd known all along.

To be continued in Cocky King ...

THANK YOU

Thank you for reading CHEEKY ROYAL! I hope you enjoyed this installment from the ROYALS UNDERCOVER Series.

Go On and STALK me at ALL the places!

Reviews help other readers find books. I appreciate all reviews. Please leave a review on your retailer's site or on Goodreads to help other readers discover my books.

Don't miss the other books in the Royals series in reading order

ROYALS UNDERCOVER
Cheeky Prince
Cheeky Royal
Cheeky King

ROYALS UNDONE * Coming soon
Prince of Thieves

Royal Bastard
Bastard Prince

NANA MALONE READING LIST

Looking for a few Good Books? Look no Further

Free on ALL Vendors
Sexy in Stilettos
Game Set Match

Royals
Royals Undercover
Cheeky Prince
Cheeky Royal
Cheeky King

Royals Undone
**Prince of Thieves* (Coming Soon)*
**Royal Bastard* (Coming Soon)*
**Bastard Prince* (Coming Soon)*

The Donovans Series
Come Home Again (Nate & Delilah)
Love Reality (Ryan & Mia)

Race For Love (Derek & Kisima)
Love in Plain Sight (Dylan and Serafina)
Eye of the Beholder – (Logan & Jezzie)
Love Struck (Zephyr & Malia)
**The Roommate Problem (Holden & Taj) (Coming 2019)

London Billionaires Standalones
Mr. Trouble (Jarred & Kinsley)
Mr. Big (Zach & Emma)
Mr. Dirty(Nathan & Sophie)

The Shameless World

Shameless
Shame
Shameless
Shameful
Unashamed
Shameless Bonus

Forceful
Force
Enforce

Deep
Deeper

The Player
Bryce
Dax
Echo
Fox
Ransom
Gage

The In Stilettos Series
Sexy in Stilettos (Alec & Jaya)
Sultry in Stilettos (Beckett & Ricca)
Sassy in Stilettos (Caleb & Micha)
Strollers & Stilettos (Alec & Jaya & Alexa)
Seductive in Stilettos (Shane & Tristia)
Stunning in Stilettos (Bryan & Kyra)

~~~

In Stilettos Spin off
Tempting in Stilettos (Serena & Tyson)
Teasing in Stilettos (Cara & Tate)
Tantalizing in Stilettos (Jaggar & Griffin)

The Chase Brothers Series
London Bound (Alexi & Abbie)
London Calling (Xander & Imani)

Love Match Series
*Game Set Match (Jason & Izzy)
Mismatch (Eli & Jessica)

Temptation Series
Corporate Affairs
Exposed
The Flirtation

The Protectors Series (Superhero Romance)
*Betrayed a Reluctant Protector Prequel
Reluctant Protector (Cassie & Seth)
Forsaken Protector (Symone & Garrett)
Wounded Protector (Jansen & Lisa)

The Hit & Run Bride Contemporary Romance Series
Hit & Run Bride (Liam & Becca)

Don't want to miss a single release? Click here!

ABOUT NANA MALONE

USA Today Bestselling Author, Nana Malone's love of all things romance and adventure started with a tattered romantic suspense she borrowed from her cousin on a sultry summer afternoon in Ghana at a precocious thirteen. She's been in love with kick butt heroines ever since.

Nana is the author of multiple series. And the books in her series have been on multiple Amazon Kindle and Barnes & Noble bestseller lists as well as the iTunes Breakout Books list and most notably the USA Today Bestseller list.

Want to get notified of Nana's next book? Text SASSY to 313131!